WITHDRAWN

INTERIOR

LOOK AT IT THIS WAY

MASAI
DREAMING

MASAI DREAMING

JUSTIN CARTWRIGHT

RANDOM HOUSE NEW YORK

Library of Congress Cataloging-in-Publication Data
Cartwright, Justin.
Masai dreaming / Justin Cartwright. — 1st U.S. ed.
p.   cm.
ISBN 0-679-43860-2
I. Title.
PR6053.A746M3   1995   94-41335

Manufactured in the United States of America on acid-free paper
24689753
First U.S. Edition

Book design by Lilly Langotsky

FOR MY SONS,

RUFUS AND SERGE,

IN THE HOPE THAT THEY WILL ALWAYS

TRAVEL PEACEFULLY

Social man is the essence of civilized man; he is the masterpiece of existence.

—ÉMILE DURKHEIM

The concept of humanity as covering all forms of the human species, irrespective of race or religion, came into being very late in history and is by no means widespread.

—CLAUDE LÉVI-STRAUSS

One thing that, fundamentally, we never foresaw was how large modern societies that have more or less emerged from the Middle Ages in other respects, could be hypnotized as Australians are by their dances, and set in motion like a children's roundabout. This return to the primitive had not been the object of our thoughts.

—MARCEL MAUSS

It is a six-pointed star having the dimensions of the palm of the hand and with black edges. It has to be in yellow material and to convey in black lettering the inscription "Jew." It must be worn from the age of six years old, and must be quite visible on the left-hand side of the chest, carefully sewn onto the item of clothing.

—EIGHTH ORDINANCE
PARIS, MAY 29, 1942

ACKNOWLEDGMENTS

I would like to thank all the many people who helped me both in Paris and in East Africa. In particular I would like to thank Daniel Friedman, John Reed, Primrose Stobbs, Marina Milmo and a certain Masai family.

I would also like to acknowledge the use I have made of books by Éric Conan, Steven Lukes, Jeremy Josephs, Paul Webster and Solomon ole Saibull, among many.

MASAI
DREAMING

PARIS

The old cinemas—moviehouses, fleapits, bioscopes, bughouses et cetera—were fine places. They had odors of their own, which suggested the nature of what went on there. Popcorn, sugary drinks, tobacco smoke, chocolate and quite a lot of semen had escaped into the atmosphere. A few hundred people sat there farting, chewing, whispering, exhaling; there was bound to be a lot of gas, moisture and aroma coming from these people in two hours. Fear, love and excitement on-screen produced complementary bodily reactions off-screen. As a result, the old moviehouses had a scent that was part canteen and part latrine.

You could also smell the celluloid overheating in the projector and occasionally even smell it burning. (It's something, like murder, you see more often in movies than in real life, in the sort of atmospheric movie, set in a small town, where the cinema stands for lost values and the elderly projectionist is a man with a past. He is seen carrying the huge reels of film to the projectors, which look like bits of antiquated farm equipment, contemplating this past. In these movies you can be sure that the celluloid will, at some point, burn, either as the young trainee makes love to a nubile girl who shares his dreams of escape to the city, or as the elderly projectionist suffers a heart attack. The celluloid develops a fatal melanoma, which spreads quickly outward as the nitrate first melts down and then catches fire.)

The cinemas along the Champs-Élysées have a glittering, Las Vegas look to them. The billboards are boldly, and surprisingly naïvely, painted, a provincial depiction of the glamorous sexual allure that the French associate with movies. I see the movie I want, advertised by a tall, nearly naked Masai warrior, looking surprisingly like the tennis player Yannick Noah, but nonetheless carrying a spear and wearing the Masai cloak of red loosely over one shoulder. This billboard is nearly fifty feet high, I would guess, and even here, among the posters of women with perfectly formed bosoms accompanying elegantly clad bastards, I have to admit it stands out: RÊVES MASAI. *Un film de S. O. Letterman.* Underneath is what should be the clincher: *Avec Mel Gibson et Julia Roberts.*

The French have been urged to boycott the film because Julia Roberts is playing a Frenchwoman. There has been a very minor scandal in the press about this and the fact that she plays a woman betrayed to the SS by her compatriots. Still, the film is doing good business.

I pass under the neon archway. For a moment I wonder if you still give the usherette a small *pourboire,* as you used to. In those days she would find your seat for you; only she was equipped with the arcane knowledge and a small flashlight necessary for this. You stumbled after her with your fifty centimes ready. Not now. The cinema has the blandness and the textures of an airport lounge. The large, comfortable seats are clearly indicated. Although the French are heavy smokers of dark tobacco, the air is clean and synthetic. It is afternoon. The cinema is not full, but there are some very enthusiastic, almost carnivorous, kissers at work. They see no need to court anonymity at the back of the cinema. The carpet on the floor continues seamlessly up the walls and the interior has been bent into smooth curves. French designers in the recent past decided that the ovoid was a shape of the utmost modernity. In French airports, television monitors are housed in eggs. Furniture is often elliptical, and there are cars here hunched into a fetal crouch, like actors improvising the shape of an egg.

The lights dim and the ads come on. French ads are full of sex. Young girls run around with their breasts exposed at the least excuse. (Their breasts have a remarkable elasticity and independence.) The world the ads portray is full of clues about the state of the nation. Over at the Collège de France they may be worrying about the rise of the right, but here they are worried about panty liners, mineral water and cheese. You won't be surprised to hear that both cheese and mineral water can be very good for your sex life, as, of course, are effective panty liners.

The main movie starts in an interesting way: the sky is limpidly cerulean—as it appears only on postcards. After a few moments, the noise of an airplane is heard. It is obviously going to enter our field of vision soon; the noise progresses from the right to the center of the cinema. But before the plane appears, another interesting thing happens: the apparently still frame of the improbable sky is actually moving, which we discover only as a mountain comes into view. It sweeps onto the screen and holds still, right in the middle. It is a curiously shaped mountain, clearly a volcanic shape, but strangely streaked with gray and white, the appearance of the dirty snow you find after the thaw. At this moment, of course, the tiny biplane appears from behind the mountain, and we realize just how high the mountain is. Up to that point it might have been taken to be a small hill; there are no trees or houses to lend scale as it stands on a bare plain.

The biplane is from that romantic era when planes and cars were thought to have personalities. (My father used to refer to his car

---

as "she.") Its wings are braced by cross wires and its single engine makes a thudding sound as it flies straight at the camera. As it comes closer, strange, barbarous singing rises. All in one shot—the virtuoso shot that daring directors like to attempt—the camera pans down as the plane banks before landing and we find a large crowd of Masai running toward the intended landing site. They all carry spears and are painted in red ochre; they run with long, somewhat awkward strides; it is from them the singing is coming, although, of course, it is apparent that their singing has been incorporated into a richer sound track, which is now swelling portentously. The plane touches down on very rough ground: its wheelbarrow wheels bounce and one set of wings rises alarmingly while the other dips. Now the Masai and the plane are converging. It's a magnificent shot: the Masai run, run, run, run; because of the optics it is dreamlike. The little plane bounces, shudders, slews and finally makes lasting contact with the ground. At exactly the right moment, as the plane comes to a halt, the Masai warriors, in a highly agitated state, reach the plane, and the camera closes on the pilot, whose face, as he removes his leather flying helmet and goggles, appears just above the bobbing red-ochre composition of plaited hair and fat-shone bodies. It is Mel Gibson, with a grave expression, which can't quite suppress his unruly Aussieness.

As he climbs out of the plane and is engulfed by the warriors, the titles roll. I often find this technique, of trying to create expectation by delaying, or even previewing, the start of the action, irritating. But here I think it works admirably, because it conveys the grandeur of the location, the intense, physical nature of the Masai, and the lonely pilot, an envoy from another world.

Now the picture changes dramatically. It is completely dark. A pinpoint of light appears, dancing and swaying in the surrounding inkiness. For a moment it vanishes and then returns. All the rich color of the African scene has gone. We see nothing but this mysterious light, a chilly firefly, coming toward us. In fact, we wonder if it is actually coming toward us. Then we hear a familiar sound, the sound of a train in the distance. The pistons of the steam locomotive are like a heartbeat, unnaturally accelerated. Now we see an outline of the locomotive. It is upon us, completely unexpected, apparently running right over us with a terrible noise, the noise of a foundry or a steel mill. Now it is going away, equally unpredictably, and we see only a small red light on the back of the train.

We are now inside the train. At first it is hard to make out what is happening. There are human shapes lying on the floor. Then we make out two people standing, their heads nodding. Now we know immediately what we are meant to know, because these are Orthodox Jews, praying and nodding, and we are in a cattle car in the night.

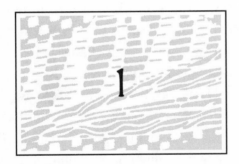

Beneath the hotel where I am based, temporarily, is a restaurant—a long, cool room with fans that move the air about, so that occasionally a fly, rising heavily from the *samosas,* will be caught in the turbulence and sent spinning away in the direction of the curried chicken, which waits in metal containers for the customers. This chicken is excellent, although the birds are scrawny, with a skin so rough it might contain a message in braille. In its containers the chicken settles in its turmeric-yellow sauce and gently disintegrates, so that the legs separate into their muscles and the stenciled skin hangs loosely. It improves as the day wears on. In this room you can get five times the official exchange rate. Very few tourists come here, but there are a number of aid workers who are regulars: locust-control officers and agricultural experts with parched, bleached children wearing Mickey Mouse T-shirts. The parents seem to feel that this display of verve—the bright shirts with happy themes—is a protection against the intransigent world in which they find themselves. Anyway, you can eat here, without fencing your currency, for next to nothing.

The tape recordings are primitive. The tape, made to some vanished standard of the 1930s, is like linen. It is textured and creased. It reminds me of a much-ironed tablecloth in a family restaurant.

Claude (Claudia) Cohn-Casson made hours of recordings of Masai song and Masai legend. I have had them transferred to little piles of cassettes. By my side I have Father Mol's *Dictionary of Masai Place-Names* and Hollis's *Masai Language and Folklore,* 1905. Evidently, Claudia was looking for the link between magic and the structure of Masai society. French sociologists and ethnographers of the first half of the twentieth century were sure that there were general rules of society that could be deduced from the study of what was common in mankind, all part of the "conscience collective" also known as *"l'âme collective."*

Other anthropologists believed that primitive—"savage"—societies were survivors of earlier stages of evolution. They therefore believed that studying them would produce useful evidence of the development of our own societies, which were thought to be more evolved. This is now described dismissively as "the time-machine approach."

I hear Claudia's voice, carefully reading the translations between each song. Her voice is clear, slightly didactic and also somewhat artificial, like someone speaking into an answering machine. I wish I could speak French well enough to get all the subtleties of her accent and intonation. Was she daunted by the uncharted reality of Masai life and the task of shaping it according to the prescriptions of Durkheim, Lévy-Bruhl and Mauss? These chaps sat comfortably in their studies or grandly ensconced in the great amphitheaters of the Sorbonne, perhaps a little fieldwork behind them, spinning their intellectual theories with airy ease.

Doggedly—on the evidence of the tapes—Claudia recorded and translated day after day. The Masai's curious, whining song stops and Claudia records her translation. This was the raw material that she planned to use to make her name in the new anthropology, a French Margaret Mead. Most of the tapes are the songs and laments of women, for example:

> I have eaten alone, miserable in my shame.
> Generous Ngai, answer my prayers.
> Do not forget all those like me who are childless,
> Whose backs are cold without a baby to carry.

My room is large and cool with a view out over some compounds—*shambas*—where banana trees are grown, and a thriving workshop, manufacturing auto spares out of other auto spares, sets up a lively clanking at dawn. The hotel is owned by an Indian, a third-generation Tanzanian. He tells me that the town was used for the location scenes in *Mogambo,* a film that starred Ava Gardner, Clark Gable and Grace Kelly. I remember her sending a postcard to my father, saying, "Be seeing you in Mogambo, Love, Ava." I was puzzled, because I wondered how she had got our address. To Amin Shah this era—he is speaking of the 1950s—was a golden era. The clocktower was functioning (his hotel is called the Clocktower and overlooks this dilapidated monument), the streets orderly, the park sprucely planted and a sense of purpose chimed every hour.

I have spent three days listening to Claudia Cohn-Casson's tapes.

> O Dieu, faites que mon mari ne devienne pas berger,
> pour n'avoir pas de fils.
> (O God, let my husband not become a herdboy
> for the want of a son.)

There are some Masai outside on the street. These are mostly the stay-at-home Masai who took up farming after the rinderpest plague devastated their herds at the turn of the century. Genuine, plains-dwelling Masai also come to town, where they wander disdainfully among the artifacts of the metropolis. They have a way of walking extremely slowly, but persistently, as though they fear the townies are going to buttonhole them if they stop to admire anything on display. However, they do stop frequently to shake hands with acquaintances, planting their spears in the ground, which is unyielding, packed by thousands of pairs of feet. As they talk to their pals, they gesture over their shoulders, or smile wryly at the urbanites. This world, bowed down—bent double—with possessions, amuses them. Perhaps sometimes they envy it. This world seems to produce in its inhabitants what the French sociologists called *anomie*. The Masai's possessions are cattle, goats and children. The children are there to look after the cattle and to keep their mothers' backs warm.

Claudia reads the song again, her voice acquiring a certain emotional timbre as she says:

> Please grant me a good baby.
> Cattle are not payment enough.
> Only a child will do.

She is catching the mood of the Masai women, plangent but also playful. It is possible this is just a quality of the ancient recordings. I find myself listening for anything Jewish in her enunciation.

Downstairs the fans are wafting the smell of chicken curry and samosas up to my room. The whole building is permeated by curry. These smells have entered the brickwork and lodged there over the years since Shah Buildings (1951) were erected. A small plaque shows that the building was declared open by the district commissioner himself, Ronald Beaton MBE. When he opened the building the curry was only just beginning its infiltration. Now it has taken full possession of the fabric. It is soothing. In a Masai hut the smell of smoke and small animals lies heavily in the air. No Masai—Claudia writes—can help but associate their warm odor with humanness. It is the nexus of humanity. Living alone here in this aromatic bazaar I am content. Sometimes I am ecstatic. I have no desire to get on with the job in hand.

Outside my window, past the shambas, is a river. It flows down from the mountains where coffee planters and fundamental Christians have set up shop, both types of enterprise providing employment, and both providing evidence of the connection between Protestantism and the work ethic. The river flows from the higher reaches, where the colobus monkey (which looks like a conventional monkey dressed up as the chancellor of a university) crashes and collides with the branches of huge trees. (It seems to me to climb trees about as skillfully as the chancellor of a university.) I can see, whenever I wish, vehicles being washed in the river. Land Rovers, Toyotas, Peugeots—strong cars—are driven right into the water and splashed down. It reminds me of the temple elephants being washed in the river at Kandy, and probably has the same ritualistic significance. A little farther upstream women are washing clothing and linen and spreading them on the rocks to dry. The cloth is a rich ochre red or a deep, inky blue. These are Masai colors. The cloth is made in faraway places, outside the Masai cosmos. All over Africa women wash clothes in this way. My own clothes have just come back from the wash. They are spotlessly clean, pressed and folded and lying now on the foot of my bed, like a well-made sandwich. I find it difficult to fold a shirt or hang up a pair of trousers; I appreciate the craft in this. Out there they are flailing away at the clothes, pounding them on the rocks, shouting to each other, loosing little rafts of bubbles and slicks of palm oil on the surface of the water, turning an everyday activity into a ritual. One woman is singing. As I play my tapes, I imagine that she is the singer, begging God to give her a baby, but as she turns, I see that there is already a baby attached to her back. When she stoops to knead and pound the clothes, the baby's head is tipped down toward the water, and then it bobs upward again as she stands erect. How many times a day is this child inverted? There may be important clues for a pediatric study along the lines of the cradled and uncradled theories of prewar anthropologists. What is absorbed by a child bobbing up and down like this, close to its mother's back in the cheerful hubbub of the occasion? You can see the attraction of fieldwork for the nimble: there is no end to the connections you could make.

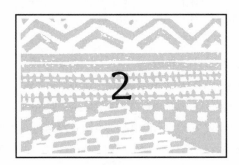

2

Trains have a guilty, uneasy quality about their movements. They are primitive; iron wheels grind on iron tracks, hoses puff and blow, water seeps from their workings, and they make strange, unsettling noises. Traveling by train at night is like taking a journey in a foundry; sleep is impossible. In my childhood I made eight long train journeys a year.

Sitting at the window I am writing on a small table.

A train lurches through the night. It approaches the Alsace region, a region that in my mind is something of a joke, all vineyards and sauerkraut and broad-faced devotion to eating. This is a troop train, but the last wagon is a cattle car. His face infrequently caught for a moment by the light of a lantern at a station or by the flaring of a match, sitting in a puddle of his own urine, is Léon Cohn-Casson, until recently the chairman (and patron) of the Hôpital Israélite de Paris. Cohn-Casson is sixty-two. He is dressed in a florid, self-regarding manner, his little vanities suggesting his wealth and connections. The yellow six-pointed star on his left breast is of silk. Yet now he is on the last transport out of France, although he does not know this.

(I hardly need describe the conditions. Although they are so frightful—unspeakable—you will not be surprised.)

Since the train left the siding at Le Bourget fifteen hours before, bewildered children have been clinging to their mothers, elderly ladies have simply defecated into their underwear or beneath their skirts, a baby has died, its mother has gone mad, a vicious fight has broken out between a Resistance fighter and a dentist, resulting in blood and, sadly, broken teeth, shots and screams have been heard from farther up the train, floating by on the night air, as sounds do in trains, appearing slowly and then rushing by.

As the train was standing in the station prior to the journey, Léon Cohn-Casson, typically, made a small speech, reassuring everyone that with the war almost over and the Allies already pressing for a tribunal of war crimes, the Nazis would not be looking for trouble. Cohn-Casson had seen how they worked, and there was nothing to fear at this late stage. The Nazis, he joked, were mad but they were not stupid. The Resistance fighters shouted him down, calling him a collaborator and worse.

The intervening hours in the cattle car have worked a change on him. Now he sits with his clothes fouled and his large face—which had previously seemed to be plumped out from within by self-esteem—is flaccid, like tripe or a cow's dewlap or a fore-skin. It has been vacated by the forces of duty, honor, seriousness and patriotism, as they came up against something more elemental. Nothing in his previous life, and he takes pride in his wide experience, nothing he had seen as director of the hospital, has prepared him to sit for hours in his own urine. Next to him, avoiding the damp straw as far as possible, sits his daughter, Claude, who has her arm around his son Georges, eleven years old.

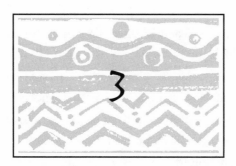

The Masai country stretches a long way. It follows the Rift Valley southward through Kenya and spills out onto the plains of Tanzania. For some reason—I am exceptionally receptive to unbidden thoughts as I stand here—it reminds me of the little funnels of sherbet we used to spill onto our hands as children. (The fizzle on the tongue, the chemical glueyness, the quick fix, which in turn reminds me of the first time Jeannie Mennen stuck her tongue in my ear.) I am standing on a high escarpment looking down into the Rift Valley, thinking about the Masai's epic journey south from their origins on the banks of the Nile, and I'm thinking about myself and my not-so-epic journey from sherbet consumer to . . . to what I have become.

Some way north is Ol Doinyo Lengai, the Mountain of God, his permanent residence. It rises from the floor of the valley suddenly. For the Masai this volcano—it sends out smoke and ash from time to time—is said to be a sacred place. I wonder, however, who knows what *sacred* means to a Masai. The sides of the valley are decked with trees and bushes. Below me there are watercourses, delineated by stands of trees—African figs, Cape chestnuts and wild almonds—so that the floor of the valley is a map, with the rivers green, the land brown and the distant mountains on the other side purple. In the bushes behind me, long-tailed birds scuttle around the branches like mice. There are innumerable bee-eaters, which flit between bushes. Tiny sunbirds poke their beaks into specially designed florets on succulent plants; one of these with glossy green and carmine feathers hovers on its delicately beating wings. Instead of filling me with wonder at the extraordinary adaptation of evolution and so on, it reminds me that it is an image easily and often caught by photographers on fast film with fast lenses. I am poised here, too, looking down on Masai country, somewhere approaching the second half of my journey.

Around the summit of Lengai clouds are gathering. They hang there in the air. I can see above them and below them, as in a Japanese painting of Fuji. The clouds are gently shunting each other; some turbulence, perhaps from within the mountain itself, is creating this movement. I can easily believe that God lives there. It is a numinous place, quite different from the other mountains, its runneled and scoured shoulders dusted with ash, so that from a distance, from where I am now, the volcanic ash looks like a light fall of snow. Not so long ago some Masai *morans* speared a tourist who dared to climb to the top. Ngai is the Masai name for God. The vowel sound *ai* pronounced "eye" is very popular with the Masai. Researchers and academics now spell "Masai" *Maasai,* which is considered more authentic and less touristy. There is no correct spelling of a Masai word, because Maa is not a written language.

Down below on the plain there are brown dots, little clusters of dried fruits. Through binoculars I can see that the larger clusters are cattle and goats and the smaller ones are gazelle. From down there I can hear the cowbells and the occasional shout of the herders and see a flash of their red robes. The huts are like upturned dinghies. This is the village—or more accurately the site of the village—where Claudia Cohn-Casson lived for a while. When Claudia Cohn-Casson set out for the Masai country in 1936, she thought that she would learn from the Masai something about the earlier stages of human life, the savage stages through which the human race had passed so unevenly, here a nation forging ahead, there a nation stuck in the Iron Age, there a nation—most notably the French—able to make elegant, entirely intellectual, confections simply out of ideas. (It occurs to me that they are similarly adept in the kitchen.) Her aim was to bring back some spark of knowledge that would illuminate the world of anthropology and, of course, help her to understand the events in Europe. It is anybody's guess what the Masai would have been able to contribute to an understanding of Hitler or Mussolini, but Claudia did not believe that anybody could take Hitler seriously. When she left Paris to live among the Masai, none of her friends thought he would last long. When they mentioned Hitler, it was with a short, dismissive exhalation of breath through pursed lips. In French literature this is written: "Pouf."

From up here on the slopes of the Rift, the countryside below looks dry, although I am surrounded by pleasant greenery. When I look at the plants closely, it is clear that they are hairy and tough, resistant to drought and heat. The plain below is showing large patches of soil, ochre red, like outbreaks of eczema. In places the soil is being sucked up into the air in little dust devils. Up here, however, the air is still, disturbed only by the ceaseless arcing of eagles and harriers, which slice effortlessly through the stillness, a stillness that is heavy with anticipation.

Victoria and I have been living together for nearly two years. Until recently we had intended to get married, but there have been complications. It is probably these complications that have been responsible for accelerating my dream life, although the origins and purposes of dreams are notoriously difficult to explain. I began to dream about the Masai one night. There they were, floating uninvited through my dreams with their long thin legs, their cloaks of red, their strangely effeminate faces, their curiously shaped cattle, clutching their spears and sticks negligently as they strode across the savannah on cattle business.

The Masai have a thousand descriptions of cattle. They revere cattle: cattle are both provider and symbol. The Masai drink blood and milk fresh from their animals. They treat the cow as a sort of soda fountain, drawing off these vital fluids as required. In my dreams I came to believe that these people knew something we didn't.

Soon the Masai began to take a grip on my waking hours too. The scents of Africa—the spicy khaki bush by the roadsides, the dry clear woodsmoke and the smell of dust—began to steal up on me as I sat at my desk. In my room I have a Masai spear and a Samburu spear. Instead of working, I would hold them in my hand, perfectly balanced. The Samburu blade was shaped like a small fish, a flounder or a sole, and the Masai like a long, heavy kitchen knife by Sabatier. The wood between the iron tips was hard to the touch. I sniffed it. It smelled still of the mixture of smoke, cow dung, blood and cattle that clings to the Masai. They live in a warm, scented mist of these odors. In my dreams I saw the Masai in movement on the vast plains, usually in twos, sometimes with a dog. I never saw the women, with their shaved heads. One night the dream acquired a new dimension: it was accompanied by the above-mentioned odors. When I woke, of course, the scents had gone. Instead there were the night smells and night noises of—of myself—and of Victoria.

I am just about to start the descent to the valley floor when two Masai women appear below me, beating and cajoling three donkeys up the steep path. They have long heads, melon heads, with big eyes and very closely cropped hair. They are wearing blue *shukas* and long skirts of the same material. They are laden with bangles and bead jewelry and their ears are stretched to accommodate the little silver arrowheads and earrings that they favor. Claudia listed all these and illustrated them with neatly drawn sketches.

I speak to them in my rudimentary Swahili, which they barely understand. They come from a kraal, a *manyatta,* some miles away up the escarpment toward Ngorongoro and are heading back from the village, where they have been buying some maize. They seem to be sisters, with a curious dazed look, as though they had been woken in the night and were not quite sure of their surroundings. They want me to give them a present of some sort. One girl has a pain in her head. I give her some aspirin and point at my head. She tucks the aspirin into her shuka, revealing half her side and her breasts as she does so. In there, in the airy depths of her clothes, her body is browny-gray, exactly the color of the underside of a field mushroom. The girls do not say goodbye or thank me, but set off up the path, chattering and beating the donkeys, which are carrying the sacks of maize in their saddlebags. They leave a gentle fragrance in the air, a distinctly human whiff, but it soon disperses. I turn to watch them climbing up the escarpment, mounting steadily, urging on the donkeys, their voices carrying cheerfully down to me for a long time.

Before I set out for Masailand, I watched a documentary made in 1938 by an American producer called Waindell Leavitt. Leavitt had intended to film the famous Masai lion hunt. He had a contract to produce features about strange lands; he would arrive, hire an entourage of colorful helpers and then film himself on close terms with the local *tubab,* sometimes watching a dance featuring lissome, and preferably seminaked, girls and then, say, at a festival involving elephants or animal sacrifices. He had enlisted the help of Claudia Cohn-Casson to set up a Masai lion hunt.

It was a disastrous venture almost from the start, resulting in the death of two Masai warriors, the killing of two lions, the nonpayment of the cattle promised by Leavitt and a serious fight between two factions of Masai, one Ilkisongo and the other Ilpurko. It had set back Claudia's work on the significance of the exchange of gifts and women's ownership of cattle by months.

Leavitt, from the comparative safety of his open Willys safari vehicle, which had been shipped to Dar es Salaam on a Greek freighter, was shouting, "Wait, wait, just a moment, wait." His headman was shouting the same words in Swahili, and another man was translating them into Masai, so that there was a time lag, as used to happen with long-distance phone calls. The Masai, like the lions, were in a highly agitated state. Just as Leavitt's cameraman was trying to engage a new magazine in the camera, the lions suddenly burst out of the bushes where they had been crouching, growling ominously and flicking their tails. Spears rained from all sides, and all three lions—young males—were struck, but none was stopped immediately. Leavitt was still asking for a few moments' grace. The cameraman was jostled by his assistant, who was dodging a spear, and the magazine fell to the ground. One of the warriors was struck by a spear thrown in the confusion and was killed outright. Two lions burst through the ring of buffalo-hide shields held by the warriors and escaped but a third attacked the son of the *laibon,* or medicine man, fatally wounding him and also wounding two other warriors, who had tried, in the highest Masai tradition, to grab the lion's tail and stab it. Much was made of the fact that the lion, which had a nascent dark mane, had headed straight for the son of the laibon. To the Masai it was evident that the lion had identified him immediately.

By the time Leavitt's camera was running again the warrior had died, one side of his face entirely missing, two lions were dead and the two antagonistic groups of Masai, imprudently brought together from different regions for the filming, were fighting over the circumstances of the deaths.

Leavitt must already have been thinking of ways of editing in some shots of lions with the scenes of chaos in front of him: in the finished film these inserts have a fatal flaccidity, reminding me of the lion attacks in Johnny Weissmuller films: lions trotting harmlessly toward the camera and wrestling playfully with the scantily clad ex-swimmer, to the accompaniment of dubbed roars and growls. (As a boy I always used to wonder what he wore under his loincloth, which miraculously stayed in place through all his jungle exploits.)

The death of the son of a laibon was marked in an unexpected fashion: his torn body was anointed with fat and dressed in a cloak of hyrax skins—surprisingly like the bulky raccoon coats favored by rich young Americans in Paris—and was laid where he fell, with his left arm folded to support his head. The dead warrior was placed on his left side and faced north, Claudia noted. Then rocks were placed on the body. Passersby would stop for a moment and put another rock in place. Within a few weeks the pile of rocks had become a cairn, and soon after a small pyramid. The other warrior was simply laid out where the hyena could find him, his cattle stick in his hand, facing east. By the next morning there was nothing except a slight discoloring of the dry, brown earth to mark his last resting place. Claudia asked questions about the meaning of this: why were one man's remains protected and why were another's recycled so quickly? (Although, of course, she did not use the word "recycled.")

Claudia refers to the making of the documentary as a scandal and a fraud, yet it had caused the sometimes slow pace of her research to speed up: she was able to witness bereavement, the shaving of heads, the changing of names, the shifts of family alignments, vicious fighting and a lion hunt in a short space of time.

———

19

The fascinating aspect of Leavitt's documentary—released as *Lords of the Savannah*—is the glimpses it affords of Claudia Cohn-Casson. Making allowances for the refractions of time, she is startlingly beautiful, her hair dark—no indication of color—and her face, sometimes hidden in the shadow of a bush hat, sometimes cast upward toward the sun (presumably at Leavitt's bidding), both young and knowing. In her writings she makes it clear that she enjoyed the filming up to the point where it all went wrong. She is seen conversing with the women, waiting with them for the cattle to appear up out of the watercourse, announced by the cowbells and a miasma of dust and the shouts of the herdsmen. Of course I am imagining the sounds as I have heard them, because the documentary was post-synchronized with bits and pieces of sound, predominantly drumming—probably from West Africa, where they have a taste for that sort of thing—to lend drama, and Leavitt's own voice reading the commentary. His voice is full, with an undiscriminating portentousness like the commentary to the *March of Time*. The most mundane event—women collecting water from a river, for example—becomes "an age-old struggle to secure the bare necessities of survival in a harsh environment." (In those days the environment had not yet acquired religious significance.) Claudia is described as "every inch a chic and sophisticated Parisienne, but a highly respected and brave chronicler of the dark continent and its most aristocratic people, the Masai."

The brother of the man killed by the lion is still alive. It is he I am going to visit. He is now a very respected laibon himself, able to tell the future by throwing pebbles onto the ground. He will, I hope, be able to tell me about Claudia Cohn-Casson. He is said to have an encyclopedic memory and an enormous store of folktales. Many researchers have visited him. I can still hear the Masai girls and their donkeys in the distance above me, but I can no longer see them. From down below on the plain I can now hear goats and children heading this way. The noises are like distant radio stations fading in and out over each other. Soon I catch sight of them, the goats fanning out eagerly, the children running behind them anxiously. From here it is not clear who is leading whom in this arrangement.

Claudia: I see her now in Waindell Leavitt's risible documentary, the chic and sophisticated Parisienne, her face turned coquettishly to the sun, her dark eyes closed slightly against its glare, and I see her walking among the goats as they flood through the gap in the thorn barriers of the *boma*. Next, Leavitt has her standing in a sea of goats beside two melon-headed Masai women who are counting them in. As I see the picture again, superimposed on the reality beneath me, the goats reaching the kraal, crowding in their self-important fashion into the boma, I imagine that under the guise of anthropology, she is looking for something more elusive. Who can look at something like this without wondering how it is that for the Masai, getting in the goats and the cattle each night should have become the meaning of life. Because these herbivores and ungulates are not to the Masai what they seem to us, merely animals: they carry a heavy load of significance.

I wonder, perhaps, if she is seeking parallels with the desert culture of the Jews.

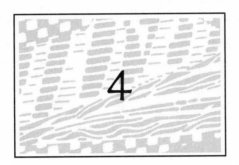

Most infidelities come to light in unforeseen but predictable ways. The routines of city life—the dry cleaners, the deliveries, the telephone company, the cab service, the post office—grind on, unaware that their mundane activities are glissading over small human deceptions. Sometimes they aid the enactment of these little dramas—the discreet hotel concierge, the well-timed postcard, the pre-emptive telephone message—and sometimes, equally blindly, they expose them without malicious intent: the evidence on the credit card statement, the delivery of a gift, the chance conversation with the taxi company. Flowers and their association with sexual infidelity could profitably be the subject of a graduate study.

Marcel Mauss, Claudia's mentor and Durkheim's faithful nephew, wrote about the significance of gifts in primitive societies. "Essai sur le don" demonstrates how the exchange of gifts helps form the social order. Claudia was particularly eager to understand the nature of cattle exchanges at all key moments in Masai life. Mauss makes the point that the exchange of goods was a moral transaction designed to maintain personal and social relationships, quite unlike the impersonal monetary system.

Owing to an oversight by Interflora, Victoria's flowers were delivered to her office a day late. Victoria was out of town and the receptionist called home to ask what she should do with the disturbingly large and exotic bunch of flowers. They were so lush that she felt uplifted in their presence, the way people respond to wealth. What she said was, "Hi. I've got the most amazing flowers here for Victoria, the lucky bunny. I'll send them round. Is anyone there to let them in?"

"Yes, me."

"They're on their way. Byee."

I had just come in the door from Gatwick, on an earlier plane from New York than I had intended because of a threat of traffic-control strikes. This is how the late flowers met the early traveler.

I arranged the flowers in a large vase of Provençal pottery, brightly colored, cheery, like the plates that restaurants have lately adopted to go along with the new, more earthy food. I put the flowers in this vase because it was a gift from me to Victoria when one of her essays on Stubbs was accepted by an art journal for a payment of seventy pounds, slightly less than the cost of the vase. That's the way it goes in art history: a private income is advised.

My luggage lay in the doorway, abandoned but also pointing significantly toward the door. The lilies—expensively hybridized to produce flowers of impertinent unreality—intermingled with the perfect pinnate leaves of eucalyptus (whose oils in my childhood formed part of a soothing rub placed on the chest to relieve congestion of the lungs). No koala had ever seen leaves more pristine: their gray-green appeared to have been waxed and polished before leaving the insect-free greenhouse where they had been raised for the sole purpose of dignifying the writhings and duplicities of lust. In these aromatic depths, a little note was buried. I opened it carefully. A computer had printed these words: "I hope you regret nothing. I don't. I have grown. Steve."

I sat looking at the television for some time. My luggage, a treacherous obstacle course, was unopened. A key turned in the lock. It sprang open with a loud, exuberant pop.

"Oh, hello, darling, you're early."

"Yes. I took an earlier plane because there was some talk of flights being canceled."

"What lovely flowers. Are they for me?"

"Looks like it."

She bent down to kiss me. She hadn't realized yet. She hadn't realized.

"They came with a note."

She read the note. Her hands trembled. Her face—I've never seen this before, only read about it—drained suddenly. Her eyelids seemed to flop open, so that I could see the reddish lining beneath the whites, as the whole intensely complicated arrangement of eyeball, socket, iris and so on was cruelly laid open, like a shellfish.

"Oh, my darling," she said, choking, "I'm so sorry."

"Do you regret nothing?"

"I'm so sorry."

"And you weren't going to tell me?"

"No. I wasn't."

"And you haven't got an explanation?"

"No. I was lonely. He was lonely. We were drunk. If it wasn't us, it would be nothing, just one of those silly things. It's awful. I'm sorry."

"Sorry you did it or sorry I found out?"

"Both. Did the bastard send the flowers here?"

"No. He sent them to the agency. They considerately forwarded them. Are you going to tell me who it was?"

"No. You don't know him. He was a friend of a friend from a long time ago who happened to be in town."

"As long as you've grown, that's the main thing."

In truth I felt sorry for her in her anguish but I was, all too predictably, stoking up my own distress. At the worst moments in one's life, at moments like this, there is a strong sense of rectitude, a knowledge that you are excused any selfish or irrational behavior. You can say what you damn well like. They owe you.

But she got in first: "I'll go now. I'll go now. You didn't deserve this. I love you, but it's better if I go. You may want me back or you may not. I wouldn't blame you. I'll just get some things."

She got up and went to the bedroom to gather her clothes. Inside my chest I was giving lodging to something that was swelling dangerously. For a moment I thought I was having a coronary. I began to cry. I sobbed like a child who has been wronged, but also—like a child—enjoying this righteous capitulation to self-pity.

"Don't cry, darling. Shall I stay?"

Her mulberry lips hovered over my—no doubt—crumpled face. They approached close to mine, more familiar to me than my own.

Then I said something that even now, some weeks later, makes my blood freeze.

"You can stay if you have an HIV test."

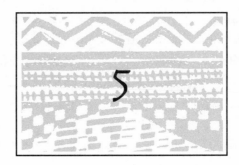

5

Claude Lévi-Strauss wrote that "myths think themselves in man, and without their knowledge." He also suggested that myths are not lesser forms of mental activity than science but the same mental activity simply restricted to the available local material. (In addition he once revealed that he received at least two requests a week from Africa for a pair of his famous jeans.) In the back of my Anglo-Saxon mind I also have a completely unworthy thought about Lévi-Strauss: *merde.* Nonetheless, as I walk with the laibon I ponder this idea.

If I understand Lévi-Strauss right, he means we are making a big mistake by classifying human mentality into primitive and advanced. I can testify that there is no profit in grading human sexual behavior in this way; it springs from an unplumbable well, a well of unspeakable and also sublime longings, which are, like the myths of which Lévi-Strauss is enamored, somehow a mirror of one's self. We are disturbed by the untrammeled self it reveals. All societies at all times have had rules about sexual behavior, and as I walk, it becomes clear why: sex is not subject to reason, and society is the product of reason.

Next to me, the whites of his eyes tinged saffron-yellow, walks the laibon. His hair is gray and he has a mustache. He is descended from the great laibon Mbatian, and there is attached to him an unmistakable potency. He wears a blue robe and carries a thin stick, a little leather container and a snuffbox. Behind us, some way back, is a warrior with a heavy spear, one of the laibon's sons. He is our protection.

If I understand the laibon right, we are going to seek a post that has been planted in a distant kraal to provide fertility for the cattle. He is to renew its potency by doctoring it in some way. For this service his payment is a goat; he has received payment in advance. The goat, troubled by presentiments of its fate, is tethered outside his hut, a small, plaintive creature with a Roman nose and tan markings.

Certainly the laibon gives no indication of embarking on a ridiculous or fraudulent mission. For him this is a routine operation. We walk along the dry watercourse, staying away from thickets for fear of buffalo, which are *umbogo* in Swahili (*umbogo* is a comical word; it sounds like the name of the faithful African tracker in a Hollywood adventure pic). Huge trees are alive with bee-eaters with iris-blue wings and chocolate-brown fronts. These colors, however, are iridescent, so that as the bee-eaters fly, suddenly swooping low—to catch bees—they seem to shimmer.

I am sweating. The laibon walks quite slowly but persistently. Let's say he was twenty in 1938. That makes him well into his seventies and possibly even nudging his eighties. His buttocks occasionally come free of his blue cloak completely. They are the buttocks of an old man, resting like a leather satchel on the top of his thighs. His thighs are old too, but they are stringy and effective. His face, however, has escaped the diminishment of age, in the way that successful actors often keep up a noble front while the rest of them is crumbling. He has a huge scar on his leg, which I already know is the result of a buffalo attack. He shows no curiosity at all about me, but accepts that I want to ask him questions. Unfortunately, I cannot ask him the important questions because my Swahili is not adequate. His Swahili isn't much good either. We talk mostly about cattle and children. When I speak about Claudia, he says that he remembers her well, although she went away suddenly and never came back. He asks me the name of the white man who organized the ill-fated lion hunt with Claudia. Leavitt. He spits. *Mzee Leavitt.*

Like Claudia, I am running a tape recorder. My contribution is going to sound like an obscene phone call, because I am panting as I try to keep up. He stops talking and I turn the machine off as he marches relentlessly onward.

Just as we near the escarpment, where I believe Claudia had a small house, we see a herd of buffalo, which run into a thicket when the warrior shouts at them. It is a disdainful noise, high-pitched and whistling. They move in a rolling, awkward way, like weight lifters out jogging. A rumbling sound, a sound familiar from Westerns as cattle are rustled, reaches us as they get up speed. The ground is littered with bones; I stop to look at the vertebrae of a giraffe, which lie there like a punctuation mark on the dry stubble of the savannah. Nothing else is left of the giraffe except a shaving brush of hairs from its tail. As I look up from the giraffe remnants, I see three giraffe in the middle distance, gazing mildly at us, possibly reproachful. I have a small bottle of mineral water, from which I take a swig before offering it to the laibon. He drains it without offering it to his son, but bids the boy keep the plastic container. A fiction is maintained that warriors neither eat nor drink. He points at my tape recorder and tells me to turn it on. Now he is speaking Maa. I have little idea of what he is saying except that he mentions Claudia frequently. For an hour I watch his face carefully. He speaks without much emphasis. Sometimes I gather that he is talking about Masai history. In any event I become very familiar with the topography of his face. Like many Masai's, his lips are sharply outlined, so that they appear pasted on. His teeth bring to mind the seeds given to caged birds, discolored and irregular. His eyes, very wide from corner to corner, are hooded and his nose is small, almost pert. His skin is lightly abraded like the skin of an orange. His ears are stretched at least four inches; large, circular lower sections hang loose and are decorated with blue and yellow beads. Higher up there are two smaller holes, through which more beads are threaded.

During our conversation—during the laibon's monologue—our escort sits silent on a rock, half turned away from us. At times he picks his teeth with a whittled twig. He says to me in English, "toothbrush tree," but otherwise he simply listens to his father. Of course the laibon may not be his natural father, because Masai sexual relations are complex and, up to a point, tolerant.

I have to stop the laibon when the tape runs out.

We set off again on our journey. We have already been walking for three hours. Behind me, diagonally across the valley, I can see the Mountain of God, its summit now clear of the attendant tugboat clouds and its flanks pale in the bright sun. Eventually we arrive at our destination, a small village high in the mountains. The huts appear to be abandoned. It is a mystery why a tall people like the Masai should live in such low huts, in which it is impossible to stand. But a very small child emerges, dressed in a brown shuka. She steps forward and stops for the Masai greeting, an outstretched hand placed for a moment on her bowed head by the three of us in turn. From a hut now comes a young woman, followed by a warrior. She stands in front of the laibon, who asks her some questions. The warrior picks up his spear, which is planted outside the hut. There is an unmistakable air of apprehension. Later I learn that this girl is the wife of the man who has paid the laibon to doctor his post. He is away at a temporary manyatta where the grazing is better. Suddenly the laibon smiles. He speaks to the warrior and the tension is dispelled. In Swahili he says to me, "She wants a baby. Her husband cannot give her."

He sends the girl to fetch the post. I am expecting some sort of artifact, but it is simply a squat, round piece of wood. From his container, which looks like a dice shaker, the laibon takes some powder. He spits on it in his hand and rubs the mess, an ochre-brown color, onto the post carefully, like a doctor applying an ointment. He allows the girl to carry it back to the center of the boma, the inner sanctum where the cattle sleep, and with a rock he fixes it into the ground. Nobody seems very excited by this magic.

A little way from the village is a stream, dribbling down some striated rocks in a thin trickle. You don't have to know a thing about geology to see that these huge rocks must have been shot up out of the center of the earth like footballs and then come rolling down from above. We rest under the shade of some enormous fig trees for a while, hectored by baboons from a safe distance. The girl, the errant wife, is wearing a huge necklace of beads. She goes off toward some rocks for a wash.

As I catch a glimpse of her washing herself between the legs her large eyes turn slyly toward me for a moment. The scene is powerfully erotic. It reminds me of one of those Victorian paintings of harems or dancing girls, whose ostensible purpose— paper thin—is ethnographic. When I look at her warrior lover gently fondling his spear, I wonder how he sees her. Does he see an impossible triangle, or does he see a one-night stand?

6

"Why are you going? That's all I want to know. Just tell me straight."

"Firstly, as you know, nobody ever tells their nearest and dearest anything absolutely straight. It doesn't work like that. The whole idea of being absolutely honest is more difficult with someone you love. It's probably quite easy to be absolutely straight with a stranger. Secondly, the question implies I have some other motive."

"Which you do."

"I don't. Honestly."

"Are you sick of me?"

"No. I'm not sick of you and I have forgiven you, although I am sure you don't need my benediction anyway."

"Do you mean absolution? I don't want to be corny but aren't you running away?"

"Why is it that everybody thinks that if you leave town you're copping out? I'm not running, I'm just taking time off. I want to go."

" 'I want to go.' You sound as if you think somehow you are going to find yourself or your peace of mind or something else."

"That would be a bonus."

"So your peace of mind has gone?"

"My peace of mind, like most people's, is very fluid. It comes and goes."

"And at the moment, it's in retreat?"

"Yes, it's in retreat. But I am sure it will come back."

"Out in the sun with the immemorial rhythms of nature and so on?"

"With dusk falling and a strange peace coming over the parched landscape."

"Are you having a midlife crisis?"

"If I am, it's a little early."

"I don't know. If you double your age, you would be very likely to be dead. Unless medical science makes a giant leap in the next few decades."

"Thanks. Have you thought about taking up counseling, which is very fashionable, almost the only growth industry in Western society, when you've had enough of advertising? You would be good at it."

"Would you like some more wine?"

"Another problem I have is I'm frightened of drink. It makes me feel bad. But, yes. Thank you."

"And then a fuck? Or are you afraid of that, too?"

"I'll manage. Why are you cross-examining me? Is it because you really want to know why I am going, or is it something more basic?"

"No. Just that."

"I want to get away because I want to do this film. That's it. I don't want to get away from you or from London."

"Or make some sort of point?"

"Or make some sort of point. I just want to try to write this script, if I can."

———

32

"Or is it that you just don't want to get married?"

"No. That's nothing to do with it. When you say, Don't you want to get married?, what you are really saying is that if I loved you I would want to marry you. As a matter of fact, that does not follow. It may even be the reverse of the truth."

"The reverse of the truth. Is that different from the opposite of the truth?"

"If we have a fuck, will you promise now not to answer any questions I may ask?"

"Don't ask them. That would be the simple answer."

"I'll try."

"And now you're getting a hard-on. Is this the only way our sex life can go?"

"Jesus, I hope not. Let me kiss you just here. I wonder why I always want to do that one first? It must be like running around a running track counterclockwise. It corresponds to some natural order."

"I wish you wouldn't talk with your mouth full."

"The old jokes are the best."

"Now the other one. It's feeling neglected."

"Just pull your skirt up."

"Do you want to get undressed?"

"No, for some reason I want to do it without getting my clothes off."

"Uh-oh."

"It's not for that reason."

"What do you think of my new panties?"

"I like black. Some people like white. Wimps. God knows why. Oh, look my finger can go right in here, just slides in under the elastic like—"

"Like Peter Rabbit under a fence."

"Yes. Or—"

"Don't say it. Turn round. Let me put it in my mouth. How's that?"

"I love looking at you as you do it. Your cheeks are sort of concave, the reverse of a hamster. Did you . . . ? Don't stop, just nod . . . How would you like someone to fuck you from behind while you're doing that? Like this."

"You . . . said . . . you wouldn't."

"I can't stop."

"Do you love me? Or am I just a sack artist as you said back whenever it was?"

"I love you. Turn over. I've got to put it in now. Lift up. I want to rip them off."

"Go on. Wait a minute. Oh, yes. Here we go. Fuck me. Fuck me."

"Is this how you did it?"

"Not now."

"Is it?"

"I'm not answering."

"Say it. I want you to."

"You don't. Don't spoil it. Please don't."

"You're thinking about him. Say it. Now. Now. While I'm doing it. Say it."

"Fuck me, Steve. Stick it in. Ram it in. Go on. Oh, God, oh, Jesus, oh, Christ. Pull it out and come on my face. Oh, yes. Oh, Steve. Oh, fuck."

"I'm coming. Put it in your mouth. Quick, swallow it. All of it. In your mouth. Gobble it up. Oh, Jesus."

"Oh, Tim. Tim. I love you. I love you. Don't go, please, stay and marry me."

"I'm sorry."

"Don't be sorry. Kiss me. Kiss me, baby. Please don't go."

"I've got to go."

"You want to go. There's no got to."

"I want to go. But I don't want you to think I'm going because of what happened."

34

"But that is the reason, really, isn't it? You know I regret it bitterly. I'm not going to try and excuse it. It was even quite good fun, it's just that it wasn't important until it came out."

"And the others."

"There are no others. You know that. If you tell me why you're going, I'll understand."

"Now you're doing what I was a few minutes ago. You're trying to pick at a wound. But there's no wound in your case."

"There will be. Believe me. It's an excuse."

"I have been dreaming about the Masai. I've got to go."

"What are they saying to you in your dreams? Get away from that dreadful bitch and come and walk the savannah with us? Come and drink some blood?"

"That's the sort of thing. Don't laugh. It's about the notion of the meaning of life."

"The meaning of life?"

"I thought you would sneer."

"I'm not sneering. I'm stunned."

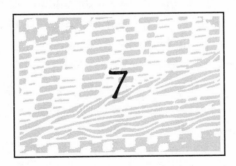

Just outside my room, next to a compound that sells retreads, they are holding a young ox. It has extravagantly curved horns, to which a tether made of strips of hide is attached. We used to call this a *riempie* when I was a boy. I haven't heard the word for thirty years, yet it takes possession of my tongue the moment I see the bullock. Riempie. One of the two men holding the bullock suddenly plunges a long knife into its throat. It starts and then subsides, hardly believing what's happening. The blood gushes out and is caught in an enamel basin by a young boy. As the basin fills, so the ox's legs begin to fail as though there is displacement taking place, the blood from the animal's legs rushing directly into the basin. The bullock sinks to the ground. Dark, aortal blood now streams onto the frankfurter-colored earth. The ox twitches and its legs, far from folding up deflated, straighten and flex and straighten again finally, like someone pulling on his pajamas.

The two men now start to skin the animal. They make a long slit from under its dewlap all the way down to the empty purse where its testicles were once housed. The knife leaves behind a white path. The fat—it must be fat—is white-white, a sort of cuisine white, the color of Normandy butter or the skin of a perfect garlic. Suddenly the ox bellows. It is a hoarse, short, stabbing noise. Even the man slicing open the belly gets a fright. He laughs. The boy has spilt a lot of the blood. The second man cuffs him about the ear, but gently so that he doesn't spill any more. The noise is the bullock's swan song.

The men now cut open the belly. Something like a seal flops out. With a quick slice they release the contents of the intestine, puréed spinach, and pull the rear of the animal clear of the mess using its tail as a handhold.

Now they start to work the skin loose with shorter knives, cutting and pulling. Soon they have the whole belly exposed. They cut up behind the front legs and relentlessly onward. The skin is peeled back so that it lies on the ground around the great white carcass like a surplice. The legs of the carcass, however, begin to show through in patches of red. Butchering the animal is a very physical job, demanding a lot of hacking with machetes and axes. The meat, cut into lumps and chunks, is placed in buckets. Across the river, fires are beginning to show in the compounds outside the shambas and the small, square houses built of mud or breeze blocks. The sun has dropped behind the mountain. From that way comes hymn singing and African pop, swimming languidly in the scented air, doing a lazy breaststroke down from the mountain toward the freestyle sounds of the town. The butchering still has some way to go, among the maize cobs and old tin cans and bits of plastic bags, which are no longer serviceable, even by the poorest.

I wonder about the destiny of the head and the horns, the only part of the animal that is intact.

There is a knock at my door. I turn from the tiny, completely useless balcony. (Architects fall *en bloc* for the same affectations year by year, decade by decade. What strange freemasonry binds them?)

"Come in."

It is one of the waiters, Edson.

"There is some person downstairs who wants to see you."

He says "parson," and for a moment I am confused because only this morning I have seen a young English priest buying something from Kilimanjaro Hardware across the street. He was wearing a gray shirt and dog collar above his shorts and sandals. The sandals were probably made for tougher feet than his; he was also wearing brown nylon socks. It struck me that he must be unaware of the important distinction between the sacred and profane in the savage mind.

My transcripts were ready. The translator and typist is called Gladys. She is a Masai from the west who works as a secretary for a German aid program. It has taken her two days to transcribe my tapes.

"Would you like a drink, Gladys?"

Within her well-fed body is the skeleton of a Masai. We drink beer in a room just off the fragrant dining room that is known as the Sundowner Bar. It has no windows and is paneled in a dark, oppressive wood. The effect is of sitting in a poorly carpentered packing case. The tables on which the waiter places the drinks are extraordinarily low, just shin height, so that as Gladys hands me the typescript and I reach forward for it, we are almost prone.

"Are they interesting?"

"Beg yours?"

"The tapes. What the laibon said."

"She's very superstitious."

This confusing of the genders, I can see, does not bode well for my transcripts. Perhaps she is thinking in German; her boss is a hydrologist from Hamburg.

"Did you find them interesting, what he was saying?"

"Not so very much. These people"—she gestures vaguely toward the savannah—"they don't go too much to school."

I've had this before: Africans who have forsaken the bush for the metropolitan life are reluctant to admit that anything out there could be of any value. Here in town, right here in this hotel, were solid things, things with some heft, that seemed to a lapsed nomad to belong to a universe different from the world of grass, hide, mud and blood. Out there everything lacked mass. A thunderstorm could wash a village away, dissolving the cow dung worked and squeezed into the framework of saplings from which the huts were made. Out there the cattle and the goats ruled; they were tyrants that demanded constant attention and, according to the seasons, migration. Families and villages moved at the whim of their cattle. Green grass—grass, for God's sake—was more important in the life of the pastoralist than religion. (It had acquired a symbolic value. A Masai pleading for mercy cries, "Green grass, green grass.") Yet what was grass if it wasn't unreliable?

Put simply, why walk ten miles for water when you can stroll into the Sundowner Bar and order (if there hasn't been a power cut) an ice-cold Simba lager?

This is what Gladys is implying. I have been dreaming about the Masai, and in my dreams they have retained something we have lost. Now I am sitting with a chubby Masai woman in a floral dress who is very keen to have another beer, and deny all knowledge of a previous life.

"Two Simbas, Edson."

"Coming up, sir."

As Edson goes through the doors into the kitchen area, I see a man entering from another direction with an enamel bucket of meat.

Victoria has her back turned to me. We are lying awake, both pretending to be asleep because we do not want to talk any more. It is almost four in the morning. I am thinking that if this goes on much longer I am going to get to the airport wrung out. I feel I need to keep all my senses fit and alert for the plane journey. Opera singers, tennis players and athletes suffer from this sort of preoccupation. Yet I am not in training for anything specific.

I can't see her very well, except of course, for the familiar outline curled up under the sheet. In truth, anybody could be under there. She breathes with a slight heaviness when she is asleep, an endearing and insouciant little snort escaping from time to time. Now she is breathing evenly.

My prick feels sore and chafed. I want to get out of bed and go and sleep somewhere else, somewhere fresh and breezy. I don't want to sleep either facing or turned away from Victoria's back. Her back, which may or may not have been presented to Steve as he mounted her. I lie here asking myself which is worse, that he mounted her from behind, with all the dispassion and contempt that implies in a one-night stand, or whether he was directly on top of her, roughing up her breasts a little as she likes, sticking his tongue in her mouth, as close in the exchange of intimacies as it is possible to get. I have asked her, breathless with the desire to know, stifled with the fear of finding out. Her reply is that details don't matter. I reply that the details are everything and that once I have had them all, I will get them out of my system. I want to know if he came on her face, if she cried out, if he fucked her violently, or—worse—if he fucked her with an insidious and ingratiating skill. She asks why I think it was such a one-sided business, why I assume she was entirely passive. She has already told me she wanted to do it, she wasn't that drunk, it was nothing important, she wishes she hadn't done it, not just because I found out, but because she regretted it immediately and burst into tears in his—his—hotel room. She only did it because she was feeling lonely. Can I understand that? But really what I most want to know is whether she was playing with his cock in the taxi on the way to the hotel or whether she was demure the whole way there. What I want is impossible. I want her to explain something completely irrational and inexplicable. What? You know what I mean. So it might happen again? Just theoretically? Theoretically it might, but then you might have an affair; you have probably had lots. What about that girl who used to come and do your accounts? Don't be ridiculous. (She is closer to the mark than she imagines. But my peccadilloes have a purely rhetorical role in this conversation, something I resent bitterly.) For two nights we have been discussing her one-night stand when I was in New York negotiating a sabbatical from *Manhattan* magazine. They did not promise to keep my job open. The pain these late-night wrangles cause me is mitigated by the intensity of our lovemaking, but it is a short-term trade. I am also thinking how sad it is that the sexual passion of our first few months together can be rekindled in this fashion.

Now it's four in the morning and I am exhausted and I have to catch a plane tomorrow, for which I feel I must be in tip-top condition. And quite soon she is going to ask me why I don't want to marry her. I can feel her back gathering indignation.

"You will never trust me again, I suppose," she says, still turned away from me, skillfully paraphrasing the question I thought she would ask.

"Things look very different out on the savannah."

"I bet they do."

We are like lovers in a French film: we have expressive backs.

"You know what?" she says. "In my heart of hearts I think you are just using this incident."

Her back appears to be oscillating and trembling. My black heart squeezes itself involuntarily, like a palsied hand.

9

The beef curry makes a change from the heavily muscled chicken. Mr. Shah has also put rump steak and French fries, monkey-gland steak and beefburgers on the menu. The French fries seem to have become contaminated by the invasive turmeric; they are yellow, like very small bananas. The restaurant is full, the overflow from an aid summit, held in the new but already weary hotel up the road. Two German children are having an argument in Swahili. The restaurant, despite its natural gloom, is loud and cheerful this evening. Mr. Shah walks among the tables benevolently; he wants to see more of this sort of thing—open, modern, fun, a mood induced by beef and by French fries and by ketchup. He is wearing gray leather shoes in a basketweave pattern and a very cheap wristwatch. There is a tendency, which he recognizes, to complacency in catering.

These aid people hold their knives and forks in a variety of ways. The Americans prefer to stab the food from above and then, having rendered it helpless, lay down the knife and take up the fork in the same hand. The British hold their knives and forks like pencils, with the diffidence of young children learning to write. The Scandinavians prod and scratch with knife and fork simultaneously, as though expecting to find something unhygienic hidden within. A French couple are not talking. They are suffering from a malaise, possibly marital, so that each watches the other eating with pain, every movement of a glass or a knife scrutinized, every ingestion critically appraised.

Gladys's transcripts are lying on the bed in my room. The print on the page is crisp and clean, beautifully spaced, the golf ball, or whatever it is the German hydrologists use, striking the page a good whack, producing a contemporary form of hieroglyphics, all presentation and no content. The laibon's words, delivered to my little tape recorder under hawk-slashed skies, have been rendered into English, but the English is nonsense, alphabetti spaghetti. The only clues I have as to what he is talking about are the frequent mentions of Claudia, which Gladys has transcribed confidently as Khlodya, and a certain person—or perhaps a place—called Fahfakhs. There are also mentions of Tepilit, the laibon's deceased brother.

Perhaps the laibon was talking in riddles, in some way not susceptible to translation or taboo to women. Gladys, I speculate as I sprinkle desiccated coconut on a second portion of curry, urged on me by Mr. Shah, may have found it embarrassing and deliberately sabotaged the translation. I have sent my tape to the university in Nairobi for another translation. I am not disappointed at the delay. I am slowing down anyway, conscious that time, which in our parts of the world is considered in some way pressing, is here no taskmaster. But I have also come to see that time in our world is not so much pressing as beckoning, touting for business: *Get some in while stocks last.* It is the anxiety of death. The laibon, out there, is telling me about something that happened fifty years ago and more. It can wait.

I am finding my mood exhilarating. My problems with Victoria are taking on the appearance of someone else's problems and so have become banal. I am no longer in the position of the aggrieved. I am my own confidant, listening to my problems with feigned sympathy while saying to myself How predictable this all is, how often I have heard this kind of thing, he'll get over it.

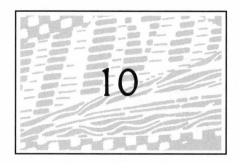

The young parson comes to visit me. He has heard that I am proposing a film about the Masai and the French anthropologist. What a great idea. I suspect that, like most people in our era who assume a personal relationship with television, he has a project of his own. If it's not too much trouble he would like a little natter. He looks less like a priest than a graduate student. His hair is thinning and very short, and today he is wearing a polo shirt with some trekking shorts. His legs and quarters are quite sturdy, so that he tapers gently outward from narrow, bony shoulders.

I offer to buy him dinner and we cross the road to the Outspan Hotel, which he recommends, as I am paying. As we cross the road I notice that we are not exactly besieged by parishioners. Still, it's early to make judgments. We sit in the courtyard under a tree, from which lizards and insects are liable to make unannounced descents, falling quite heavily onto the table. This tree is said to be the very tree where the German explorer Adolf Siedentopf first encountered the Masai back in 1875. It was not a happy meeting: Siedentopf had to flee back to the coast, harried most of the way, to return with some heavy armor and a lot more copper wire. The young parson—Darren Wiggins— is a student of local history. In an aviary nearby are some dispirited birds which, Wiggins tells me, are the rump of a collection started by the last British DC, Ronald Beaton MBE, the same man who opened Shah Buildings, a great sportsman and—is Wiggins envious?—a legend among the Masai. The collection was comprehensive, including a representative of every single species of bird in the area. Beaton, in the breaks from administering justice, produced *Beaton's Birds of Masailand,* now a collector's item. The few incarcerated birds that have survived the neglect of the hotel owners and the almost complete indifference of the locals look very similar to the birds on the outside— ring-necked turtle doves, superb starlings and cattle egrets. Still, I have seen a small zoo in Africa that has four or five baboons in a tiny cage in a place plagued by wild baboons.

Wiggins is ordering. He recommends the lake perch, but I know how far away Lake Victoria is and how slow the roads are, and opt instead for chicken, the stringy variety, which is always served, shriveled and brown as a walnut, on a paper napkin in a small, locally woven wicker basket. Wiggins now orders some wine: "I hope you don't mind?"

"No, no, go ahead. Red will be fine."

"What is your film going to be about? Not another one about the lords of the savannah and all that stuff, I hope?"

"Are you an Anglican?" I ask.

"I am. It's a burden that we were once the established religion. The locals expect a bit more of me than I can deliver. You're a journalist, aren't you? You do that Letter from London for *Manhattan?*"

"You're well informed."

"Tim Curtiz, Letter from London."

"I've taken a sabbatical."

"I've been out here for three years and I now can't believe I have been to London, although I was brought up in Hitchin, almost in the suburbs. It's bizarre."

Before he can put his alternative Masai film treatment to me, I ask him to give me a rundown on the religious activity of the town. He is against the fundamental Christians who have set up shop on the slopes of the mountain. They are creating an economic dependence, which is dangerous because of the flakiness of their religious beliefs and their eagerness for converts. They pay for converts. The Lutherans and the Catholics, a legacy of German rule, are okay, if a little stodgy. Unlike the Anglicans, they set a lot of store by liturgy, which to him is fine in context but pretty silly in a place that has plenty of perfectly good rituals of its own.

"The trouble is, what they really want is a nice old-fashioned vicar in a suit. They are really buying into England. They all think I can get them into college in Durham, or get them a job in London. They get quite pissed off when I tell them they wouldn't like London. The truth is, my conscience wouldn't permit me to send them off there to be humiliated."

He has a good appetite. He finishes my French fries and orders some more bread.

"What do you know about Claudia Cohn-Casson?"

He takes a while to reply. His mouth is full. He has trouble eating, as if he finds it painful. As I watch him I wonder if various eras produce their prototypes, free of genetic influences. Of course, this Lysenkoism is impossible, but if our age has a type, this is it: a sort of peri-urban man, whose values and opinions are previously owned, received entirely from the seminar and the television set and the newspaper. A determinist, if there are any left, would probably say that this is a class brought up in the eddies and backwaters rather than the turbulence of history.

"Claudia Cohn-Casson was an interesting woman," he replies. "Very advanced for her day. Very advanced."

"What do you mean?"

"Sexually. Not that we in the Church are supposed to know about such things, of course."

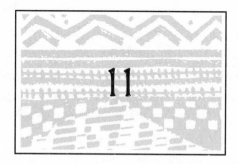

I now have a small camp of my own, a "fly camp," which I can set up with great difficulty. I have hired an old Land Cruiser from a safari firm that is facing ruin, thanks to the growing fear of travel. This fear springs from the realization that the natives are no longer as amenable as they were. They are liable to do anything for religious or monetary reasons, or just for kicks. I note these expenses carefully. My pre-production budget is seventy-five thousand dollars, which is to cover the cost of the first draft of the script as well as all the research. Film producers have faith in this process because it suggests a cooperative venture. It gives them the opportunity to take part in the inner workings of writers, a form of mumbo jumbo designed only to confuse.

S. O. Letterman, my producer, certainly believes that his ideas will blow away any mystique that may be attached to the writing process. I am the draftsman, but he is the I. M. Pei of this project. My contract is for the technical stuff, the actual research and getting the script down on paper—in his mind, the easy stuff. Writers are a dime a dozen. Of course, he has never said anything quite as crude as this. He's a plausible, overweening chap, with a personality that hovers on the edge of the ridiculous, but that he has trained himself to apply in a very effective way to the business of making films. In restaurants he makes special demands on the waiters—rare vinegars, fat-free cheese, please, may I see the bottle before I choose the Pauillac, no monosodium glutamate in the soy sauce, high roast arabica only, finger bowl with the *quaglie al spiedino,* it's the only way to eat them, *certo, signore,* a kir made with framboise and lots of ice, et cetera, et cetera. No meal goes by without some demand that demonstrates his singularity. Yet waiters seem to take up the challenge, because he displays a certain familiarity with the ways of the world, which writers, by and large, lack. Writers spend too much time thinking about the ambivalences. In the course of our discussions and negotiations, we dined or breakfasted about thirty times. We had breakfast at the Connaught, dinner at Lasserre, lunch at the Savoy, two breakfasts at L'Hôtel, lunch at the Plaza and many outings to restaurants (on both sides of the Atlantic) where fish were blackened or vegetables grilled or polenta fried in accordance with some diktat that had come to his notice in the mysterious way these things happen.

I had written an article on the Nazi round-up—*la grande rafle*—of Jews in Paris at Drancy, and that is how I had come to his notice. By a strange coincidence, he had just been thinking about a movie based on the French Jews when he read my piece. He called and the voguish feasting commenced.

12

It's no news that memory is deceitful. I have tried to explain that in Claudia's case memory is particularly treacherous, but Letterman likes the idea of ambiguity. He sees it as European, a kind of intellectual chic, useful to our story.

He has come a long way since he worked as a production runner with James Wong Howe and Martin Ritt in a coal-mining village in Pennsylvania. I suspect his own memory is a little unreliable; in his telling he was Martin Ritt's right-hand man and Sean Connery's golfing partner after just one week. He is self-deprecating but all his anecdotes feature his achievements. Whatever the ostensible subject matter, Letterman—as clapper loader, assistant director, coauthor, executive producer—emerges from the narrative undergrowth muddied, festooned in foliage, sometimes even bloodied, but always victorious.

Muthaiga Club, where I am staying, releases forgotten gusts of memory, like those lilies that exhale their sweet perfume only at night. My father was happiest in places like this. He loved clubs and wardrooms with the predinner drinks, the discreet signing of chits, the smiling elderly waiters (from a class almost extinct now, men who lived to serve other men). I remember arriving in my father's Pontiac at clubs just like this, sweeping (not always silently; the car was old) down to the front door to be deposited and greeted, to be called "sir" by elderly black men. I remember running on the rolling lawns of Kikuyu grass before dinner, the night noises of the exceptionally vocal African insect life striking up as it quickly grew dark, night unrolling from the ground upward; bullfrogs—in fact all manner of Rana and Bufo—frogs the size of a pair of rolled-up rugby socks, toads with great horned eyebrows, and tiny, reddish, darting amphibians, starting to howl, shriek, growl and purr, a backdrop to our dinner on the terrace, to which we have been summoned by the stirring, thrilling beating of a gong hung from a pair of tusks. We sit straight, elbows tucked in, endless soup spoons, fish knives and butter knives to deal with. "A gentleman is a man who uses the butter knife even when his wife is not at home," said my father, only two-thirds joking. The dinner itself, a ritual of many courses, begins to emerge in relays from the swing doors of the kitchen, the food bland and unexceptionable, but plentiful and somehow sanctified by being served by the immaculate waiters in sashes and gloves.

So Muthaiga Club is instantly familiar. My room looks out over a croquet lawn, at the end of which is a pond thickly planted with papyrus—the plant always mentioned by schoolteachers in any history of written language—in which, I know with certainty, all hell will break loose as dusk falls. High on the wall of my room, near the open window, waiting for the lights to come on, a gecko is clinging hopefully to the knobbly plaster. Unlike other members of the reptile family, the gecko is a benign creature, cheery, opportunistic and patently useful.

I am troubled by the thought that this familiar world, into which I am able to slip without a moment's readjustment, is a vanishing world. The club is now written up in style magazines;

models are photographed with the headwaiter. (Models are often photographed surrounded by nearly naked Masai warriors.) The world of fashion and advertising (from which Victoria has not quite made her escape—she is like someone with one boot stuck deep in the mud, unable to move either way) now uses places like that as themes for new looks or as inspiration for "lifestyles." S. O. Letterman has something similar in mind, a re-creation of colonial Africa, as seen from Santa Monica Boulevard. Right here, in Muthaiga, colonial Africa lives on. But does it live self-consciously or blithely, as it did when I was a child?

I am as aware as anyone of the changes going on in the world. I earn my living by observing them and commenting on them. But coming here has made me realize how much time has passed since, as a small boy, I used to set off with my father for dinners and functions. I have probably not heard or read the phrase "bee-tle drive" in my adult life, yet on the notice board of the club, just under the list of aspirant members duly proposed and sec-onded and posted, is the announcement of a beetle drive, a kind of homespun bingo, in aid of the library fund. The notice is signed by Sir Thomas Fairfax, Hon. Secretary, Library Commit-tee. I remember the frenzy of a beetle drive, the wings, the lit-tle legs, the stubby pencils, the cries of "beetle," the powdering of the noses, the soda siphons fizzing.

Proust (who was a near neighbor and acquaintance of Léon Cohn-Casson) thought that memory could unlock the imagina-tion. He was always searching, rummaging: *Les vrais paradis sont les paradis qu'on a perdus.* I fear it can throttle imagination. The memories summoned here in Africa seem to me like tendrils of vines attaching themselves to me. They have in them presages of mortality; I have a feeling that there is now more of my past life than of my future. And I am aware of my past life; I feel it loom-ing up behind me, breathing lightly on the nape of my neck. Nineteen fifty-eight, small boy arrives in Pontiac at club. Ser-vants bow and scrape. Khaki shorts replaced by abrasive long trousers for the evening. My father, exuding his insubstantial charm, his hand-me-down cosmopolitanism, signs us in.

"Good evening, Shadrach."

"Good evening, sir."

"This is my son."

"Nice boy, sir. Big boy now. Before, small."

Shadrach—can he be this pleased to see me?—smiles as he cups his hands to indicate the tiny creature I was previously.

"Too big now," he says.

Muthaiga has the same system. The privileged sign in at a large book attached by a thin chain to a sort of lectern. The headwaiter already has my name memorized.

I take a stroll in the sonorous gardens. There is a sudden flurry outside the main entrance, a Gothic porch. The evening is closing, a mist rising in the hollows of the golf course. The waiters are folding napkins, the insects are tuning up vigorously, the first croaks and ululations rise from the pond, the damp earth breathes out aromatically, the exotic flowers pump out their night perfumes, the sky in the distance over the knuckles of Ngong, the direction of Masailand, flails with electricity. (It seems more like buckets of thin paint dropped from the sky than lightning.) In the Delamere rooms a pianist is playing "Young Love" and from the kitchen comes a waft of roasting meat. The flurry is caused by the arrival of an old car, of a type that retains a kind of dignity as it ages. Lady De Marr arrives every evening, God willing, in this old banger. I watch her arrival. She knew Claudia very well; they used to go to parties together dressed as boys. Now Lady De Marr staggers through the front door, saluted by the guard, the *askari,* disdaining the proffered help of the majordomo, who wears a fez and a sash. Another man drives her car away to park it. He does this gravely, perhaps fearing—with some justification, from what I can see—that the whole thing might collapse like a car in a Laurel and Hardy movie, falling absolutely flat onto the ground in its component parts. I hear her voice complaining of the bad manners of the police at a roadblock. It is a voice unaffected by the changes in articulation that have taken place since the 1930s. She pronounces the word "damn" with a little gurgle of amusement: "Dem cheek. Bloody roadblock outside the club. Silly arses. Somebody should tell them to bugger orff and catch some criminals."

Nobody can reproduce this intonation. Actors and actresses produce a version of Noël Coward when they try. I move after an interval toward the entrance. The frogs are already deafening.

Claudia Cohn-Casson often had dinner here when she was in Nairobi. She sometimes had dinner with Sir Thomas Fairfax, who tonight is having dinner with Lady De Marr. I wish to observe this, because I find the prospect of two octogenarians having dinner in the middle of Africa moving. The intensely familiar surroundings, the froggy air, the starched linen earnestly folded, even the little fake candleholders on the wall with their chintz shades, shunt my real life, my sexual wrangles with Victoria, my work, to one side. This uninvited, almost uncontrollable welling of memory is like finding a hard splinter in the soft, flabby flesh of my real life. But also I am suffering a pleasurable and painful feeling, a feeling so often made banal by film, of time reprieved and relived. Here I am, for Chrissakes, about to dine alongside two people who knew Claudia Cohn-Casson, in surroundings she knew well, in an ambience that I know all too well, although I have only just arrived. After dinner, like some cultural tourist, I will introduce myself to these envoys from the past.

A gong booms. The sound makes small silverfish run down the back of my neck. I am, as my father used to say, going to have the works. I start with a consommé Lady Curzon. Even in the soup, the old order is commemorated.

13

"Ningependa brandi kwanza. Rémy Martin. Do you like brandy?" asks Fairfax.

"I do. Very much."

"Tatu. Rémy, Jephson, not Kenya brandy, kufahanu?"

I can't stand brandy. Here it is drunk with soda before dinner and straight after. Fairfax and Lady De Marr have already had a few by the time I join them.

"Germans shit on a little ledge and look at it for hours before flushing," says Lady De Marr.

"Off on her favorite subject," says Fairfax.

I wonder which part of the sentence he is referring to.

"Absolutely obsessed with poo-poos. Strange buggers, really. What are you, a journalist?" she asks.

"Yes. I write for an American magazine. Now I'm writing a script for a Hollywood producer."

"We were both in that ghastly film *Out of Africa*, weren't we?"

"I thought you liked it," said Fairfax.

"Absolute tripe. They wheeled us on in the background like a couple of fossils. The whole thing was nonsense from start to finish. Denys and Tania would have been turning in their graves."

"You both knew Claude Cohn-Casson well, didn't you?"

Fairfax glances at me. With his small mustache, each hair separated but thick and glossy, he looks like a shrewd seal, like Walter Cronkite. The brandy arrives, tumblers half full. Lady De Marr, Camilla, lifts her glass and holds it, abstracted for a moment. Despite the spoor left on her face by the climate and her age, it is essentially the face of an Englishwoman from the counties. I feel I could pull off the cruelly applied latex prosthesis and find there one of those untroubled faces from the frontispiece of *Country Life* or *Tatler*. These women loved horses, dogs, the countryside and unsuitable men.

"On safari Count von Gottberg wanted us to install a shelf in the long drop."

"That's enough about poo, for God's sake, Camilla," says Fairfax cheerfully. "Camilla believes that you can tell a great deal about a nation by its lavatory habits."

He holds his nose and gives an imaginary lavatory chain two tugs. He has a good amount of strong, gray hair. (There is no doubt that a good head of hair gives a man a wholly unjustified appearance of moral authority, witness certain Supreme Court judges and senators.) His face, however, is discolored on the right side, faintly purple.

"Stroke," he says, catching me looking. "Oxford blue."

"The French are always washing their fannies. We even had a portable bidet for Maurice Chevalier's safari. Down the hatch," she says, swallowing deeply, "happy days."

"Bottoms up. To our dear president, the richest man in Africa. Jephson, nilete brandi."

The brandy is racing around my body, looking for signs of weakness. It has hardly passed my lips when I find it prospecting the inside of my head.

"Claudia, Claude was her real name, of course, but we couldn't be doing with that, was an anthropologist, although she called herself an ethnographer, I remember," says Fairfax.

"What was she like?" I ask lamely.

"What was she like? Jewish, for a start. She looked quite Jewish, didn't she, Camilla?"

"Who, sweetie?"

"Claudia."

"Very Jewish. But exotic. Levantine. Lovely gel. I say 'gel' but she was a year older than me at least. Fucked like a snake, you know."

"Camilla, for God's sake, belt up."

"I know it's hard to believe when you see us now, but we were all at it. Chronic. Even Tom."

"Ethnographer," he says, like a man reading a wine label. "I've never read a word she wrote, you know. Not a dicky bird. She left here in 'forty-three, or was it 'forty-four? Anyway, I was in the army and that was it. I wanted to read her thesis."

"I've read it," I said.

"Is it translated?"

"No. It's in French."

"The French women had the most beautiful clean fannies in the world, so Denys used to say. Tasted of soap. I told the director to put that in his film, but of course he thought I was just a mad old teapot."

"Which you are."

"Which I am. Gallet. It used to be beautifully wrapped in tissue paper. Now we can only get Lux made locally out of God only knows what."

"Boiled-down tourists, I should think. Tatu brandi, Jephson. Have you seen the tourists? All dressed up like bloody Christmas trees, fat behinds covered in pockets and zips. What do you think they keep in all those pockets? I mean, bugger me, all they do is sit in little Toyota vans all day, bouncing around taking pictures of Tommies."

"They take pictures of me," said Camilla. "Oldest living inhabitant."

"Taking a picture of you, my dear, is something anyone with any taste or sense would do," said Fairfax. His eyes, deep in his seal face, are dark.

He turned to me: "I would like to read her thesis, although my French is a little rusty. Could you let me have a copy?"

"I have got a photocopy you can read."

"Is it good?"

"It belongs to a certain time, but it's been highly praised."

"You're too young to belong to a certain time yourself," says Lady De Marr. "It's a painful business."

Actually, I have begun to think that I do belong to a time, but it is separated by so many decades from theirs that I reproach myself.

We were almost the last to leave. The waiters are still standing attentively among the mahogany and chintz. Neither Fairfax nor Lady De Marr notices them, but drunk as I am, I feel them imploring us mutely to go away.

"Must go, I suppose," says Fairfax finally. "Do you want me to get your car?"

"All right."

Fairfax calls a waiter and orders the memsahib's car to be made ready for the short journey to Warthog Manor, her solid but decrepit stone house.

"Silly old bugger," she says suddenly, as Fairfax, in the way of elderly men who have once been very athletic, hobbles and skips to the lavatory, trying to shake the easily accumulated stiffness out of his limbs, as though by this display of sprightliness he can somehow leap out of the tethers fixing him to the earth.

"Silly old bugger, but my only friend on earth. I'm afraid I can't tell you anything more about Claudia, really, but I'll try and jot down some memories, if you like."

She has become suddenly lucid.

———

"You haven't told me a thing, if you don't mind my saying so."

"Haven't I? At our age you can no longer remember in what order things happened. Fact is, after a couple of glasses of Kenya brandy, you can't remember anything anyway, and a damn good show."

She looks at me appraisingly.

"We can't afford Rémy Martin. It's just a little game Tom puts on for visitors. The waiters play along. We have a few tricks left, you know."

Fairfax reappears.

"I can't pee anymore. It takes forever. Don't get old if you can avoid it. Your car's ready, Camilla."

"Everyone falls in love with the Masai, you know," she says as we, the elderly general and the attentive subaltern, along with a few askaris, attend the old lady at her departure. "Big mistake. Biggest bloody liars in Africa. Night-night."

I wonder briefly why they speak in this telegram way when they have something important to say.

The air outside is cool. The car sets off in a series of lurches across the gravel, for a moment blotting out, or perhaps silencing, the night life.

"I'm off too," says Fairfax. "I have a cottage in the grounds. I'm going up-country tomorrow, but do leave a message for me here if you would like any more information."

I wake up. The brandy has poisoned me. I feel its toxins in every part of my body. (Victoria has this sensation about a variety of apparently innocuous substances: she claims to be poisoned daily by wheat and dairy products; she can detect the presence of fertilizers in carrots and mercury in shellfish.) I try to turn on the lights but either there has been a power cut or the club's generator has been switched off. I find, a blind man discovering his latent tactile abilities, the candle provided for such occasions and try to strike a match. The matches are made of a wood so flimsy that it reminds me of the balsa with which I tried, unsuccessfully, to build model airplanes. The little blobs of phosphorus flare briefly as they fly off dangerously in various directions. My head is very painful. I can feel a vein standing out on my temple. Eventually a match lights. The candle reluctantly comes to life. These are forgotten rituals of our civilization, creating a living chiaroscuro in a room. Lit in this way a room is a simulacrum of a dream world. As I stand up, heading for the bathroom, I see a piece of paper under my door. It is the club's notepaper and written on it are these words:

> One had to forget—because one could not live with the thought— that this graceful, fragile, tender young woman with those eyes, that smile (those gardens and snows in the background) had been brought in a cattle car to an extermination camp and killed by an injection of phenol into the heart, into the gentle heart that one had heard beating under one's lips in the dusk of the past.
>
> These are not my words, they are the Lolita chap, Nabokov's, but they express better than I ever could my feelings. One had to forget. As I am sure you already know, I loved her. But I had to forget. I ask you not to cheapen her life in your film.
>
> Yrs
>
> Tom

14

I picture the old man hopping and pacing to his cottage, finding the paper, finding the passage, transcribing it, bobbing back to the club and slipping the note under my door, in order to set the record straight; I find myself close to tears. The candlelight in the room wavers in a warm draft. In the shadows and its gentle movement I believe I see the firelight that constrains and defines the Masai night. Beyond the firelight there is the unknowable. Why do we persist in trying to know everything there is to know in the belief that one day, presumably quite soon, we will succeed? *One had to forget.* Nabokov's words, Fairfax's words. They could easily be rephrased: one could not understand.

And he was right. I had discovered some time ago that he had loved Claudia Cohn-Casson.

When I wake the candle has burned right down, so that in the enamel holder there is nothing but a lava flow of wax. Outside I can hear a sound that is also achingly familiar to me: someone is trimming the grass with shears. They chatter and stutter in the never-ending colonial quest for the perfect lawn, which is, of course, a reproach to the disorderly lives and vegetation on the outside.

S. O. Letterman has entered into a very personal contract with tennis. However well he does, however badly he is beaten, he contrives to incorporate the result into his bildungsroman. Like Marcel Proust, he is making art out of his life, and tennis is an important element. When we played at his club in Westwood and I beat him comfortably, he discussed the result with his friends in such a way that it was clear that he had deliberately thrown the match in order to contribute to our personal relationship. In the locker room—no ordinary changing room this, but a soft paradise of fluffy towels, hairdriers, lotions, masseurs, electronic scales, isometric drinks, cardiovascular scans and congratulatory attendants—he told a well-known (everyone in this club is said to be well known) producer that he took the first three games off me in each set. And then he added that, of course, writers had nothing better to do most afternoons, and since I was now writing a movie for him, he knew how to keep me happy.

"You can't let these guys get depressed," he said. "Writing is a mood business."

Somebody told me that Letterman had had five hundred tennis lessons. It was said with a "whaddya expect?" kind of intonation. Not everyone, it seems, has bought his bill of goods. Certainly his tennis has an entirely synthetic look to it. There is a small, and often fatal, time lapse before he plays each shot, as he recalls the instructions concerning grip, feet placement, racquet position and so on. Nonetheless, his tennis has high ambitions. He has all the latest equipment—vibration dampers, elbow restraints, luminous head and wrist bands, and bicycle shorts under his strangely textured tennis shorts. His racquets—there are many—are transported in a bulging bag inscribed with a crocodile, given to him by Michel Piccoli.

"Very brave man. He signed a petition, you know, against Mitterrand and Vichy. Real shame our movie never got past first base. Anyway, this bag is a little souvenir. Mitterrand wrote articles for a Vichy newspaper before he joined the Resistance. Did you know that?"

He has had plenty of flirtations with European directors and writers and claims to be a great fan of Louis Malle and Alain Resnais, but when it comes right down to it, he doesn't believe that a European sensibility sells tickets at the box office. Yet he can work both sides of the street. In argument about the treatment of the script—these things process in ordered stages—he is just as likely to enlist Bergman as Schwarzenegger as supporting evidence. Like his tennis, his moviemaking seems to lack instinct, but half an hour in the locker room and lunch on the terrace tells you everything you need to know about the constraints under which he operates. Papal bulls issued from the Hollywood Vatican flutter in the air. There are prescriptions concerning actors, restaurants, religious sects, fads, social issues and automobiles, which you ignore at peril of excommunication. The insiders—and Letterman is right on the inside track—pick up these changing signals constantly; they have no patience with outsiders' skepticism.

I am reminded of Letterman's tennis because as I stroll through the grounds of the club, waiting for the arrival of my transcripts, I come upon a red-earth tennis court. The surface of these courts is made with a clay brought up from underground by termites, the insects that create the famous anthills of the savannah. Nobody is playing as yet, but the lines have been freshly painted, a large old roller is being stored by an elderly man with tribal scars on his cheeks (like the marks made by French grill pans on *bifteck*) and a big jug of lemon squash is standing in the shade of a little thatched tennis house, protected from the desires of wasps and flies by a beaded lace doily. Beside the court a bed of yellow canna lilies, with leaves the color of red cabbage, is being doused by another retainer, this man with a little ornament, beaded like the doily, in one of his ear lobes. The water bounces off the waxen leaves.

It was Letterman's idea to use the awful journey from the house in the avenue Hoche via Drancy to Auschwitz as a recurring, dreamlike image in the film. Letterman had previously told me that flashback is a device that must be used sparingly, yet now he was a plausible advocate for this treatment. It appeals to me, too.

The final, defiant round-up by the retreating Nazis, in which Claudia and her deluded father were caught, the train journey and the selection process at Auschwitz will all be treated in black and white, in order, if I get Letterman, to increase the realism and to reduce the melodrama. I can see that his aim is to make these scenes so powerful that they will go beyond any fictional treatment of the death camps that has ever been tried before: the train rolls through the night, the outcome, although certain, appallingly delayed by the shots of the iron wheels and the crude pistons; the final scene of the five chimneys pouring their shameful smoke over the Polish countryside, intercut—this is my contribution—with the smoke rising from the savannah.

Letterman confided to me after one of our tennis games that my pieces in *Manhattan* had always struck him as somewhat trivial—artifices—until he read my piece "Drancy, Antechamber of Death." The mundane details of the denunciations, the decrees against Jews using the telephone or traveling on the Métro and so on had brought home to him that the French had both suffered by and been complicit in the Holocaust. (I forgave the fact that he was merely paraphrasing my final sentence. He has a way of drawing you into his enterprises, which is flattering.)

Still nobody comes to play tennis. The lines are painted, the canna lilies watered. The lines are perfectly straight, their whiteness defying the ochre ant-soil. On the cabbage leaves of the cannas, huge, shining droplets of water repose.

Letterman told me that he once saw Steffi Graf playing tennis at Wimbledon. He was seated at the back of the court, initially angry that someone had screwed up with the tickets, but he quickly realized that every few games he was almost directly behind her. Each time she bent to receive serve he found himself staring mesmerized at her derrière. Binding me with his confidences, he said that viewing the wonderfully athletic Aryan rear of Steffi Graf made him understand how the camp inmates could believe they were indeed *Untermenschen* in relation to the SS. He was joking, of course. He squeezed my arm to make sure I got the point.

The grounds of the club lead to a golf course, but this, too, is still, except for the attentions of green-sweepers and grass-cutters. The first fairway extends up over a gentle rise and into a forest of huge native trees. These are the only trees around the town that have not yet gone for firewood. The town has an edgy, vicious hum. The poor see the lumpy, soapy tourists and they harbor thoughts of separating them from their possessions. A short walk near the university produces the dispiriting impression that urban life in Africa is hopeless. In their smart uniforms the police have a lethargic menace. A large Mercedes rushes by with outriders; the other traffic—held together with recycled parts, bits of wire and home engineering—is swept aside dismissively, mere twigs in the path of floodwater. I wish to run up to the window of the Mercedes and shout at the general sitting there: *Wake up, you fat bastard. Can't you see how you look parading in this cemetery like some overstuffed SS officer in Birkenau?* Yet when I take a taxi back to the club, the driver tells me that the Indians will be getting it in the neck soon. They are to blame for the misery and squalor.

Here in the club, gardening is still practiced with religious intensity. In the Third World gardening is absurd. Why grow things you can't eat? Why water luxuriant canna lilies and fast-flowering, even faster-fading roses, trained on ropes to make living swags around the croquet lawn? Why trim the grass so short that not even a goat could get its incisors into the chlorophyll? Why spend money on fertilizers and ant poisons and petrol for the mowers and whitewash for the tennis court—and incidentally any stray rocks that need it—and why build great steaming compost heaps of the by-products of the above?

The answer is that gardens re-create a corner of paradise. For a Masai, paradise is a vast savannah, dotted with beautifully marked and horned cattle. For a Westerner entering this harsh, insected and vipered landscape, a small sanctuary of parterres and walkways and pergolas and graveled paths was evidence of faith. As the town began to grow and at the same time fragment in strange, squalid and unforeseen ways, the gardens became symbolic in a different fashion. This garden (protected from the road on one side by huge, untidy gum trees in a permanent state of reptilian slough, the discarded bark hanging from the newly emerged, silvery trunks) has for me so powerful a charm because it returns me to my childhood, with a complete collection of odors, insects, fragrances, ponds and overvigorous plants. But there is more to it. The texture of the sounds, the little ant-bear funnels, the twittering of the water sprinklers, the unnamed but instantly familiar birds, the patient devotions of the gardeners, the numberless frogs (now in caviare-eyed repose on water lilies and ledges), the huge, lazy tadpoles, the dragonflies on their biplane wings skimming the water, the busy red ants returning with baguettes of grass (the same ants that used to run up the shorts of children and sink their vicious fangs into unwary little scrota) and now the distant thwack of tennis balls and the inevitable muted cries of anguish—all these impressions play so strongly on my memory because they leap thirty-five years of my life in one bound.

It's pleasurable and it's surprising in its detail. The question is, What on earth does it mean? Why are these memories so strong and so personal? I am sitting now in an arbor of rust-colored bougainvillea, drinking lukewarm weak coffee, brought to me in a stainless steel pot by a waiter in a starched white uniform, thinking in an aimless way about this puzzle, when I see the waiter returning. He is holding a round copper tray under one arm like a subaltern with his cap at a passing-out parade.

"Telephone, sir."

I walk up to the main building along a path of large brown stones with the shape and texture of unleavened bread. Within their surfaces are tiny specks of quartz. This is the rock—I am not sure of its name, geology being a closed book to me—of which the clubhouse is built and which the early settlers favored in their pursuit of the substantial.

Taking a long-distance call still causes a certain turbulence here. I am ushered reverently into a cabin and pick up the quaint handset, which has an additional round earpiece for clamping over the spare ear, so that I see myself reflected in the glass like a radio operator or a session singer. The call fills me with apprehension.

Over the airwaves and under the sea, or however his quavering voice reaches me from LA, I hear S. O. Letterman.

"Jesus, where were you, on safari?"

"In the garden, reliving my childhood. I'm the Proust of the savannahs."

"I didn't get that last bit. This is a fucking awful line. Do you want the good news or the bad news first?"

"I'll take the good."

"The good news is that Paramount has gone for it."

"And the bad?"

"The bad news is that they want to see a first-draft script within three weeks."

"Anything else?"

"Isn't that enough? How's it going? Okay?"

"Fine. I met her ex-lover last night."

"Jesus, he must be one helluvan age."

"Seventy-six. Imagine Robert Redford with a blue face in twenty years' time."

"You been drinking?"

"Yes. I have. Brandy. Kenya brandy."

"At my house you told me you didn't drink. You refused all my drinks. Listen, are you pleased?"

"I'm elated. Well done. Congratulations."

The truth is, I don't feel elated. I wander back out to the garden, but the magic has gone.

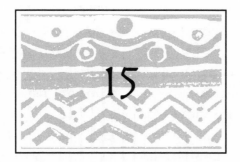

The professor's secretary, who is wearing fluffy aquamarine slippers, asks me to wait at the end of a blank corridor. After a few moments the professor himself appears from a doorway.

Northern European faces don't necessarily age well. The early freshness, the attractive blondness, the amiable, even features, can become anonymous as the hair thins and the face subsides into middle age. Like a bust of a minor general in a park, his weathered face has no edges. His hair, similarly, has collapsed onto his head, so that at first—I see him at the end of a corridor—he appears to be completely bald. He has very fine hair, resting timidly and lifelessly on his skull. He is a man of about fifty-five, with a quick, nervous manner, as if he had pressing engagements elsewhere, which seems unlikely: the university has run out of steam and its faculty members are all jumping ship if they can.

Uitsmijter has made a study of Maa. He holds his translation of the laibon's monologue. It is on curious shiny fax paper. He hands me the manuscript, about fifteen pages. I hand him the agreed fee, in dollars, and for a moment we are suspended, directionless, outside his office. The transaction seems to embarrass him, because he insists on carrying it out in the corridor, out of sight of his secretary, whose fluffy blue feet have just slipped and slid back through the door of his office. I wonder what this casual, sexy skating along the linoleum says about their relationship.

"Is it interesting to you, as a scholar, I mean?"

He speaks English in a curious way, that improbable Dutch-accent tongue slapping down hard on the vowels, like shoe leather on a dry pavement. He has also adopted African pronunciations of some words, with a savoring of random vowels.

"What you have here is a traditional account of Masai origins, but also mixed with the arrival of this woman—I am assuming, although it is not my business, the ethnographer, Claude Cohn-Casson—yes, okay, well, there was an incident during the war, a famous incident as far as the Masai are concerned, when a British official was killed in a very small dispute about cattle. Your man, Saibol ole Saitoti, is linking this incident to Mademoiselle Cohn-Casson. He also refers to Fairfax, he means Sir Thomas Fairfax, who is still alive, you know, who was a friend of Mademoiselle Cohn-Casson. I find it very interesting that your laibon knew Fairfax.

"The rest, I must say, is confusing but very interesting for me. Saibol speaks Maa in a way which tells me that he comes from the Kisongo of the Ol Doinyo Lengai, yes? Yes, good. He makes some allegations which I can't understand. I have tried to translate them for you. Mostly he is talking about a period before the war, but he also refers to the uprising against the Germans in 1915, and some events immediately after the last war, and to a man he describes as his brother. Wait a minute, I have almost nearly forgot your tape."

The social sciences building is free of students. The prodemocracy rallies and protests at the rigged elections have led to government disappointment with the behavior of the students. The university has been under curfew and restraint for months. The antidemocratic movement, which calls itself the antitribal movement, is considering widening the net in its search for suitable replacement students. People without any education at all seem to offer the best hope.

Uitsmijter returns with my tape.

"You should go now. You won't find in Masai stories linear logic. You have to understand that the whole linguistic system of signs, signifiers—are you familiar with linguistics? Well, I don't blame you—all these are different. It's not what you would say was logical but it is very complex. The old settlers thought the Masai were liars. So, if I can help you again, please tell me. Goodbye."

He pauses briefly to watch me leave. I look round as I reach a junction in the corridor and he quickly pops back into his office. I wonder if his jumpiness is a result of the university's troubles or sexual intrigues, which can wreak havoc among the middle-aged.

I walk through a cut-price version of the groves of academe, a concrete path overhung by jacaranda trees, set in a termite-ravaged lawn.

In his desire to make sure that I do justice to the Masai cosmic vision, the professor overestimates my attachment to the logical.

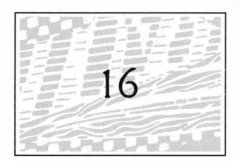

16

The club is very quiet. There is a period of what seems to be enforced idleness in the afternoon. It reminds me of provincial France, where you can drive through a village on a summer's afternoon and wonder if the place is inhabited. No tennis-ball-thwacking. No lawn-mowing. No clatter from the kitchen. Only the drugged flies lumbering and buzzing through the air and the idiot, eager frogs bellowing recognize no siesta. I pull back the candlewick bedspread and lie on my back with my manuscript.

The laibon kicks off with a creation myth. The first man, Kintu, visited the sky where God, Ngai, lives and was given God's go-ahead to create the Masai people. (I had been led to believe that God lived in Ol Doinyo Lengai. Perhaps he claims the airspace above as well.) From Kintu sprang all the Masai, whose life was to be a great odyssey. The Masai were expressly charged by God with responsibility for the world's cattle. Cattle, says the laibon, must be praised. Every Masai thinks constantly about cattle. Every Masai sings hymns to cattle. The world is framed in the image of cattle. (My words, not his.)

This is the Masai's special task on earth. There is no contradiction—as Claudia pointed out in her thesis—between this task and the fact that other tribes have cattle: other tribes have stolen them. They are not entitled to them. These other tribes were ordained by Ngai to be farmers, wretched people obliged to scratch the soil, just as the Ndorrobo were specifically entrusted by Ngai to produce what the Masai need—spears, shields and useful vessels. The Ndorrobo were not allowed to own cattle so they had to hunt the unappetizing wild game, something a Masai would never do.

Many white people, says the laibon, did not understand God's commandments and tried to change things. (You don't need to be a trained anthropologist to spot the seeds of conflict in this theology.) And now the fat bellies in the cities are carrying on where the white folk left off.

(I can picture the laibon as he told me this, his son sitting behind him on a rock flossing his teeth.)

The Masai moved from the great river of the north, freely interpreted as the Nile, says the professor in a note, down toward their present location. It was a terrible journey, reducing the Masai nation to a few hundred survivors. (Our own time provides the television simulacra of this march in Somalia and Ethiopia.) The march took many years, perhaps more than a century. Time in those days lacked urgency or precision. But the plains, savannahs, rivers and hills, all the way from Samburu down to the Masai Steppe, proved fruitful, and the Masai built up their strength through the acquisition of women and cattle so successfully that they chased out the other tribes, who were obliged to cling to the mountains or secrete themselves in the forests, land useless for cattle.

When the white man came (what a familiar and mournful phrase), the Masai were not allowed the same freedom to repossess their cattle. It became a crime, punishable by lashes under the Germans and by fines under the British, to take the cattle of other tribes. This was a gross injustice. The laibon speaks of the Masai uprising against the Germans in 1915 and of the last great war waged against the unspeakable Bantu tribes around Lake Victoria, *who ate fish*. The warriors in those days, he says, preferred to die rather than return home without dipping their spears in blood. Warriors now know nothing of war and cattle-raiding. They are similarly ill equipped to deal with lions. Some poison lions that are troublesome, rather than kill them with a spear. It is a shameful thing. Now the Masai are torn by the need to go to school (*schule* in Swahili, a leftover of German occupation) and the understanding that young people who go to school are lost to the traditional ways. Women are particularly vulnerable to the false promises of city slickers. (I think here of Victoria.)

After a short discourse about women—the need for the dowry of five animals and three useful articles to be maintained, even for schoolgirls—he speaks of Claudia. She came to live among them. His father was the laibon at the time and he had five brothers. His father wore a cloak of hyrax skins, which he received along with other tools of the trade—pebbles, containers and more important, the ability to use numbers to foretell the future. He is descended directly from Kidongoi, the first laibon, who was given supernatural powers on the mountain by Ngai. (Although the tablets have been transmuted into handier, pocket-size pebbles, the kinship with Moses seems too close to be a coincidence.)

As I read, I am struck again by the laibon's sense of being at the center of the universe. He lives near the mountain of God, in the Rift Valley in a paradise of rivers, lakes, mountains and plains. People who come from the outside world inhabit the periphery, where they have no cattle and live an inferior life. Claudia came from that world. At first, he says, people did not understand what she wanted, but she came to learn about the Masai and write it in a book. She wanted to attend the *eunoto* (the warriors' graduation) and the women's circumcision and understand everything about betrothals. She soon knew all there is to know, more than many Masai men, about the exchange of gifts, cattle and goats that always accompanies these ceremonies. At first people were suspicious; they could not understand why she was so interested in these details, which she wrote down in a schoolbook. Soon she could speak Maa. One day she brought a voice box. (Uitsmijter has written a note: "probably a Uher, commonly used by researchers.")

Les vrais paradis sont les paradis qu'on a perdus. I am struck by anxiety. How quickly can one learn a language? My Swahili, such as it is, comes from a Berlitz tape and a phrase book. In Claudia's time very few Masai spoke Swahili. As I get older I find myself tormented by anxieties of this nature, the anxieties about things one will never do. They are the anxieties of our times, born of the idea that the individual must in one way or another (any damned way, as a matter of fact, even confessing to having been abused as a child) express his uniqueness and fulfill his potential. Durkheim, Claudia's inspiration, said at the beginning of the century that the problem for twentieth-century Western man was the anomie created by the breakdown of the old certainties. What he could not see was the restless, self-centered consumerism it would produce. Nor did he see another consequence, as his nephew Mauss confessed, shortly before going mad: "how large modern societies, which have more or less emerged from the Middle Ages in other respects, could be hypnotized as aborigines are by their dances and set in motion like a child's carousel. This return to the primitive had not been the object of our thoughts."

The club is quiet. The gardens outside my window are bowing down to the heat of the afternoon, but my mind is racing in this stillness, like a dust-devil on the apparently windless plains. I see myself drawing closer to Claudia Cohn-Casson, but not necessarily in the way that S. O. Letterman is expecting of me. The club and Fairfax and Lady De Marr and now the laibon's tale seem to me to have pulled us together. It's absurd, but I feel we are all protagonists now in the same story. I have heard her voice and spoken to her lover and been walking with the Masai who was present at the farcical and tragic lion hunt. I no longer believe that I am just writing a treatment of her life. I feel as if I am poised somewhere on the edge of a slope and am about to slide down when I am supposed to be climbing up. It's crazy, but I feel as though I have no life outside this one I have found here, complete with silly old colonials and Masai witch doctor. I haven't thought of Victoria, whose sexual peccadilloes gave me such pain, for days. Yet even as I remember Victoria, I feel keenly the unsettled state of my mind. How could I possibly have neglected to think about her, when a few weeks ago I could think of little else, in lubricious detail? I find myself instead picturing Claudia, her dark eyes turned to the sky. I see her crouching at the entrance of a hut (*olpal*), looking in at, perhaps talking to, the shy bride within, who does not want to leave her father's village (*engang*). I find myself attempting to memorize the Masai words as she did. I see her walking with the bride to her new village, being teased by the escort of girls. I see her, as she described, catching sight of the husband's village. And I imagine these same dark eyes catching sight of the five chimneys of Auschwitz-Birkenau.

The laibon now talks about the famous incident when a district officer was killed. The British had insisted that the Masai sell some cattle to pay for schools and clinics and—there was clearly a hint of blackmail—to contribute to the war effort. Many Masai resisted this tax, but they had no choice. The laibon says that his father saw the sense in it. He didn't want the Germans back. A young man called Tepilit ole Saibol, the laibon's brother, tried at the last minute to withdraw one of his cattle from the sale. The district officer in charge, known to the Masai as Tombol (Miles Turnbull), refused to allow the animal to be withdrawn and ordered his askaris to restrain Tepilit. In the presence of a few hundred Masai, the young warrior hurled his spear right through the district officer's heart. The blade appeared out of his back. Watched by the crowd, Tepilit withdrew his spear and walked away. He was eventually arrested. He did not hide and he said that he would do the same again. The bull in question had markings of which he was particularly proud. He had offered an alternative. The laibon says that his family offered forty-nine cattle in restitution, but the British took Tepilit to the coast and hanged him there. What was achieved by that? However, some members of his family were glad, because it meant they did not have to produce cattle.

Uitsmijter in a note says that the Masai have a system of fines, multiples of seven. Forty-nine cattle is the highest possible penalty.

The young man who was hanged was a special friend of Claudia. He wanted to marry her. Fairfax—Fahfakhs—who was a big man in the government, had come down to the little town where Tepilit was held. Fahfakhs was wearing a uniform. He and Claudia spent a long time talking to the police and to the accused man. He, the laibon, had heard Fahfakhs shouting at the accused man in the cells at Ewaso Narok police post before he was taken to the coast. (Fahfakhs spoke fluent Maa.) The laibon's father had explained to Fahfakhs that the family was ready to pay compensation, up to the full amount possible. He had told Fahfakhs that the young man wanted to marry Claudia, and perhaps he thought that the district officer was laughing at him and treating him with contempt. Tepilit had asked Claudia, in the proper way, to see if her father, wherever his village was, would accept gifts. He had given Claudia a necklace to wear in the meanwhile and called her *pakiteng*. (Uitsmijter explains that it is an affectionate name meaning "heifer" used by betrothed people.) The laibon still could not understand the point of hanging such a man. The district officer's family got no cattle out of it either.

Fahfakhs explained that Native Law did not cover this case. The laibon told Fahfakhs that Tepilit had actually killed a lion for the film that Claudia was making with Leavitt, whose name I had reminded him of. Tepilit had risked his life for Claudia. Two morans had been killed, and still Leavitt had not produced the promised cattle. After Tepilit was taken away to be tried, they never saw him again. Soon afterward Claudia said she was leaving. Some said that she was going to be the wife of Fahfakhs. Many people were very sad to see her go. He, the laibon, was not so sad because he believed that she had caused many upsets. But she spoke to them all and said she would never forget them. She was going back to her father's house to show people what she had written in her schoolbooks about them. She would come back as soon as she could. She was leaving their country with a heavy heart.

Professor Uitsmijter has quite a deft touch in translation. I find myself able to place the words, in all their moving directness, right into the laibon's mouth as he spoke, with Ol Doinyo Lengai away in the distance looking like a steamed pudding, its runneled slopes lightly coated with cream, poured from above but vitrified before reaching the base.

Some time later they heard that Tepilit had been hanged. After the war was over they heard that Claudia had died. How had she died? He would like to know what happened to Claudia and her books. Nobody had ever told him. If I knew, would I tell him? Did she marry Fahfakhs?

"Now we must go. We will go to the engang up there by Kitumbeine."

And so, monologue complete, we had set off.

The thin paper in my hand flutters as I drop it onto the bed. The ridged and tufted counterpane has been carefully and frequently laundered. The onset of the cooler hours is announced by the first thuds of tennis balls. After they hit the racquet they make another, more resonant sound, as they bounce on the ant-soil surface, a sound you can hear on television when tennis is played at Stade Roland Garros. There is no sign of Fairfax and no message. I eat alone in the dining room and the next morning set off early back to Mr. Shah's hotel. The journey takes seven hours.

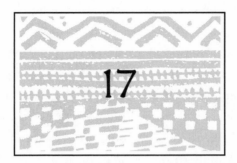

As usual there is chicken lolling in the metal trays of the dining room, like unhealthy continentals in a mineral bath. For all its *Last Year at Marienbad* qualities, I choose the chicken again. Mr. Shah is solicitous. He wants to know about Nairobi. Did I see anything of the riots? I tell him that some Indian shops have been burned, according to my taxi driver. He shakes his head sadly.

"They blame us for their problems, I mean even though we have lived here for many, many generations. They always do. But it's not so bad down here. Some pickles and chutney?"

Léon Cohn-Casson believed that the sooner all Jews lost any traces of separate identity the better. He agreed with Émile Durkheim that Jewish ethnicity would wane with the advance of secular society. The only way forward was on secular, scientific principles. Sociology and anthropology were the application of these principles to understanding how people behave. For this reason he had encouraged Claudia to enter these new, modern sciences. He had cultivated Marcel Mauss, Durkheim's nephew, so that he could personally convey to her the importance of understanding the springs of human action. Mauss had come to their house in the avenue Hoche for dinner; like most academics—I am guessing—feeling a little shabby when confronted by the glowing paintings and rich Aubussons and complex dinner settings. Claudia wrote about his quiet passion. He could pluck examples of the universal spirit from any number of societies he had studied.

What a queasy period those interwar years now seem (I am looking at the chicken curry), the old hatreds and prejudices simmering and bubbling nicely, with all the dark, irrational fears surfacing in a way that rational people like Cohn-Casson believed had long ago been rendered obsolete by the evolutionary nature of society. The modern order, because it was based on industry, would produce a rational society. What a delusion.

Cohn-Casson was born in 1882, not long after France's humiliation by the Prussians. He had spent his life, as many of the French intelligentsia had, looking for a basis for order in society. France is a country that has grave doubts about its moral fibre; it sees its national character as being as permeable as a colander. It was for this reason that Léon Cohn-Casson became such a fervent advocate of a secular morality. He disliked the arriviste Jews because he felt that they were provincial and superstitious and liable to arouse hostility; nor did he believe that they would be loyal to France. But Cohn-Casson also found it impossible to side uncritically with Jews, because to do so would deny modern thinking by placing tribal loyalties above the mandates of science. Léon Blum, the new prime minister, said of people like Cohn-Casson: "They secretly curse those who put them in the hands of secular enemies."

And here is Mr. Shah. I can't tell him of the analogies I am cheerfully fabricating. He wants me to have some tinned pears, which have come in from South Africa. Or I could have lychees.

18

"Women make us poets; children make us philosophers." This is one of Letterman's aphorisms. He has a number, many quite apt, which he is liable to produce to lend substance to his conversation. His conversation is a finely wrought sales pitch. He is selling himself. It has been his life's work. The events of his life are constantly incorporated into this spiel. For example, he has been married and is still on very good terms with his wife; their divorce unlocked her true potential, and she is now a part-time feminist studies lecturer at USC. Letterman implies that he had to divorce her for her own good; he could not bear to see so much life force confined in marriage. Their son, Dylan, who is twelve, lives with her but there are no custody conflicts and they have a wonderful rapport. Dylan helps him see things in an honest fashion, without all the crap. This is the philosophical side. On the poetic side, he has had many good relationships with women. He thinks that a part of his nature is more in harmony with women than men. He sees himself as having an intuitive, feminine aspect. Although he mentions it to me, he finds he is unable to display this aspect to men. It comes out only in his dealings with women. Personally, I think this is another of his sales pitches.

I walk up the track past the fundamentalist missions, way above the coffee plantations, up into what is nominally a wildlife reserve. I am proposing to ponder the question of Letterman's script up in the higher altitudes.

A sign reads CRATER RESERVE. PLEASE STAY IN YOUR VEHICLE. This sign has been painted on a piece of board and is listing badly. Some small boys come down the track toward me. They are laughing and chasing one another. When they see me they become strangely still and respectful. They probably think that, like most of the white men in this evangelical belt between the coffee plantations and the colobus monkey habitat, I have religious connections and perhaps even powers, the sorts of powers that cause money to come to pass. This is the white man's greatest achievement: he has learned how to get his mitts on the money. (There is another argument, nowadays timidly advanced only by a few academics of the old hair-shirt tendency, that the white man has fixed the game, making it almost impossible for the others to get in.) The connection between religion and wealth is clear: the religious people have almost as many vehicles, servants and supplies of electrical goods as the aid community.

I give these children my benediction. It is delivered in the form of a few coins, which bear the likeness of the last president, a pleasant utopian who retired of his own free will. The children, their faith reinforced, run down the hill to tell others of their good fortune as I stride up the track toward the forest. The forest is cool. I ask myself why the people don't live up here in these glades beside the rushing streams. Life would be so much more leafy. It would be almost European.

At a great height I catch sight of a colobus. These monkeys are used in the manufacture of household articles and headdresses by all the tribes in whose domain they are found. This is the sort of relationship between man and animal that Westerners find hard to accept: the use of a monkey as a flyswatter. In my excited state, as the trees close over my head, I see this kind of thinking, this desire to reshape the world into something reassuring, as having many applications. For example, S. O. Letterman sees Claudia's story as a vindication of the human spirit, to which, professionally, anyway, he pays tribute. The human spirit, in this estimation, is always on the move, restlessly upward, like climbers on K2. I am under notice to find a suitably uplifting ending for our movie. The smoke rising from the five chimneys of Auschwitz-Birkenau is a downer, although he thinks there may be something in my idea of complementary smoke rising from the savannah.

"It's crazy, but people just won't go to the movies if the thing ends on a downer."

I don't argue with Letterman. Why should I? He's an expert on popular taste. He sees Claudia as brainy, beautiful, romantic and symbolic. The last part of the proposition still needs some work. I have decided to broaden my idea of the savannahs with smoke rising from the Masai villages. I see the camera closing in to find her old Masai friends gathering after a day, another of the infinite number of days, spent caring for the cattle. The ex-hunter, aviator and war hero Tom Fairfax, who was her lover, is approaching in his biplane. First his small plane is seen searching the vast plains for her village. The sky is reddening, reminding the viewer of the ghastly hues of the night sky above Auschwitz when the ovens were working at full capacity. Down below, fires are being lit and the cattle are being driven gently into the enclosures of thorn bushes. Music rises on the sound track. Fairfax's plane circles once and then comes down to land bumpily on a piece of gazelle-inhabited ground. The warriors come loping for news of Claudia. Fairfax climbs from the plane and walks, surrounded by the tall warriors, across the darkening savannah to the laibon's manyatta. The laibon, dressed in his traditional finery, a cloak of fur on his shoulders and carrying a thin stick, walks across the enclosure, now thick with the strangely blotched cattle, their huge horns gently meshing and unmeshing, to greet Fairfax. The moment is prolonged and intensified almost unbearably. (The music, I will suggest, should be based on Masai chanting.) Anyway, this music rises hauntingly. The laibon and Fairfax face each other.

They speak in Maa, but with subtitles. Fairfax tells them that Claudia is dead. There is a throaty murmur, a sort of groan. The laibon asks who killed her. Fairfax says she was killed by the Germans. He takes a piece of paper from his pocket, a letter from Claudia, smuggled to him from the Drancy camp in Paris. He tells them that Claudia has written them a last message. He clears his throat, which is suddenly somewhat congested, and reads: "Whatever happens to me, I shall always be thinking of you and hoping that you will have green grass for your cattle." From the Masai this deeply human murmur rises again. Night is falling. Fairfax stands surrounded by warriors with their spears, women holding their children, cattle and goats jostling; the music rises. The subtitles now roll over this scene. They tell the audience that Claudia Cohn-Casson, born 1912, is believed to have died in Auschwitz on or about April 20, 1945, fifteen days before Germany surrendered.

I am panting now. The air is thinning. There is nobody in the forest, although it is loud with calls and cries. A small antelope races away into the bush. For a moment, before it separates itself from its surroundings, I catch a glimpse of its round eyes, beautiful but stupid, taking in the sight of a forty-three-year-old writer wearing shorts and a faded polo shirt, his face somewhat craggier than he sees it in his mind's eye, his waist a little more solid and his eyes bright with the thoughts he is generating. Almost immediately it has vanished, able somehow to *levée* and *jetée* through the undergrowth without a sound. Farther away I hear colobus monkeys again, crashing about like drunks after a party, but all I see is branches in motion, semaphoring their passing.

I think that Letterman will go for my new ending. I am light-headed, perhaps from a mild attack of altitude sickness. Through a gap in the trees I can now look down over a green vegetable pointillism of treetops, falling away *down* to the town. It takes me another two hours to reach the top, which provides a view down into the crater, which looks, from this height, like a small, almost perfectly oval park with artfully sited clumps of trees and lakes. On the other side of the rim I can see way over the savannah in the direction of the Mountain of God, which is reduced in size, so that I can't be sure which of the outcrops on the horizon it is.

From below, in the Bible belt, I hear hymn-singing.

19

Victoria is thirty-two now. She is wary of platitudes and would never use the magazine phrase "biological clock" but, like Captain Hook, she is prone to hearing a fateful ticking.

She resents being prey to such banal anxieties. But we both know, although I haven't said it, that the consequence of her unfaithfulness is that I have been able to take the high ground. We also know that this is unfair.

I have hardly thought of her for at least a week; I am free of the little stabs of pain and the scudding dark clouds that had a habit of appearing from nowhere, uninvited and unexpected. I now see the whole episode (do I know everything?) in the way that Victoria paints it: a minor sexual frolic that, without the mistimed floral tribute, would have meant nothing. But my new detachment is bad news for Victoria's cause. As all lovers know, the other's unease is balm for the soul. I feel guilty about having engaged her for weeks in close and autoerotic questioning. So I settle down to write her a letter explaining my erratic behavior. I am proposing to dress it up a little, as in Joyce's letters to his Nora, as a symptom of high-mindedness. In these matters, high-mindedness takes a holiday: Joyce wanted to watch Nora crapping.

I write to her with my window open to catch a breeze that is coming from over the plains, where the short rains are expected. They are announced by atmospheric restlessness: papers in the street below suddenly dance and the trees on the mountain ripple. The Masai feel the air, hoping that the rains will produce nutritionally supercharged grass, which will return to their cattle the smooth, lustrous flanks and moist eyes that they love. Can I tell Victoria this? Can I explain to her that I am fully in sympathy with their monomania?

I tell her of my travels, although none of them is to a place you could easily find on a map, and of the people I have met. I then reassure her that I have forgiven her, although I am aware that the word "forgiven" implies that I have absolution in my gift. (The truth is I don't want to forgive her, because it will free her from the grappling irons I have on her. Also, I don't want to forgive her because it will suggest that I have settled for something.)

After a few minutes I realize this letter cannot be written truthfully. Instead I write half-truths. I tell her of my trip to Nairobi and the contacts with the laibon, but I am unable to explain to her how my personal relationship with the subject matter is developing. I gaze out of the window and see in the distance a flash, like a tourist's Instamatic, of lightning. I make a determined effort to rummage around in the jumble of our years together for some of the intensity of feeling I had for her. I would like to be able to find at least an oddment of eroticism. But I can only retrieve her lips, those lightly ribbed, juicy lips, studded and patterned in close-up like a mulberry or a raspberry, their almost leathery texture if you were to brush them with your fingertips or tongue tip (that snaky little organ equipped with ideas of its own). Nothing else. Her lips, like a Man Ray picture or a New Age sunrise, straddle the horizon of my imagination.

All our conversations—we have been great talkers—have now been dumped to join the countless other discarded conversations, arguments and recriminations. There must be some evolutionary purpose to this constant verbal skirmishing and foraying. What I see now is the complete futility, the gross overproduction, the immeasurable waste of emotion and words. It is as though we had to talk in order to reassure ourselves that we were living. Maybe it is radar, coming back to confirm the solidity of objects around us.

But then our conversations took a dive into the murky waters of sexuality and jealousy. I am glad to be free again.

The clouds have dropped down over the mountain, so that the evangelicals and charismatics on the first contour above the town have vanished into the mist. With their invisibility comes silence. The mist has doused their singing. I try to write, but we have run out of words. We expended them too recklessly. The ones that are left are lifeless. Instead, I find myself wondering what Tom Fairfax was concealing behind the seal face and marine eyebrows.

Then I remember the unopened letters, the reminders from the gray and fogbound north. They are in a drawer of the flimsy wardrobe.

Reluctantly, first examining the postmarks at length for clues, I open them. S. O. Letterman's office sends me the announcement made at Cannes of the imminent Franco-American production of the moving story of Claude Cohn-Casson, to be called *Masai Dreaming*. I am credited as the internationally known journalist and writer. Casting is in hand in Paris and Los Angeles. A number of well-known directors have expressed an interest in the script, which is in first draft. My bank also writes about maintenance payments.

I leave Victoria's letter to last. It contains a doctor's certificate, declaring her free of HIV.

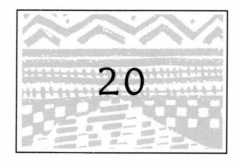

20

There is no question, you can be ready for death, even wish it to hurry up.

Saibol's brother, Tepilit, was ready to die because he realized that he would never get justice. Claudia pleaded with him to make some defense. Why should he make a defense? He had done nothing wrong.

The cell where he was held was, like a prison cell in a spaghetti Western, built of mud. The bricks were formed from unleavened mud, dug from the shallows of a nearby stream. The public works department, a heroic collection of people with strange provincial accents and manners, had a mold into which the mud was poured and then pressed from above. The roof of the cells was made of corrugated iron, imported from Birmingham. These little buildings were spreading out over the savannah in a game of checkers, with the goal of linking all the pieces into a chain of sound administration. The building program was halted during the war by the scarcity of corrugated iron.

It was very hot under the tin roof. Tepilit sat on the mud floor. He would not speak to Claudia; in despair she sent a message to Tom Fairfax in Nairobi. He spoke Maa fluently and he had unrivaled connections. As women do, she probably knew that she had made an impression on him on the two or three occasions they had met at Muthaiga.

Claudia could see that locking up a Masai for a crime he did not understand was cruel and inhuman. Also, her relationship with the accused man had been—I am wondering to just what extent—quite intimate. After all, he had felt able to call her "heifer" (*pakiteng*). Claudia, who was all too aware of what was happening in France—foreign Jews rounded up, her own father hopelessly compromised, labor camps from which none returned—wrote urgently to Fairfax to come and get this man out of jail. It seemed to her ridiculous at such a time "to ask this man to make a defense. It is like asking a Jew to apologize for being a Jew." What Claudia had in mind was some coloring of the evidence so that the district officer, Miles Turnbull, a harassed, overworked but popular man, who was dead—*bien entendu*—could be seen to have acted rashly in asking his askaris to point a gun at Tepilit, which Tepilit naturally interpreted as meaning they were about to shoot him.

But Tepilit refused to accept any suggestions that he had not killed the man deliberately. Far from it. As he sat on the mud floor of his cell, disdaining the bed, he said that he would do exactly the same again. His official statement, which bore his thumbprint, confirmed this. Fairfax, who was wearing his army uniform, soon lost patience. Despite his familiarity with the

Masai, he found Tepilit's obduracy insulting. He had made a long journey, borrowing fuel for his plane. It could all be resolved quite simply. After a few months in jail for manslaughter, Tepilit could be released: the war effort encouraged flexibility. But Tepilit could not follow the reasoning.

Fairfax was a farmer, a hunter and a figure in the colony's legislature. He had been to Sandhurst and served in a cavalry regiment before going to Kenya to farm. Like so many others before him—Blixen, Finch Hatton, Berkeley Cole—he preferred the life of safari. At the start of the war he had taken up his old rank of captain and was now a major in the King's African Rifles. He was dressed in that uniform with its fancy red flashes when he came to Claudia's aid.

They became lovers. Perhaps she had known it would happen, perhaps he had answered her call for the same reason. For about six weeks before she set off for France, the long way via Cape Town, they made love feverishly. In the meanwhile Tepilit was transferred to Dar es Salaam and hanged in the fort one morning at four-thirty.

I have in front of me some photographs from a collection of settlers' memories. There they are, sitting on their fast horses, gathered with their hounds, posing next to dead animals, picnicking by crocodile-inhabited rivers. In these photographs are ghostly presences, Masai and Kikuyu and other tribespeople. Sometimes they are blurred because, not being part of the composition, they are moving, carrying the sponge cake or the gun case or the canvas water bottle. At other times—included in the composition—they stand rigidly to attention, hardly breathing, their faces a frozen rictus. Fairfax could fit into any of those photographs seamlessly. (In fact, he is in one as a very young man accompanying the Prince of Wales on safari.)

Fairfax looks like Walter Cronkite. I see that behind the bluff little mustache and the liquid, fish-liver eyes—in my photograph the eyes are turned toward the Prince of Wales (himself a rather ghostly figure under a solar helmet)—shelters another presence. Perhaps this happens to us all as we age: our past lives detach themselves and stand to one side hesitantly, hardly believing the corporeal links to a former self.

The records show that Tepilit was hanged on March 18, 1944. After he was transported by train to Dar es Salaam, nothing more was heard in Masailand until the official notice was posted in the district commissioner's office in Ewaso Narok confirming that sentence had been carried out. This news was passed to his people, who burned his few possessions and redistributed his livestock. There were arguments about procedure because he was the first Masai from the area to die in this way. None of the simple rituals could be observed, but in the tradition of warriors who have performed brave deeds—say, the grabbing of the tail of a lion before spearing it—Tepilit was remembered and spoken of. It was also widely believed that he would have become the laibon after his father's death. The day of the death of the white man is still a big item in the folkloric memory.

It is this that the laibon, his brother, wishes to bring to my attention. For him there is a sense of unfinished business. He hopes that I may be able, in some way, to plug the gap in his family history. This gap is still letting in the wind; he cannot see distinct segments of time past. I also wonder if it is possible to close the account. Here S. O. Letterman and I are at odds. I have suggested that we could leave the story open-ended, but he clearly thinks I don't understand the nature of movies very well.

He quotes: "Movies are about two huge faces on the screen coming together and eventually embracing."

But Letterman has sent me warm approval of my new ending. He likes the idea of the universal spirit. What he sees is not what Durkheim had in mind and what Claudia was trying to detect. Instead he sees the big idea of this movie: all people are linked by the universal spirit. Claudia, we suppose, died in Auschwitz believing in it. He suggests we emend Claudia's last message, delivered by Fairfax to the Masai, to include the words "the universal spirit." Fairfax should now say to the assembled Masai: "Whatever happens to her she will always remember that it was the Masai who showed her that the human race shares one, universal, spirit." He also agrees to my request to take Fairfax on board as historical adviser and fixes a meeting in London in a few weeks to review progress.

London. I hear the chimes striking in the gray sky. From here London seems to be a menacing, alien place. I have lived there for fifteen years, but the moment I leave I feel it closing the doors on me with indifference. In London Victoria is living in my flat, driving my car, using my bank accounts, washing our sheets. Nursing her resentments.

Here, the short rains have disappointed. A quick curtain of water fell across the plains, but by the end of the day they were as dry as ever. Up in the mountain, the Bible belt was drenched and from my window I can see the river running strongly as a result. The car-washing and laundry activities have had to move some way up the bank.

Mr. Shah is impressed by my long fax from Letterman. The heading "Letterman Productions, Hollywood, London, Paris," with a movie-camera logo, seems to me to come from a comic book, but it obviously reminds Mr. Shah of his brief association with Ava Gardner, Clark Gable and John Ford. I ask Mr. Shah to fax Letterman in LA and Fairfax at Muthaiga. He likes these contacts with the more substantial world and happily hurries off in the direction of his stationery shop and fax bureau, where I know he will encounter many difficulties. A moment later he comes back.

"Time difference about eight hours with LA, yes?"

"I think so. Behind. They're behind."

"Okay. I thought so. No problem."

• • •

The universal spirit is quite adaptable, even protean. Claudia's thesis on the exchange of gifts attempts to confirm the presence of the universal spirit at work in the Masai. But she is very aware of what Marcel Mauss called "the total social fact." She doesn't, of course, mention it, but as a researcher living among the Masai she must have become part of the total social fact herself. By allowing Tepilit to engage in the formalities of gift exchange, she may have been able to observe at close quarters how it worked, but she was also entering into the drama. Mauss had suggested that by an exhaustive process of observation and recording, it might be possible to establish unchanging laws of human behavior. But, he warns, this universal spirit, which his uncle, Émile Durkheim, had airily postulated, can be recognized only after taking into account psychological, religious, magical and pragmatic factors. This is clearly impossible. Only a professor at the Collège de France could imagine that anyone (let alone someone who had exchanged bovine nicknames with a Masai warrior) was capable of any such omniscience. This is the nature of sciences and pseudosciences, always striving for a set of rules and final solutions.

Claudia probably took heart from another of Mauss's strictures, that the ethnographer should not only observe the particular but keep in mind the context. Her thesis has its gaze on the exact detail of the exchange of cattle, goats, blankets, gourds and snuff, and it tries to establish by the comparative method that these customs are part of universal human practice. The details of the comparative method are a little sketchy, but she claims that Melanesian practice is very similar. The poor anonymous Melanesians, famous only in anthropology.

As I look out of my window—the scene is as interesting to me as a Canaletto—I see the clouds suddenly begin to rise off the mountains. They appear to be vacuumed downward at high speed, like a milkshake being drawn up a straw, the top layers, the fluffy stuff, going last.

I wonder if she had sex with Tepilit. I reproach myself at the same time. Who is to say what it was like living out on the plains for months on end, at first in a tent and then in a small house, not much more than a hut, built of saplings, mud, and cow dung, which she equipped with Somali fabrics and safari furniture? I suspect what Claudia really discovered about the universal spirit was more personal than scientific. The Masai believe that when a woman has sex with a younger man (in truth I have no way of knowing the relative ages), the woman becomes younger and more beautiful. Perhaps this, too, was part of the total social fact. As I speculate about Claudia having sex with a Masai warrior, I wonder if Fairfax was troubled by these thoughts.

Letterman's notion of the universal spirit has a commercial aspect: it stands for that human striving which exists as a counter to the banality of human life in the suburbs and malls of our countries. According to this flattering theory, the audience are players in a bigger drama. The human spirit is trundled on to reassure them that they are still party to the heroic, which cynical people might think has departed the suburbs some time ago.

21

The walls of the police cell where Tepilit was held are still visible. On one side they are at full height. The distinct lozenges of mud have gone, worn down by the weather, but it is possible to see their outlines in the dissolving walls. They are like sugar lumps in tea, moments before they vanish. Near the old police station is a compound of very tall barbed wire, with a collar pointing outward to prevent intrusion. It has no purpose as there is no gate. In this compound a huge piece of road-making equipment, a Hanomag grader, rests on breeze blocks. It has lost its tires and most of its engine; what is left is the crude metal, as simple as a wheelbarrow. It looks as though it stopped work a decade ago. There was a period of austerity in government fiscal policy when spares could not be imported.

The police have moved to another town farther up the river that gives Ewaso Narok its name, Black River. Now Ewaso Narok is, apart from the stranded earthmover, home only to two bars and a shop selling soap, maize meal and other staples. Masai elders enter these tiny shacks, elegant in their cloaks and blankets but looking to me—from the dusty, baking cab of my Toyota—shifty. You see these people, the ones who have overdone the booze, in all tribal places, confirming, like some Victorian temperance tract, the dangers of drink. Their eyes are yellow, their focus unsteady and their stride is either exaggeratedly purposeful or shambling. One elder in a blanket rests his sticks against the wall of the former jail and has a pee, contributing minutely to the eventual disappearance of the police station. In front of the former police station is a weeping pepper tree and some huge but untidy cacti, giant fibrous plants. It is possible to reconstruct the police post in the mind's eye, a small building, tin-roofed, with a verandah and a line of large white painted rocks that contained a garden of cacti and the youthful version of this lachrymose tree. I am thinking of a scene at this police post, the arrest of Tepilit, the intervention of Fairfax, the impressive dignity of the accused and the relentless, incomprehensible workings of the white man's justice.

The track out of Ewaso Narok is hard to follow. It soon unravels like thread falling off a spindle. I take what I hope is the main path. Really, I don't care if I get lost. I have no fear and, despite the deadline Letterman has conjured up, no sense of urgency. I stop to give a lift to two young warriors, who are fully made up in ochre, topped by headdresses. Hours of work have gone into their plaited hair. They have a curious way of sitting on the backseat, unfamiliar with the correct posture. As the Toyota moves forward they fall backward. One reaches over my shoulder and cranes his neck so that he can look at himself in the mirror. In Swahili I ask them where they are going. They are heading for a gathering at a place I cannot see on my map, but they seem content with the direction I have chosen. From them comes a smell that I find achingly familiar; they and their spears and shields give off the scent of Africa: woodsmoke, hides, cattle and dust. We travel almost in silence for a few miles. They inspect any other Masai they see on the track closely. Only then do they speak. One of the boys bangs the seat right behind my head urgently, and indicates that I should stop to pick up another couple of young warriors. These two boys say nothing to me as they get in, first handing their weapons to their friends.

We come to a river, absent from my map, where suddenly I see the plains and both banks smeared with color. A few hundred Masai are gathered, the later arrivals dotting the savannah to the south, advancing in pairs or small knots of red and purple. The plain is like a field of poppies, with the flowers growing most thickly near the river. The boys get out of the Toyota. One sticks his head in my window and says, "Thank you." He is practicing his English, without any reference to the meaning of the phrase.

A hunter turned safari operator, Oskar Koenig, describes a ceremony he calls the Festival of Love, which he purports to have witnessed: "One of the young men knelt by the cowhide near a hole in the ground, which, as I knew, was meant to resemble the vagina. His young body reared in sexuality, when he performed the act of fecundation . . ." According to Koenig, this led to a month-long orgy involving virgins and she-asses garlanded for the occasion. (The asses probably owe something to Koenig's native Bavaria, where uxorious cows are garlanded and brought up to the Alpine pastures each summer.) Koenig, concealed behind some rocks, watched this ceremony for some hours. He was deeply impressed by the monumental nature of this sexual feast, Wagnerian in its scale. He concludes: "So although at first it is also natural for civilized people to condemn out of hand what I had just witnessed as disgraceful heathen bestiality, they too, if they were honest, might come to feel it was at least partly redeemed by the genuine religious conviction on which it is based."

I have found no mention of this Festival of Love in any other accounts of the Masai, but there is something blatantly sexual about the warriors. They are like heavy metal rock stars primped and primed for sex. Yet—like my friend S. O. Letterman—they have a gentle, effeminate side, a dandyism and a preoccupation with details of appearance and decoration.

The plain stretches all the way to Lake Natron, which lies sunk below the hills, with its dead still ether water and its atolls of flamingos. From this apparently empty country, the Masai are streaming, bright rivulets. There is no one to tell me what is going on. I imagine this is how Claudia felt. I walk closer to the river, where there are some huts. I can see now that they are dancing and processing around the boma. I wonder if they will ask me to go, but apart from a few curious glances, quickly snuffed, they ignore me. I am floating here completely alone in a Masai universe.

The warriors now form a line and skip into the enclosure. A second group approaches from the other side and lines of girls form in the middle of the enclosure to admire and tease them. One of the warriors is in a fit. His friends carry his rigid, moaning body to one side and an older woman splashes him with water. The warriors, their spears resting on their shoulders, take very small steps and chant in time, breathy snorts—*"Hooh, hooh, hooh"*—as they circle the girls and pass the second line of warriors, moving in the opposite direction. The girls are singing now, a high, nasal whine that sounds more Arab than African. They seem to find the sexual promenading of the warriors amusing. They are laden with beads and their breasts are bobbing and rippling with static.

After an hour or more the dancing stops. Some Masai are drifting away. Again the plain blooms. I move on. Nobody takes much notice. The sun is low now and I need a lot of time to pitch my tent where I am headed, the dry watercourse near the laibon's village. I drive along the track, my heart full. I have left behind a perfect segment of the universe we inhabit so blindly. Claudia must have seen something like this many times—dances, endless dances, meaning what? Perhaps meaning nothing until you come along and ask what they mean. I have an overwhelming feeling that these dances, which have been going on unchanged for hundreds, perhaps thousands of years, are truer to the "*âme collective*" than our restless, critical, self-obsessed quadrilles. Yet even as I think it, I know it to be a ridiculous thought. We are all dancing hopefully and blindly, in our own way.

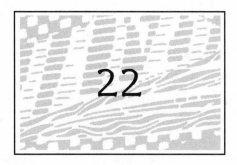

The canvas of my tent (to be exact, not canvas but a green plastic material) is flapping in the breeze that comes over the plains and stirs the dry leaves where they lie on the bottom of the dry river. Outside, the embers of my fire glow as the breeze fans them. A lion roars in the dense thicket into which the watercourse runs. Over at the laibon's engang they are bedded down behind their own thicket of thorn bushes, the cattle jammed together in a large boma and the goats in a smaller one right in the middle, as far from the athletic leopards as possible. My travel alarm glows in the dark. It is four-thirty in the morning. I am out here alone, unprotected, only a thin piece of plastic canvas away from lions, buffalo, leopards and hyena. But I am more disturbed by the sharp, diving whine of a mosquito, which produces an anticipatory tension by its frequency alone, just like the moment when the dentist turned on his drill and swung the whole clumsy contraption over my youthful, gaping mouth.

I wonder if the children in the engang are frightened. Our own children are now so far removed from danger, at least of the primal kind; these Masai are so close to it that you would expect them to be cowed and fearful. Outside the engang is a night world into which the Masai never venture. It is a combat zone that they concede to the predators until morning, when they drive out their cattle again past sleeping lions and strangely reticent hyena. The children are left out on the plains with a few goats from a very young age. Yet as they step forward for a greeting, receiving the palms of your hands on their springy hair, they show no sign of fear or anxiety. With their monsters and wolves and unpredictable dangers, fairy stories are supposed to prepare children for life in some symbolic fashion. Here the dangers are real. In the few weeks that have gone by a boy from the village has been killed by an elephant. If my understanding is correct, the boy was looking for a missing goat on the edge of the thicket when he was charged by a cow elephant and killed. There is no mourning for children; by the next day the body was eaten by the hyenas. There is a compensation scheme, and the laibon wishes me to drive one of his sons fifty miles to a small town to collect the papers. My arrival and my anticipated help with the paperwork have been fortuitous. I don't like to ask how much money they will receive from the government, but the laibon tells me: seventy-five dollars, the price of two new cows. I realize that the forty-nine cows that were offered to the district officer's relatives was a huge sum, however you measure it. And the district officer's family got nothing.

Dawn is approaching. The roof of the tent begins to glow, like the mantle of a gas lamp turned up very slowly. It is cool outside as I throw a log on the gently breathing embers. I put the kettle, already nicely blackened and battered, into the pile of ash and climb back into my camp bed. Wakefulness at this time of day is notoriously unsettling: in London it brings balls of anxiety to the gut as the sodden city outside sneers at the sleepless. Here I feel awake and ready, compelled to be on my feet when the sun reaches us, and the cattle, fretful and peckish, are released in a torrent of bay and brown and white, their huge horns gradually unlocking and separating as they spread out into the plain. The warriors always accompany them when they must travel long distances to find green grass. Green grass, green grass.

Predawn. Claudia lying in her hut listening for the first sounds of life. A satisfying pile of notes and tapes accumulating. The tapes, the same ones I have back at Mr. Shah's cumin-scented hotel, neatly stacked on a shelf made from a tea chest draped with Somali cloth. Over at the engang they are starting their fires into life. Is Claudia longing for her Masai lover? When and where does he visit her? The emptiness of the landscape is illusory; there is no privacy here. A warrior will plant his spear outside one of the small huts to indicate that he is inside and should not be disturbed, but I can't imagine Claudia, chic Parisienne, et cetera, allowing her relationship to be semaphored in this way from outside her own hut.

As I lie here under the green, seaweedy tent I remember, from some trite television interview, a remark made by Brigitte Bardot, loopy Parisienne, namely, that in all her many love affairs she was off at the first sign of the waning of passion. Perhaps Claudia grew tired of Tepilit. Perhaps the cultural divide was emphasized by their being lovers and she quickly found she had nothing to say to him.

Victoria and I have undoubtedly passed that milepost. Victoria thinks that I am not sufficiently in love with her to want children. Even the most liberated women believe that there is an evident connection between sex and children, a notion whose truth is tested only after the event. After her unfaithfulness, I found the connection severed. If the purpose of sex is to have children, then is there a special sort of casual, slightly illicit sex with near-strangers that has nothing to do with procreation and is also more exciting than the other steady sort? (The wronged one feels entitled to the interrogatory role.)

"What do you mean?"

"Was it more exciting?"

"Don't."

"You know what I mean. The whole business. Getting clothes off, zippers, panties, his cock, what he wants to do to you and you to him."

"You make it sound sort of mechanical."

"Oh, so it was not sort of mechanical, but quite tender with a lot of cozy conversation? How nice."

"Oh, Jesus."

"What I mean is, why can't you just admit that it was wonderfully exciting to fuck somebody else?"

"How stupid do you think I am? If I say it was wonderfully exciting, you will wonder when I am going to do it again, and if I say it was a mistake, which it was, you are going to ask me under what circumstances it might not have been a mistake."

"Actually, I could ask you a lot more interesting questions than that."

"I know, like how big his cock was and so on. But these are not questions that come into it."

"Did he come in your mouth?"

"Please. I have apologized, I have groveled. I can't do any more. I just hope it will pass. That's the accepted wisdom."

" 'Time is the great healer.' The trouble is I don't want to be healed."

"You don't want to be healed because it means you don't have to justify running away."

I'm the injured party, yet she is suffering more than I am.

The sun is now striking the tent and the trees around, producing an underwater effect on my green tent like kelp swaying in a tide. I clamber out of bed. I have to make a great effort to keep the tent tidy. It's amazing how quickly my few possessions become disarranged. Claudia lived here for nearly four years, creating a small, domestic homestead. Often she would go to Nairobi or the coast for a break and to get supplies.

The fire burns evenly with a thin hot flame, as though there are no oils or resins in the wood. I am drinking my coffee from a tin mug and toasting a large slice of bread on a fork while bacon fries in the pan and scents the air, and the bee-eaters begin their busy day and the vervet monkeys start to squabble. Although I know that in these matters there is almost no limit to what people will do, I am horrified that Victoria should have subjected herself to an AIDS test and—as I have heard happens—the offers of emotional counseling and financial advice. My heart, however, does not respond in the desired way to her letter and certificate. I see it as a silly gesture springing from her work in advertising, the promotion of appearance over substance. What she won't want to hear is that I am cured of the madness that kept me from sleeping at night and the imagination that played havoc with my peace of mind during the day.

This seems to be the way it is with men and women; buckets of water from a well, one drawing deep while the other is empty, and so on, as if there were a physical law governing the amount of emotional nourishment available to a couple. Bardot with her crazy affection for animals, Claudia and her unspeakable death, Victoria and her AIDS test: I see them all linked in some fashion. I see women as closer to the tragic than men because of the frailty of their expectations, which have no solid foundation in the world. I see their hopes like Masai villages, impermanent and leaving few marks on the landscape. Of course, I could never tell any woman these thoughts. Perhaps, like Letterman, I think of myself as having some useful feminine understanding.

The bacon is strongly scented, very porcine; in the pan it is not going brown but looking more like a slice of pig than bacon should. I prod it with a fork and brown it on the fire before introducing it to the thick slice of toast. Another cup of coffee is ready as I bite into my breakfast. It's surprisingly good even though the presentiments of pig are confirmed by the taste. I throw the rind, as thick as a pencil, in the direction of the vervet monkeys, but they show no understanding of my offer. Nobody has ever donated anything to them before.

From across the open stretch of ground hemmed in by the watercourse and the thicket, at least half a mile away, I can clearly hear the engang preparing for the dam burst of cattle. I hurry over in that direction. I am impelled there. The grass is so dry it seems impossible that it can ever come to life again: yet the huge acacia trees along the riverbed are putting out blossom, delicate sprigs of green in anticipation of the rains to come.

Mana. The old anthropological concept dreamed up in the universities to describe the potentialities of nature as understood by primitive people. As I stride across the plain I feel I have a glimmering of what it means. It means a nervous dependence upon nature, a relationship with a stepparent who can never be entirely relied upon. Nonstop vigilance and propitiation are advisable. The importance of trying to keep in nature's good books is plain as the cattle call and stamp impatiently.

Today the laibon is expecting me to take his son in the Toyota. His son is standing near the main entrance, ready for the journey, carrying a stick, a spear and a small leather bottle, similar to the sort of thing drunken youths use to squirt wine down their throats before braving the bulls in Pamplona. (I have done this myself, although no bull came anywhere near me.) The cattle are thin and some are listless, but so far there have been no deaths. The young men split the cattle into two groups and head off to find pasture. Two girls are loading the donkeys with water containers and sacks. They greet me, but they are amused by my appearance. I see them discussing me; one of them doubles up. They compose themselves as the laibon appears and suggests we sit down for tea. With a few whacks and some loud whistles, they drive the donkeys out of the enclosure.

The laibon's face is always troubled, as though the thoughts that are his special preserve are weighing on him heavily. He drinks the tea brought to us by the grandmother, the *koko,* gravely, and makes exasperated noises.

The laibon's son, Paramat, and I walk back to my camp. He is tall and has an elongated, finely made face, a Masai face, lending some weight to the myth that the Masai came from the Nile. When he smiles, he looks slightly goofy, the skin pulled tight over his cheeks, like the face children make by sticking their fingers in the corners of their mouths.

Mr. Shah's fax machine has been working overtime. Faxes have arrived at all hours from LA and London. As I pull up at the back of the hotel, Mr. Shah is waiting with a folder full of them; his expression, although friendly, contains around his mouth a little reproach that I should have been away from the action for so long.

"I've been up to my ears," he says.

There have been many diversions. It took us some time to get to Kitumbeine, and the district officer had knocked off. We found him drunk in his bungalow. With the promise of money he accompanied us to his office for the forms. He had trouble finding them and managed to catch his finger in a filing cabinet. There seemed to me no chance of the necessary chain of events being completed. The office, which displayed portraits of both the last president and the new one, was filled with stale air. It was air into which farts and old food odors had been released, but which was completely inert, as though in some way lacking ions or ozone, because the air conditioner had not worked for years and the windows were sealed. If the telephones had rung, you would have taken fright. They were Bakelite and dusty. Bundles of papers and box files were stacked on termite-proof metal shelves, but their labels had faded. Paramat stood by the doorway with the attitude of a tourist at the shrine of an exotic religious sect. He was both eager to adopt the right stance and unnerved by the strangeness of it.

The lodging of a compensation form, a simple enough matter, here required a respect for ritual. There had to be more to it than simply filling in a few spaces with a ballpoint; greater symbolic weight required. The money dispensers in the capital could be approached only through their acolyte, whose job it was to demand some offerings and make the right moves to ensure success. The district officer wanted to know if suitable precautions had been taken to avoid the elephants. I inquired about the nature of these precautions.

"They are ferocious beasts," he said, "and these people sometimes are ignoring the law of the jungle. Some of them are even looking out for compensation."

Eventually the police certificate was accepted, the forms were filled and stamped, and placed in a tray marked "Out." I felt they might have a better chance of getting to the capital if they were folded into paper airplanes and launched out of the door.

So I have been away longer than I said I would be, and Mr. Shah is a little surprised at my dereliction. To him the outside world, in particular Los Angeles and London, is humming with importance. I would hate to have to explain to him the true state of affairs. He hands me a brown manila file and a handwritten invoice, which I imagine he is giving to me now while the connection between the reams of faxes and the many noughts, in local shillings, of his invoice is still fresh. He asks me about my safari, but I know that what happens out there is of no interest to him. Out there—not so far, as from it happens the center of the town—a realm of nothingness exists. From out there, however, the view is very different.

There are some new faces in the dining room, a Danish family of mother, father and four small children. The sun has crabbed their gaze, so that when they turn to me I see a row of puppies squinting.

When I returned to the laibon's village with the paperwork, he was looking out toward Ol Doinyo Lengai, waiting for the sound and the dust and the cries of his cattle coming back. We handed over the stamped forms, which he gave to the koko for safe keeping. The newly born goats were kept in a pen under her bed. I wondered where she would keep these papers.

"Fahfakhs is coming," the laibon said in Swahili. I didn't know if this was a question or a prediction. I had told him that I had met Fairfax. He wasn't surprised that Fairfax was still alive. Now I have his message: "Glad to help if I can. Stop. Memory not what it was. Stop. Please contact me at Muthaiga. Stop. Thomas

Fairfax." So perhaps the laibon's pebbles, worn smooth by his hands and his predecessors' right back to the great Mbatian, had told him. The laibon asked me to sit in the boma, and pointed to my tape recorder. He had much on his mind.

I lie down on my bed and remove my socks before looking at the folder. Letterman would like to see a first draft by the time I meet him in London. My legs are shaded by the dust that has gathered over the past few days, so that the contrast is like a Coppertone ad, with the puppy pulling a little girl's panties off. I look at my legs critically. God knows how much time we spend in our lives scrutinizing our bodies. My legs are now pleasantly brown, quite well formed, I believe. I am happy to see them in this workmanlike state. It confirms to me that I am far from the northern climates, the habitat of the Brussels sprout, where something sickly was spreading over my relationship with Victoria— just like the smell of overcooked vegetables. When I think of Victoria, now not very often, I no longer think of her lips in fellatio with a stranger in a hotel room; instead I remember their former, *framboise* state. I don't feel that churning, dread longing anymore, which seemed like a curse from an irrational and limitless supply of malevolence. I couldn't bear to be in its thrall for another day. I had to go. I don't suppose she will understand this, or the connection I am making, tentatively, with Claudia's fate.

Here in Mr. Shah's hotel or out on the plains I find myself making all sorts of airy leaps and connections effortlessly. I seem to be free of mundane anxieties. I can see now the attraction of those religions that exalt the achievement of personal tranquillity above all else. Really they are invitations to live the life of the mind, however ill equipped the mind may be.

24

Professor Uitsmijter has suggested what at first seems a crazy solution to my translation problems: I place my tape recorder next to the phone, he records the laibon's words in Nairobi and he faxes back the translation. He has some electronic equipment, originally intended for the language laboratory, that enhances the sound quality. As a result, my telephone and fax bill is much greater than the bill for board and lodging. Mr. Shah is becoming concerned: he sees something unbusinesslike in me, which I accept must be visible to others. Victoria says I have "blind spots, quite amazing blind spots about the real world for someone who likes to think he is so aware."

I have made more progress with the script. I have written the ending, incorporating Letterman's new lines. I have also started to write about the lion hunt organized by Claudia for Waindell Leavitt. But already I am running into problems. How do you make a film of a man faking a documentary about a lion hunt? How will Letterman fake that? And on that subject, how much of the unknown and unknowable can I sketch in? Elie Wiesel said a novel about Auschwitz is either not a novel or not about

Auschwitz. What about a movie where the main character ends up in Auschwitz? This is not supposed to be fiction, but as I write I find myself obliged to make a judgment about Leavitt. Leavitt's bombastic, trivial films were completely phoney. Claudia must have known that.

Modern audiences—I can hear Letterman saying this—won't go for the idea that Claudia, who is in some senses—although we're not spelling this out, okay—a new woman, would take part in the killing of lions for a documentary. Instead we must present this sequence as entirely Waindell Leavitt's folly, into which Claudia is drawn in some way to protect the Masai against manipulation. Leavitt becomes that stock character, the insensitive male exploiter. But Claudia's notes tell another story: she was intrigued by the whole idea and even suggested to Leavitt where they might find lions. It didn't take her long to regret taking part.

Also, I am wondering what part Claudia's lover, the laibon's brother, should take in this. After he is wounded in this staged hunt, perhaps she could be seen to nurse him daily with iodine and Mercurochrome, out of remorse, but in the process establishing the first physical contact. I have suggested that we use Maa with subtitles (I am thinking of *Dances with Wolves* and *The Last of the Mohicans*). This scene could convey the burgeoning friendship and even love effectively. The initial, halting conversation would be about Masai bravery and the importance of showing no pain. Tepilit would question her about her interest in Masai women and why she seemed so concerned with their unremarkable tasks. She would explain the nature of her interest, so awakening in him a wish to know more about what goes on outside Masailand and also opening his eyes to the fact that the white folk see the Masai as childlike. Of course Claudia is sensitive to the nuances.

She tries to warn him. She says that the outside world has plenty of its own problems. The audience, but not Tepilit, understands by now her father's situation in Paris, so her warnings are poignant. But he is keen to join the King's African Rifles and go off and fight. She discourages him. After a few days he is well enough to travel, and one of Leavitt's Willys safari cars takes them home. I plan a scene here in which the car makes its way through the vast landscape, the wounded Masai lying in the back. As they approach the valley overlooked by the Mountain of God, he asks her to accept from him the gift of a necklace. Before she can answer, they are engulfed by a crowd of young warriors, who want to hear the rumors of the lion hunt and the fight that it provoked confirmed. In this way, she has become part of the total social fact, but we will present it as part of the age-old conflict between love and duty.

Then I must consider the nature of their—of course—doomed love affair. Again I wonder how much Fairfax knows. Is it possible that in 1943 or 1944 she would have told him, liberated Parisienne that she was, the details? Would he have cross-questioned her? (I am probably too influenced by my own feelings regarding Victoria.) I can see that for the purpose of our movie any relationship between Claudia and Tepilit will have to be clouded in romanticism. I consider the question of kissing. Is it likely that they would have kissed? Of course Red Indian (Native American) women have often been kissed in movies by cowboys and soldiers, but how do we think a six-foot-three-inch Masai, almost naked, kissing a French woman will play? I compose a fax to Letterman. I need guidance on how sensational he wants the script to be. I also want to establish the degree to which he wants to be true to the facts, such as they are. I feel sure that Claudia would have shown Tepilit, if it was necessary, some of the metropolitan refinements of sexual practice. And yet, how can I know? Perhaps the Masai have taboos against fellatio and the other things the French, with their gastronomic traditions, favor in the sexual realm. I also wonder if she feared syphilis. Bror Blixen, Karen Blixen's husband, had syphilis, and it was said to be common among the Masai. But then the settlers—settlers in all countries, as it happens—were particularly receptive to uninformed rumor. The unruly, incomprehensible natives were very quickly mythologized. Until 1942 there was no reliable cure for syphilis, too late for Karen Blixen.

This is what happens: you start by wondering whether two people kiss and it leads away into the unknowable.

I see now that the simplest reconstruction is fraught with difficulty. And yet there are two witnesses—three, if you count Lady De Marr—still alive. Of course, there are no witnesses to what happened at the other end of her journey.

Pondering these problems, I stand by the window. The river has been flowing quite violently recently as the clouds (which the laibon was scanning each day) collide with the summit of the mountain, up above the religious suburbs, to produce rain. There has been a scandal up there, too. One of the missionaries has been badly beaten and stabbed. It is said that he was interfering with the choirgirls, some of whom were betrothed. My informant is the Anglican vicar. Out here, being white still counts for a lot. It is a serious matter, attacking a white person, let alone a white minister. I wonder, however, if they are beginning to have suspicions about our parking-lot creeds and oven-ready ideas. This local Swaggart, who has tears in his eyes as he preaches the gospel, is tormented by the rows of large, bobbing girls in front of him as they sing the bouncy gospel renditions of traditional hymns. As they sway and raise their arms, he sees thirty pairs of large breasts, and he imagines the same quantity of round thighs rolling and separating under the cassocks that he has had sent from Raleigh. In the vestry and in his bungalow, under the pretext of extra rehearsal, he has been fondling these big brown girls and offering them cigarettes and money for sex. Perhaps he has succeeded. The vicar says that a young Larusa, Masai, after all, has stabbed him and beaten him with a stick, and the whole town is talking about it. Some are waiting for God to express an opinion.

The stakes in the religious free market have been raised. My friend the vicar is uncharitably pleased. There is something gossipy and gay about him. His conclusion is that a religion that counts its success by numbers of converts is suspect. He seems to be implying that sound religions are those that are hereditary. I can see some truth in this. Anyone who converts must have a motive. Many of Léon Cohn-Casson's contemporaries converted in order to be more French. They believed, all rational men believed, that Judaism was simply a tribal leftover. To be French required a Western European faith. It demanded a leafy, abundant, ovoid religion, not a stony, nomadic, ascetic religion. The Jews from Alsace, the intellectuals, were convinced that a separate Jewish identity was on the wane anyway. Rational thought was the product of rational ways of organizing industry. Yet here on the mountain in the last decade of the century there is a supermarket of discount religions.

Claudia detects a relationship between religious thought and the way Masai society is organized. In her thesis she writes about it, but she also—I surmise—sees the downside (as Letterman says), namely, that none of these religious beliefs will be sufficiently adhesive to hold Masai society together once the other solvents get to work. And what Claudia was to find is that our century has proved that the irrational and the immaterial have as strong a hold as ever. *This way for the showers, ladies and gentlemen. Your luggage will be delivered later to your quarters.*

I get an idea for another scene: Claudia makes a desperate journey to see the governor to try to have Tepilit reprieved. He is charming and urbane, naturally, but refuses to help. He has no grounds for interfering in due process. He suggests that the rule of law is, in these troubled times, more important than ever, but the audience gets the impression that he is a pompous prick, giving a foreigner a little lecture about how things are done in the Empire.

In desperation she tells Fairfax that she and Tepilit have been lovers. He is outraged. He asks her to go to a doctor to be tested for syphilis. A new cure has been available in Europe for two or three years, he says coldly.

This quarrel is the cause of their separation, which is to end so tragically.

The koko served us tea as we sat in the middle of the boma after the cattle had gone. (We were probably sitting on about three feet of friable dried dung.) She poured the tea into large enamel mugs. I had seen the donkeys plodding reluctantly up the escarpment to fetch water miles away. Donkeys are not natural enthusiasts; they walk as if they have arthritis. I felt guilty that this hard-won water should be wasted on a tea ritual when I had gallons of mineral water at my camp. But she ministered to us as the tape recorder whirred. The tea was loaded with sugar, and milk from a gourd was added in a thin stream like milk being drawn from a cow's udder. As she was pouring the tea it occurred to me that maybe she knew Claudia too. She was the first of the laibon's four wives many years ago. Now the old lady is a benign presence who gives the engang a heart.

· · ·

I am now reading Uitsmijter's transcript of what the laibon had on his mind. The owl of Minerva flies as dusk is falling: the laibon believes he is not long for this earth. He has had some revelations that he wants to pass on to me. They are that the rains are going to cease falling and, because of the restrictions placed on their movement, the Masai will not be able to follow their tradition of moving on. As I read, it seems to me that this is not his literal meaning. He is voicing the complaint of all old people about the closing down of their universe. Death is the removal of all the possibilities that sustain us in our lives. But also, I guess, he is exercising his right as a laibon to prophesy. Headmasters, senators, judges, priests, all see themselves as having a particular duty in this regard. A politician invited to make the wedding speech can be relied upon to dish up some predictions along with the eternal verities. The laibon retells the accounts of his illustrious ancestors of the great migration from the North. He wants me, for some reason, to realize that he knows the lights are going out in the Masai world. He sees that finally the Masai myths have been overtaken. He tells me of a great battle his ancestors fought near Lake Victoria. He speaks of a battle against the Germans. He prophesies a war of the Masai against the townies. (I wonder if he realized that there are serried ranks of townies behind the front line that he has encountered.) The pebbles he has thrown have shown these things.

The uprising against the townies will take place after the next eunoto, which is the gathering of warriors at the end of their time as morans. Thousands of warriors collect from the huge Masai district to have their heads shaved by their mothers before undergoing rituals to launch them on their new—somewhat dull—life as elders. There is no music, only the hoarse, erratic bellow of a kudu horn and the chanting, a strange noise that comes from inside the earth itself, as though the rocks and the soil were singing as best they could.

The infinite possibilities of Masai life, on the face of it, a simple desire to wander the earth following the cattle, have been denied. Every single thing the Masai value depends upon this possibility. This is the object of life. It is life.

Uitsmijter, under the academic compulsion to explain, adds a note about the nature of prophecy among the Masai and— the comparative method—among other tribes such as the Dinka and the Nuer. Prophecy is expected of the laibons. It is usually expressed in the vaguest terms, like a horoscope in the newspapers.

Another disciple of Nostradamus, S. O. Letterman, has been throwing the pebbles in LA and finds the omens good. So far no progress with the female lead. But Mel Gibson likes the treatment, which Letterman himself has had to work up a little. In principle he would like to do the movie, but you know how it is with agents. (I don't, as a matter of fact, but this is the chummy method at work.) In many ways the time is right— fiftieth anniversary, uncertainties in the world, French self-examination and so on—for just such a movie. It feels right. The response is good. He is off to Paris to interview actresses.

This sounds like a wonderful opportunity for Letterman to bring to bear his feminine understanding on eager actresses, although something tells me that his Californian slightly absurd boyish middle-aged charm will not go down well in Paris. I wonder if what Mencken called "the usual hypocrisies" aren't too well understood by women in Paris. I am sure that Letterman would like to have some of Polanski's assurance with young women, a knowingness that makes the Californian mania for self-presentation look quaint. The success—I am looking out of the window at the thickly carpeted mountainside—comes from the knowledge of shared weakness, the weakness of both men and women in matters of sex and passion. It does not arise, as Letterman imagines, from impressing on women your sympathy and sensitivity to their imagined plight. This is why bastards continue to score heavily with women who should know better. For all his working of the flesh and his golden suntan and his deployment of pop philosophies and credos, Letterman is too contrived an individual to be successful with the sort of Frenchwoman—my gaze descends from the mountain to my backyard, where they are pegging out a goatskin—he wants to play the part of Claudia. But I can't be sure.

The interviews are conducted at the St. James's club off the avenue Foch. Letterman has filled his suite with striking vases of flowers. He has a few modish novels, a collection of articles by Paul Bordieu, a copy of *The New York Review of Books* and some scripts lying on the table in front of the sofa, where he sits with a bottle of St. Yorre—never Perrier—and an ice bucket of champagne, sacramental, in front of him to greet the actresses as they are shown in. He has plenty of time for these creatures. He feels himself to be privileged. Casting enables him to ask all sorts of personal questions, which give him an insight into the kind of life that young, beautiful French actresses live. In his own way he is something of an expert on the private lives of actresses. Young actresses dwell in a quandary. They are strongly moved to express themselves outside the confines of their lovely bodies, while, of course, conscious that a large part of their appeal lies just there. They are very aware, too, that what Letterman is presenting to them is not just a script and a lot of money, but an intimate relationship with himself. This relationship is evidently not to be confused with a sexual relationship; it is just that once you have entered into an artistic liaison of this intensity, the sexual shenanigans are likely to follow.

But young actresses in Paris have boyfriends who are successful composers, video producers and photographers. Even the very young in Paris are successful. It is a French talent. From poverty to Giorgio Armani takes no time at all, and in that brief time, if there is some uncertainty and a few wrong turns, they are contemplated over elaborate meals in good restaurants. So Letterman has to burnish his act. He is, of course, holding a few cards: this is a movie with a woman in the lead and it will largely be in English. (Letterman likes my idea of using Maa and subtitles very much; he was hoping I would suggest something like that.) It is also a movie that is likely to be controversial in Paris. This appeals to the actresses he is interviewing. All the actresses think that it is vital that France should, as they say, engage herself with the past. Their analysis may not go any deeper than that, but it is expressed in a way that impresses Letterman, a sort of passionate commitment to the power of the idea, which he has—subversively—been advocating in Hollywood for years. So he says. He mentions Alain Resnais and Louis Malle as influences.

There are nine actresses to see in the first run. Letterman closets himself with these women all day. Occasionally he has to call in his assistant, a young Algerian Parisian called Farwaggi, to translate, but most of Farwaggi's job is to make sure tapes are delivered, CVs collected and taxis ordered. He is expected to give his opinion only when asked, although even these requests are tendentious. Letterman likes him because he is neither too elegant nor too assured. In a curious way—Letterman thinks— he bears the same relationship to Parisian life that the Hispanics have to LA life. Letterman is a believer in the immigrant mentality. His grandparents were immigrants themselves, from Frankfurt. His father was born in Germany, and was a teenager when they brought him to Detroit. They took ship as soon as they saw the way things were going in 1934.

Farwaggi is also in charge of ordering room service. Letterman likes to pander to the actresses' wishes. Getting behind their personal defenses is part of his strategy. Farwaggi, his Arab provenance showing in the bluish (Camus-esque, thinks Letterman) stubble that grows stronger as the day progresses, a gentle mycological stain spreading on his eager, almost good-looking face, spends all day either on the phone ordering variations on the club's menus or rushing to and from the fax office. Letterman's activities are characterized by bustle and urgency.

He is looking for an easy rapport, but he does not want it to be too easy. In his mind's eye he sees a girl who has brains (although he knows that some very dim actresses can read with all the appearance of intelligence, and the converse), who has a slight resistance to the Hollywoodification of Claudia's life. He wants to be able to use her independence of mind—"attitude," as they say—to advantage. He also wishes to engage in a good argument with her about the nature of the character. After the opening pleasantries—"What have you been doing? What movies have you been in recently?"—he asks each of them what she knows about Claude Cohn-Casson. "How would you treat the question of the collaboration of her countrymen and -women in her death?" he asks. "Because this is something we are still thinking about, the extent to which it should be part of the story."

"France must engage with her past."

"Do you think movies should, in some way," he says, leaning back, consciously preparing himself to listen, "start out with this kind of dialectic?"

The French like the word. The Minister of Culture uses it when he's in a conversational hole. To Letterman, who was once a fan of Marcuse, it is a distinctly toothsome word. In that one word, he sees, you have a basic tenet of European thought, namely that ideas are antagonistic and aggressive. Ideas are like negative atoms—or does he mean ions?—rushing around attempting to resolve themselves. (Nobody, he has noted, seems much interested in the promised synthesis.)

For ten hours he watches the lovely squirrel lips, the high, *paysanne* cheekbones, the smoky eyes, the darkly glowing hair, the nervously crossed legs, the *langoustine* fingers, the half-risen *brioche* breasts. This one uses the word *niveau,* which he does not know, as though it is an English word, one of those border-hopping words like *ambience.* She is making a distinction between parochial films and films on a global *niveau.* Her belief is that to reach a very wide audience one must establish character first so the audience can identify itself with the issue, through the character. This is her opinion, anyway. She makes a small, dismissive explosion with her lips, like a gentle fart. She smiles. She knows his game. There is none of that fake girlishness that young women employ in California. If anything, Letterman thinks, these women have a compulsion to reach a higher plane of conversation that strains credulity. Women can't win, he reflects, sympathetically.

He soon realizes that these actresses also have a distinctly French notion of Hollywood. He sees that many of the Hollywood films they admire have undergone a metamorphosis in France from straightforward studio fare to art. These movies have been carrying, like a sealed train, the bacillus of high art. Letterman resists the temptation to sneer at what some might consider pretentiousness. He recognizes that this willingness to fillet the intellectual and thematic from even the most ho-hum work is absent from the Anglo-Saxon world, yet he also thinks that he understands it because of his own (despite the tennis lessons and jogging) Jewishness. Even Hollywood's banalities and excesses have mythical appeal to these women. Places like Malibu and Beverly Hills glow in their imagination. They want to be degraded by the system and die in a pool of their own vomit in a motel, where rooms are rented by the hour to cowboys. (This is how he tells it later after some disillusionment has set in.)

The day has passed quickly. Despite the notes, and the Polaroids made by Farwaggi in his anteroom, and the trays of fruit, club sandwiches, *croques* and so on—the cheerfully arranged *amuse-gueules* ordered from the kitchen for each girl—he finds he is becoming confused about their identities. Instead of seeing the person depicted on the duckpond surface of the Polaroids, he sees an amalgam: this one's slightly dark upper lip, this one's nervy legs, this one's role in *Le Médecin malgré lui* at the Comédie Française (where he has recently sat through an excruciating evening of seventeenth-century high camp), this one's intensely white-and-brown eyes, this one's professed love of Shakespeare, this one's part in an erotic thriller (he can remember her buttocks from that movie, but he can't fix them to the right actress without his notes). It would be absurd to say that they have become one. No, he will be able to sort them out into a shortlist of three or four for further interview. But Claude Cohn-Casson has been subsumed by their physical selves, right here in the room, as sexy as hell. And the issues, as he sees them, have also been hijacked. These French women are in favor of contentious art. But they think that art has a quite separate existence from fact. They believe—and he finds the argument chic, too—that art is the final judgment.

He decides at this stage not to ask any of them to dinner. He is not quite sure that they would all accept, but that is not why he holds back. He feels, in the light of the subject matter and the seriousness of their conversations, that he should exhibit some seriousness of purpose, although he solicits their opinions about restaurants to show that he is not all big issues. But also these young women make him feel old. Now he is poised here in Paris, sipping a champagne so dry it tastes like flint, on the brink of old age. He will be fifty in a few years' time. He was born almost as the events of the movie were taking place. When they talk about these matters and the need to engage oneself with one's history, he realizes that "history" is the operative word. But he understands. He is cursed with this understanding. When he was growing up in Dearborn there was a succession of sad-sack, embarrassing (to a fan of Earl Morrall) Old World relations with funny accents who were constantly bellyaching about the war and—of course—the dreadful death and displacement that had taken place. To him, even then, it had been history, and it somehow deserved ill fortune; in the heedless fashion of the American suburbs, it seemed right to look down on the refugees from an old, superstition-riven world.

So he understands. They think people were different then.

He dismisses Farwaggi. It is eleven. Farwaggi moves toward the door, almost shuffling, a satrap by inheritance. He offers to return at eight.

"I'll call you," says Letterman. "I want to think a little first. I'm playing tennis and then I'll call you. You done good, kid."

The idiom means nothing to him, but he gets the idea. He smiles shyly.

"It was okay?" he asks. ("Eee"—sudden swoop—"twashokay?")

"Just great. Food for thought. See you tomorrow. Not before ten at the earliest."

Camus sets off into the night. This boy has studied at film school. He loves the films of John Ford. Letterman thinks John Ford films are ponderous nonsense. Particularly *Stagecoach*.

He runs a bath. The day, the expenditure of emotion—the oyster knife he has been inserting into these women's lives—

have tired him. He feels clammy. He undresses. His body always seems to bulk up after a day like this: he can see increased sponginess around his waist and chest. (One of the cruelest ironies of the death camps is that Jews were never meant to be thin.) He lies in the bath scented, marinated by the little sachets and ampoules of emollients he has tipped into the water. Not far away is the street where Claudia was brought up. It inspires him to be so close. He has found her house, which overlooks a park. In the park is a children's playground with a carousel.

He sees this movie now as his own story, his own personal work. His *oeuvre*. He is *l'auteur*.

I am waiting for Tom Fairfax. For an elderly man he has a great many demands on his time. He is a polo umpire, a judge of horseflesh, adviser to the Farmers' Union, a stalwart of regimental dinners and a confidant of opposition politicians.

Letterman sees the role of historical adviser in the way that he sees the role of writer, only less so. The historical adviser is there not to ensure verisimilitude, but to be an accomplice in furthering the aims of the producer. When I tell him that Fairfax seems to have played a very big part in Claudia's life, he doesn't see any problem. Great news, he says. As far as he is concerned, nobody cares how accurate our portrayal of Claudia's love life is. He cites *Out of Africa*. But Karen Blixen did not end up in Auschwitz, I reply. We are not making a documentary— get him on board if you can. Fifteen thousand for the research. Mr. Shah, although he does not comment, appears less concerned about my bill now. Letterman's expansive style is getting to him.

But I don't bring up the subject of money with Fairfax immediately. I ask him to come down for a few days and I also invite Lady De Marr. I offer to book them into the hotel, owned by an airline, which carries on a heroic but losing battle for French standards. The hotel operators are here only because of some trade-off between governments. This has resulted in a restaurant that serves the regional specialties of France to bemused locals. One woman, a party official's wife, is said by the Anglican vicar to have eaten twenty-one *croustades* of morels in a sauce of cream and truffle, with a *vapeur* of Armagnac, in the belief that she was fostering international relations. (The vicar ate the other four. Absolutely delicious.) But Fairfax has made his own arrangements. He will be staying at a coffee plantation on the edge of town. Lady De Marr will not be coming.

Letterman tells me that casting in Paris is going well. He has a shortlist. Candice Riberon who was in a thriller called *Le Métro* is his favorite so far, but there is a long way to go. I have seen *Le Métro*. It opens with a very long sex scene in a small apartment. On the bed lies Candice Riberon. For a few agonizing minutes the camera holds on her face as she experiences—she hardly seems to be enjoying—sexual attentions out of the range of the camera. Her face is very mobile. Her eyes close, open, close again. Her lips move in an anguished chewing motion, so that her mouth widens and closes, a fevered sea urchin. Now the camera begins to move down her body, over her breasts, which are lightly beaded (and quite widely separated) although it is hard to tell in the chiaroscuro created, as we are soon to find out, by the shutters of the apartment. As the camera moves down her body, which is undulating beneath its gaze, almost vibrating, and leaves her navel behind, it comes to a dark, tousled shape, not clearly visible in the low levels of light. Immediately the audience believes—I certainly believed—that somebody is eating her pussy. We do not see his face, but we see her hands clutching his head. It is moving up and down in an ever increasing tempo. She climaxes and pushes the face away. It is turned in this action toward the meagre amount of light, light which has a density and texture not often seen in real life, created by filling the air with smoke and piercing it with tungsten light. The camera holds this face. The eyes are open but they are unseeing. There is blood coming out of his ears. The camera cuts to Candice, dressing. Her body is boyish, her breasts quite full, a very dark, dense thicket just disappearing as her skirt is pulled up. The titles roll: LE MÉTRO. *Un Film de Jean-Claude Reed.* It is a shocking scene, because it starts by involving the audience in its raw eroticism and then turns on them, so that they feel guilty for the stirrings they have inevitably been experiencing. After this virtuoso shot, the rest of the film is disappointing, often silly, but I remember thinking how well Candice Riberon handled the rather artificial dialogue. I remember, too, her strangely spaced cheekbones and severely cut hair. She is a serial killer who picks up men in the Métro. I can imagine S. O. Letterman being drawn to her.

I try to see her as Claudia. In this movie she adopts a coldly dismissive tone with men—her lovers and *les flics*—which is supposed to be chic, and she is placed rather artificially in perfectly arranged and photographed surroundings. Her ostensible job is something in advertising or public relations, but this is laughable: people are always rushing off to catch planes or to have show-downs with clients or engage in unmotivated conspiracies to deceive the public. There is something so fatally trivial about this movie in its elevation of appearance over substance that I feel an irrational resistance to her as Claudia. Of course I know that movie actresses often cannot choose their roles. For a start, they are in a race against the clock: by the time they have the clout to choose the right roles, they are too old for them. Producers and directors adore very young women. Like the Masai, they think you can stay young by sleeping with young women. The filming of young actresses is a sexual act. But I can't prevent myself thinking that the person who is to play Claudia should possess a clearly defined personality of her own. This is crazy, because I have not yet been able to decide what Claudia was like. I want Fairfax to tell me, but I don't hold out much hope.

The hotel is quiet. Outside, the cottage industries have taken a rest as the heat of the afternoon settles heavily on the town like an unwelcome blanket. The earth throws off the heat it cannot accommodate. As I lie on my bed I can feel it coming in the window. It is like an open oven in a kitchen, giving off gusts of heat.

I am almost asleep. I think of Claudia and Victoria and Candice and I compare their facial motions in an impertinent fashion.

Mr. Shah wakes me. I am drained and startled. The mountain outside is darkening. He apologizes and hands me a note: Sir Thomas Fairfax is expecting me for dinner at Folly Farm.

"I am afraid I have come to the conclusion, reluctantly, that the different people and races of the world were never intended to meet. For thousands of years, hundreds of thousands, they stuck to their own backyards. When they did run into each other on the borders of their territories, they usually tried to kill each other. Primitive people regarded themselves as the only humans. In their languages they described themselves as 'the man' or 'the human.' The idea that we all belong to one human family is a relatively recent one. Of course Claudia believed it."

Fairfax and I are sitting on the verandah at Folly Farm. He is able to re-create his own world wherever he goes. He has no taste for the new world, either in Africa or in Europe. He was once a director of the company that owned this coffee estate, and he seems to have squatter's rights here for life. The manager is on holiday at the coast and Fairfax has seventeen rooms and six servants at his disposal. The verandah is long and overgrown with climbing plants, which are wrapped around the varnished poles that support the tin roof. Our drinks are served on elephants' feet, which make good side tables and were once popular as souvenirs. You can't give them away now.

"I think," he says, "that the Germans had convinced themselves that there was something noble in their quest to clean up the world. They were acting in the interests of Western civilization. When I was in Germany at the end of the war, I met hundreds of Germans who tried to explain this to me. They were upset that their efforts had been misunderstood. It was quite offensive really, particularly to me, this desire for a pat on the back."

We are edging nearer to the subject of Claudia, who, so far, has not been mentioned by name. We are silent now. The insects are egging him on.

"Look, old chap, I'm sorry about the note at the club. I must have been tight. I hope you didn't mind."

"I was touched. Please don't apologize."

"Tell me what you want to know from me and I'll see if I can oblige," he says, after another pause slashed and stabbed by the insect life.

"I want to know what she was like, and I want to clear up some questions that have been puzzling me and that don't appear on the record."

"Fire away. Or perhaps I had better have another brandy first."

He rings a bell. The mountain rises above us, now completely black against a sky that is spangled (what a charming, folksy word) with jagged sugar crystals.

"Do you want one?" he asks.

"I don't drink. Despite what you saw at the club. I gave it up a few years ago."

The servant, a white-coated padder trained for the infrequent appearance of people like us, goes off on the long march to the kitchens. We sit here, comfortably wrapped up by the night. I can see that England would be anathema to Fairfax. Here, with his little mustache, each hair as thick as a fishing line, and his noble, gelid face, he counts for something. There, he would be another old person elbowed and nudged by the hordes in their restive wildebeest migration in search of gratification.

But we can't start the serious business until the brandy arrives. We are like small boys on a high diving board, making excuses.

"How is Lady De Marr?" I ask.

"Camilla is a wonderful woman. By the way, she has sent some letters and notes for you. She and Claudia were very close for a while. But she hasn't been well. She has a problem with some little gland or other, which can throw her right off balance. There's no proper treatment out here but she refuses to go home. Home. I can think of nothing more awful than England for us. It's a nightmare. I can't understand a word they're saying on the television and the streets of London seem to be full of people in tennis clothes. I nearly married Camilla in the fifties, but it wouldn't have worked. We were friends, never lovers. Can I ask you one thing?"

"Please do."

"Is there any money in this historical adviser business? I didn't like to ask earlier."

I tell him the amount Letterman has promised.

"Bugger me. Well, I'll be blowed."

My mind turns, trivially, to the shot of Candice Riberon having posthumous oral sex.

"Have you got time to come out and see the laibon with me?" I ask.

"My dear Tim," he says, "fifteen thousand dollars is slightly more than my annual pension."

The brandy arrives. His whole life, like my very early life, has been punctuated by these soothing ceremonies. Servants throw a reticulation over the day, giving it some order. They are always busy with the morning coffee, the lunch, the tea and sponge cake, the drinks, the dinner. The Masai, I have read, cannot understand our preoccupation with eating; it fills our day. In France every other truck on the road is carrying food—*poulets* from Bresse, melons from Cavaillon, Camembert from Normandy. There is something risible about this mania.

"Where do you want to begin?" he asks. His right eye is tired, so that it lags minutely behind the other. He bombards the brandy with a violent infusion of soda from the large siphon. The brandy releases its poisonous fumes into the air already richly scented by unknown blooms.

"Where shall we begin?"

28

Nairobi. We start with a young man, Thomas Fairfax, in military khaki and flying jacket, climbing into his old biplane and taxiing down a runway. He adjusts the flaps, zips up his jacket, pulls down his goggles. The runway is simply a strip of grass, cleared of rocks. The plane lurches into motion. It bounces alarmingly as it gathers speed. A few Africans, clutching sticks and wearing skins, watch the plane as it turns, pauses, and then accelerates, leaving a cloud of dust. The plane climbs reluctantly, one set of wings dipping drunkenly. Soon it is passing over the spectacular Rift Valley. There is no sign of civilization, but herds of zebra and wildebeest and clumps of elephants marble the valley floor.

Ol Doinyo Lengai. A group of Masai is clearing stones from a stretch of grassland, in the shadow of the Mountain of God. A large white cross has been painted roughly on the ground. Claudia Cohn-Casson is sitting under an enormous African fig tree nearby, at a camp table spread with a Somali cloth. She has in front of her a typewriter, her recorder and her notes. A servant is preparing lunch on a fire. Claudia hears something. She looks up into the sky in the direction of Ol Doinyo Lengai.

We catch sight of a small plane circling the mountain. It dips its wings in acknowledgment of the landing strip, and circles, preparing to land.

Claudia stands up. She checks her appearance in a mirror hanging on a tree. With her lower lip she tucks the upper lip into her mouth for a moment. She is wearing a long, fitted skirt of khaki. She adjusts her hat, a round bush hat, and walks toward the makeshift landing strip. The plane is taxiing, pursued by a group of running Masai warriors, glorious in their red and purple robes, ochred hair, lion headdresses and so on. Claudia walks over toward the plane. She holds her hat on her head with one hand. The plane is still now, surrounded by the warriors. Fairfax is securing its wheels with rocks. He looks up to see her approaching. Behind her is Ol Doinyo Lengai. Its strange shape has become familiar to us. His face is still dirty from the dust and oil, except that around his eyes is a white patch where the goggles were. The Masai begin to sing. It is a strange, otherworldly noise. Claudia and Fairfax approach each other. The moment is unnaturally, poignantly, delayed. In his uniform, jacket unzipped, he is handsome and smiling. The singing of the Masai and the overwhelming landscape are thrilling. Claudia and Fairfax come closer. She is serene. He is perhaps surprised by her composure. She kisses him, three times.

"I am so glad you came."

(Her accent is very French but she speaks English fluently.)

"Anything to help a friend."

Fairfax is awkward. He would like to say something more graceful.

"Your face is dirty. You look—how you say?—as a raccoon."

Fairfax laughs. He wipes his face with his sleeve.

"Sorry."

"I have prepared the lunch."

She touches his arm lightly. They start to walk the short distance to her camp. The throng of Masai surrounds them. Her servant brings a bowl of hot water for Fairfax. He washes his face. The Masai watch all this.

Fairfax and Claudia sit down on camp chairs. The Masai stand a short distance off, curious, but self-absorbed.

"What would you like to drink?"

"Can you manage a brandy and soda?"

"I think so."

She speaks Swahili to the servant.

"Now, do you want to tell me all the facts?"

"As far as I know them. Yes. The Masai who has been arrested, Tepilit, is from this district. These people are from his engang. He was supposed to deliver a bull to the district officer, it was about three weeks ago, and he decided at the last moment to replace the bull with another one. But the district officer, Miles Turnbull, would not accept it . . ."

Her face, as she removes her hat and begins to speak, is startlingly beautiful, although not conventionally. Fairfax watches her. As she talks the servant brings the drinks and then the lunch, a grilled fowl with some preserves.

As she speaks we see a Masai market. Spread around are hundreds of Masai men and women. Some of the women are in robes of blue, others are in brown leather skirts. The older men have blankets loosely slung over their shoulders. Almost every man is accompanied by a goat or a cow, held on a short leather thong or controlled by a thin stick. Those animals are accustomed to the Masai. There is, incongruously, an open car to one side of the market. From it, into the colorful throng, appears a young British district officer, Miles Turnbull. He is carrying some papers and is accompanied by two askaris with rifles and an interpreter, dressed in khakis. The askaris wear military sweaters, Sam Brownes, shorts and socks. On their heads they wear fezes.

"The whole thing was ridiculous and tragic. This man was very much liked by the Masai. But he was overworked. He had to collect the cattle and make sure that every boma was contributing its fair share. His district stretches nearly one hundred and fifty miles. I liked him, even though he was a little bit boring. He was so English. He could not speak Masai so he always was accompanied by this man, a Nandi, who, I am afraid, does not speak Masai very good."

"Very well. Sorry."

"Very well. So the laibon's son from up there, up the valley past Lengai, he is a descendant of Mbatian, the great laibon, he tries to persuade Turnbull to let him take out his animal from the ones that have been selected."

The young warrior, Tepilit, is arguing with the district officer. He is still vividly scarred from his recent encounter with a lion. His face is painted and he is carrying a spear. On his head he wears a headdress of lion mane. Turnbull explains through the interpreter that time is short; it is late; there is a great war on

130

with the Germans. He cannot wait for the proposed exchange of animals. But he tries to be reasonable.

"How long will it take, anyway?"

"Tomorrow it will be ready. I will bring it."

"It will be too late. Tell him that I am very sorry but I cannot make exceptions. He has had plenty of time."

The Masai warrior, Tepilit, is excited. A number of other Masai gather round. He says that this particular animal is a favorite. He strokes its side, which is white and marked with round patches of black, like islands on a naïvely drawn map. It is a beautiful animal, with huge, curved horns.

"I will bring you two cattle tomorrow. I will go now and deliver them myself to Narok."

"Tell him I am very sorry, but I must fill the quota."

Turnbull busies himself with his clipboard as his reply is translated.

"Take the animal now," he says to his assistant gently.

As they move forward, Tepilit, without warning, hurls his spear at the district officer from a few feet away. It is a heavy weapon. Between the knife-shaped iron blade and the tapered tail of the spear is a rounded handle made from a particularly hard tree. This blade enters Turnbull, so that he is skewered. A fountain of blood at first pours from his chest, but soon subsides to become a steady trickle. Tepilit watches as the district officer performs a brief jitterbug before falling facedown. This drives the spear almost completely through his body. Nobody moves. The watching Masai begin to walk away after a long, contemplative moment. They seem to be weighing the incident carefully in their minds. The askaris panic. They cock their rifles and fire into the air. Now they guard the body, which is motionless in a lake of blood that is rapidly drying, drunk by the thirsty, insatiable soil. You can almost hear the soil gulping.

Tepilit drives his bull away. He walks without a backward glance. He has a stick in one hand and is followed by a thin dog.

This little group begins to mount a hill. Nobody makes a move to stop him. The strange singing of the Masai rises. From a distance we see Tepilit, walking steadily toward Ol Doinyo Lengai with his animals. They are tiny figures in a huge landscape.

Fairfax has finished eating, but Claudia's food is untouched.

"The next day he presented himself for arrest."

"Did you know this man?"

"I knew his family well."

"Did you see him after the killing?"

"He came to my house and told me what had happened."

"And you told him to give himself up?"

"Of course. What else should I do?"

"I'm just asking. If I can do anything I must know the facts."

"The facts are not so clear. This man, Tepilit, was injured helping me with the filming of a lion hunt. Now I must help him."

"When is the trial?"

"It's not arranged yet. But I have tried to talk to him, to persuade him to say that he thought the askaris were going to shoot him or that it was a misunderstanding, but he refuses absolutely to excuse himself."

"I'll talk to him. I'll talk to the DC. I heard about the lion hunt. Sounds a bit of a balls-up."

"A balls-up? It was worse than a balls-up. It was a disaster. His brother was killed. All for a film. And that bastard, *un vrai salaud*—do you speak French?—Leavitt walked away very happy."

"He was the producer?"

"He was an exploiter. He didn't care about the Masai. He wanted blood, any blood. Lions, Masai, all equal."

"Why do you think he did it? The moran, I mean?"

"I don't know."

There is a pause.

"Shall we take some coffee now?"

Claudia summons her servant, who brings a coffee pot.

"I'll go and see him tomorrow. Don't worry."

The jail at Ewaso. It is a small police post with cells at the back. In front of the building is a row of white-painted stones and some cactuslike sisal plants forming a circle around a patch of grass. In the middle of the grass is a flagpole, from which the Union Jack hangs. A car pulls up outside. An askari salutes as Fairfax steps out of the car in uniform. He enters the building. A young white policeman appears from his office reluctantly. He straightens up and salutes Fairfax.

"Sorry, Major. I'm Sergeant Jeavons, sir."

"Major Fairfax. I want to talk to the Masai man you are holding. I have the papers."

"Are you the defense, sir?"

"No, I'm here to make a report to the governor." The sergeant's face is elaborately composed.

"This way, sir."

In a bare, mud-walled cell, sitting on the floor, is Tepilit. He does not appear to be disheartened. He looks at Fairfax without fear.

From behind the sergeant, an askari shouts at Tepilit. "Stand up man. Attention."

Fairfax speaks to Tepilit in Maa.

"I hope you are well, Tepilit ole Saibol." Then he turns to the policeman: "That's fine, sergeant. You may leave me here."

Fairfax shakes hands with Tepilit and sits on a small stool. Tepilit squats on the floor.

"How are you?"

"I am fine."

"What age group are you?"

"Botorok."

"Is your father the laibon?"

"Yes. He is descended from Mbatian."

"You have killed a lion."

"Hooh. I am praised because I held it by the tail."

"Does your father have many cattle?"

"We are owners of many cattle."

"I am happy. Do you know me?"

"You are the friend of Claudia from the government."

"I am a friend of Claudia. I am a soldier. At the moment, as you know, the white people and their friends are fighting with the Germans. This is a very big war."

"Our people also fought the Germans."

"Your people fought very bravely."

"The Masai are brave."

"We know this. We honor the Masai above all people."

"What do you want to discuss?"

"I am here because I was asked to come by Claudia. She wants me to talk to you."

"There is no need. I have told her everything that happened."

"She is unhappy. She does not want you to be tried by the government."

"We are betrothed. She is my little heifer."

Fairfax is stunned. It takes him a moment to regain his composure.

"You are going to be married?"

"She must first ask her father, who lives far away."

"Do you realize what will happen to you if you are tried?"

Tepilit makes a gesture by placing his hand to his throat and cupping it.

"I can't see any point in that. When you killed the district officer it was an accident."

"I killed him on purpose."

"What I want to say is this: there was a misunderstanding. I will tell the government. You thought the Nandi, the fat belly, wanted the askaris to shoot you."

"No. I did not. The white man told the askaris to take my animal after I had offered to exchange it. He took my best animal, even though I offered two in its place. That is why I killed him. And now my family have offered forty-nine cattle to his family, but the government will not take them to give to his family in England."

"White men have different customs."

"They don't like cattle."

"Some like cattle. I have many cattle on my farm."

"Are they milk cattle living in a house as I have heard?"

"Not all. Many are Masai cattle. Tepilit ole Saibol, I have a heavy burden. Only you can help me. I have to talk to the governor. I have to explain to him what happened. The Nandi man has run away, frightened. I can say to the governor that you misunderstood the order and tried to defend yourself. Not the district officer's order, but the translator's, who spoke too fast without proper consideration, as Nandi people do, and the askaris pointed their guns at you. You threw the spear wildly. Unfortunately the district officer stepped forward. If I tell him that they will fine you."

"Many of my people saw me. They know that I killed him on purpose because he took my best animal."

"If you say that at your trial, they will kill you."

"I have offered cattle to his family. I can do no more."

Fairfax stands up.

"Think about what I said. I will come back."

"Go in peace."

"Please God."

Tepilit does not stand up. He seems content.

The sergeant meets Fairfax outside the cell.

"All right, sir?"

"Not really. Has he made a statement?"

"Yes, sir. He admits killing the DO. No excuses."

135

"Can I read his statement?"

"I'm afraid it's gone off to the High Court, sir."

"You haven't got a copy here?"

"We haven't had any carbon paper for two years, sir."

"Was it taken down by a policeman?"

"Yes, sir. By me, sir."

"Do you speak Masai?"

"No, sir, but we got the Larusa translator in. He's the official police translator, sir. We read it back to the man twice. It took me most of a whole day, sir."

In the cell Tepilit sits motionless on the floor.

At Claudia's camp it is almost evening. The light in the sky is there by courtesy of the vanished sun, but the tops of the mountains are still golden, as though honey had been poured lightly over them. Fairfax's car appears, the lights hopping and bouncing down the track. Claudia rises. Fairfax steps out of the car. Claudia comes to greet him and kisses him lightly on both cheeks.

"How was he?"

"Stubborn."

"He would not agree?"

"No."

"Would you like something to drink?"

They are approaching the fire. Fairfax stops.

"He told me you two were pakiteng, little heifers."

"It's true. I didn't know what it meant. I did not take it seriously."

"Did you accept any gifts?"

"He was very sick after the lion got him and he gave me his necklace. He was in a fever. I had no idea he wanted me to marry him when he had his head shaved."

"What a balls-up. Claudia, the problem is that one Masai, cruel as this may sound, is not considered very important. I have flown my plane with cadged army fuel six hundred miles. I am supposed to be at GHQ. They won't hold up proceedings while we talk to him. I've only got until tomorrow."

"Please, Tom."

She touches his arm.

"Please, Tom. It is completely crazy. There's a war, the Germans are trying to kill every Jew in the world and you are going to hang one Masai because of a misunderstanding."

"There's no misunderstanding, unfortunately. He seems determined to die."

"Determined to die. Can you talk to his family?"

"I will try. I will also get the translation of his evidence. Maybe I can put some doubts into the governor's mind about its admissibility."

A boma near Ol Doinyo Lengai. Fairfax and Claudia are meeting the Masai. They are sitting on stools in the middle of the cattle enclosure talking to Tepilit's father, Sentue. Around them graceful Masai women in long leather skirts are sweeping the boma and plastering the huts with cow dung. In the distance we can hear cowbells. Sentue is a grand, dignified figure of about sixty-five. He is wearing a blue tunic and around his shoulders is a fur cloak made of the skins of the hyrax. In his hands he holds a snuffbox, shaped like a small quiver, and a thin stick. Two warriors, one of whom is Saibol, Tepilit's younger brother, stand at a distance. Sentue is speaking. It is clear that he has been speaking for some time.

"We have many problems with the government. They want to take our cows to pay for the war. We give them our cows. Every time they collect our cows they promise to give us something in return, but the next time they ask for more cows. Our cows are our life. I am a rich man. I have many cows and many children. I have offered many cows to pay this man's family. But the government wants to take away my son also. Why do they do this?"

"This is the way our law is. You cannot kill a man deliberately."

"If you have been reasonable, if you are offering your own wealth, two cows instead of one, and he will not listen, if he thinks you are a small man and will not listen to your suggestions, why not? You must kill him."

"You can't kill a white man in this way."

"A white man has blood, red blood also."

"The white man has blood. That is true. But the white man does not believe that cattle are payment for taking someone's life."

The Masai, Sentue, finds this hard to believe. He turns his old head wearily, as if to indicate to his family the kind of people he has to deal with these days.

Claudia speaks: "Your son must say it was an accident. Major Fairfax will speak to the government."

"I told my son only trouble could come from being your pakiteng."

The old man says this without rancor. It is, in his mind, a fact.

Claudia is upset. She touches Fairfax's arm for support.

Fairfax shouts: "You are a stupid man. This woman has come from far away to write about your people. She did not understand what your son wanted from her. Why does he want to marry a white woman? Does he think she will spend the rest of her life milking his cows and goats? Don't be stupid."

Sentue takes a few moments to reply.

"There is nothing wrong with milking cows and goats."

Claudia interrupts. "Ole Sentue, I agree with you. I have to go to my country to see my father. I am sure he would wish me to marry with someone in our tribe. But in any case I cannot marry your son. In our country to exchange gifts does not mean the same thing. I was a stupid woman. I did not understand."

"Because you have come here my son is going to be killed. Hanged like a chicken by his neck, in town."

"No, no, please. Major Fairfax will help him. But he must help himself."

She is weeping. Fairfax approaches very close to the laibon, between them. The laibon speaks to Claudia, ignoring him.

"How can Fahfakhs save him? Your people do not believe it is right to offer cows to his family. Fahfakhs said that. They want to kill him. He did nothing to them, but they want to kill him. I have looked at the stones. They will kill him."

Fairfax grasps the old man by his wrist.

"Laibon, great-grandson of Mbatian, you must think again. The white people are having a war with the Germans. The Masai have been good friends. The government will help your son, but he must not say that he killed the white man on purpose. Ole Sentue Simel, you must speak to your son."

The laibon simply looks down at the floor of the boma. He is not prepared to discuss this dishonorable argument. His face is adamantine. Claudia rises. She offers her hand in the Masai manner, her head bowed.

"Stay in peace. Tom, we must go."

"Go in peace."

They leave the boma. The laibon stands to watch them go. They walk together toward their car. There are tears in Claudia's eyes. She turns to Fairfax.

"He will not talk to his son."

He strides stiffly and angrily.

"Claudia, you are supposed to understand them. What can he tell him? Can he say to him, 'You must stop being a Masai. You must tell lies like the *muzungus*'? I will try to get him off. But I'm not so sure now if it's possible."

"You must do it, Tom. My work here will be finished if he is hanged. I can't support it. It's too terrible."

They climb into the car and set off. Behind them, Ol Doinyo Lengai is catching the late afternoon sunlight. They drive down into a dry watercourse and are surrounded by hundreds of cattle returning from their grazing, driven by children and young warriors. They cut the engine to allow the animals to pass undisturbed. Claudia sits with her eyes downcast. A child greets her, but a young warrior strikes the child with a stick.

"My heart is breaking," she says.

Fairfax turns to her. Her face is shaded from him in the failing light.

"I will do what I can, I promise."

She kisses Fairfax. They sit in the dust of the vanished cattle.

"Claudia, you are beautiful. You look so beautiful. I can't bear it that you are unhappy. Did you love him? I have to ask."

"You know that is an impossible question. In one way I loved them all. I have lived here for nearly five years. Sometimes for many months I was the only white person for hundreds of miles. I was very grateful to him. I was guilty because he was nearly killed. Another man was killed in the ridiculous filming. I believed I owed him some debt. That boy will do anything for me, even up to getting himself killed by a lion. So I loved him. Yes, I loved him, but I loved him in my Masai self. Do you understand me? Do you know what my professor said? He said that the most important thing in the world, I mean our world, is to live *la vraie vie*. I believed I was the first anthropologist in France to understand what this means. I was trying to live the real Masai life."

"Is that possible?"

"Obviously not. But at least I was not trying to stand completely outside this life with my little notebook. I can't leave this district with one man hanged and another killed and somehow because of me. I can't. My life would be finished. You have to help me, Tom."

29

S. O. Letterman has rented a small apartment in the rue de Beaune. It is above a *traiteur* and as he makes love with Candice Riberon, they are bathed, marinated and fêted by the scents of the food from below. At the back is a school where small, elegant children play in a courtyard.

Candice has a husband, who is a physician at the hospital in Montparnasse. She makes love with her eyes closed, as though she is trying not to look at him. Her lips move constantly, as if she were remembering a text, like a Hasid at prayer. Letterman thinks that he is falling in love with her but he has the impression that she is using his cosseted and linimented body in some sinister fashion. He thinks of that great opening shot in *Le Métro* and he realizes that her lips are moving in exactly the same way, her face pained as he does his practiced best. He congratulates himself, however, on auditioning successfully for a part in this Parisian cinema.

Since he has offered her the role of Claudia Cohn-Casson, she has introduced him to journalists, scriptwriters and directors. But this world is kept separate from their lunchtime encounters in the rue de Beaune. She makes no acknowledgment of their affair in public and he understands that he is not to refer to it with these new acquaintances. (He thinks of Marlon Brando in *Last Tango.*) There is a brutality about her lovemaking. Her feral body takes its own route, grinding, convulsing, swallowing. She ends up sitting on him, facing the small window from where the children can now be heard playing, so that all he can see is her lean and sculpted back, the ridge of her spine showing like knuckles on a fist. He fears, as this moving tableau blots out his view, that she does not want to look at him, but then, just as he is allowing himself this painful thought, she turns and kisses him on the eyes before taking his cock in her mouth. (He is sometimes disturbed by the readiness of young women to do this; perhaps it is a dietary taboo surfacing from his past.)

All the time she is in a mindless frenzy, he is thinking, comparing and second-guessing. He is cursed with this evaluative frame of mind. He wonders in how many of the little windows in all the voguishly crumbling buildings beneath all the mansard roofs sex is taking place. He asks himself how many of these encounters can be as tricky as his own, with the gorgeous actress Candice Riberon. In Paris, he is certain, there is a level of sophistication about sex absent in Hollywood. Yet sometimes he feels nostalgic for the Californian variety, just as an honest man dining in the Tour d'Argent can decently long for a cheeseburger.

But this little flat is magical. Farwaggi found it in the *Herald Tribune.* It belongs to a journalist absent in Eastern Europe, and it is really just a large closet with a marble fireplace and a tiny bedroom and a bathroom where Candice sits across the bidet unembarrassed, much as she sits across his body. He has two or three bidets in his house in Beverly Hills, but he has never seen them used in this way, with gusto. There was a vogue for bidets in California some years ago, but he thinks they are primarily symbolic, as Jacuzzis have become. As soon as he sets foot on the elaborate stairway, which rises three floors from the dark hall, itself leading off a gloomy cobbled courtyard, he has the feeling that he is leaving for a blessed hour or two his insubstantial world. (There are many sneering adjectives: *plastic, cardboard, artificial, disposable, tinsel, polystyrene, cutout.*) Yet he has an instinct that this synthetic world is more in tune with the way things are going in the hierarchy of ideas than the Parisian world of half-wild ducks cooked in their own *jus* and ideas located on different *niveaux.* (He now knows what it means.) These ideas have, anyway, suffered a Gallicization, which places the French at the center of the cosmos. On a more parochial level, his mother adopted a similar approach: Eisenhower was responsible, in her estimation, for causing her to have her hair bobbed. She blamed him personally. Letterman has forgotten the exact circumstances.

He finds, in talking to Candice's friends, that the topic of collaboration during the war has become for them either a means of attacking the government or a subject of high-minded discussion. The *intellos* do not see themselves as in any way related to the past. They operate on a different plane altogether. This is their job.

When they have made love—it is unbearably intense for him—clouds scud across Candice's eyes. She does not see him at all. He is troubled for two reasons. The first is that he has got her into bed so easily and the second is that it seems to mean nothing to her. Perhaps the two worries are related. Although she obviously enjoys the physical stuff, he would like her to bring some spiritual qualities to the performance. These are absent, saved for conversation in restaurants, where she talks with great animation, but on a plane that seems to have nothing to do with her sexual avidity. He is, he thinks, some sort of sexual experiment for her. Sex is part of her embrace of an exotic culture; it goes with the territory, as they say. She returns from the bidet and dresses quickly. His tennis-trim heart quickens to see the black parterre where he has so recently expended himself disappear beneath her skirt, pulled down in one deft movement. Thinking cinematically—there is, he believes, a whole philosophic category of filmic vision—he sees the moment played in close-up: the camera moving slowly up her beautiful legs, brown and restive, reaching this little mysterious delta just as the short, dense skirt descends.

"We must eat," she says. She turns her back to him to look in the mirror beside the cherrywood armoire. He sees her narrow hips, her lean back, her lustrous hair and—over her shoulder, in the mirror—her lips making quick whore's movements to spread the lipstick evenly.

"Sure. Let's eat. You've got some appetite. Then I got to get back to work. You look beautiful."

She turns toward him briefly and she smiles, her famous smile piercing him.

"Allez, allez."

She laughs now as he bounds off the bed, aware that his hairy—*poilu*—parts are comical. He showers. A bidet is not sufficient to remove the tinctures that must be clinging visibly to him. They make their way down through the courtyard, past the concierge's busy-lizzies and geraniums in their cluster of terracotta, and out onto the street, where the Mercedes and driver are double-parked, squeezing the traffic to an irascible trickle. Candice likes this conspicuous consumption. She slumps, her legs sprawled, as they inch out into the traffic, heading for a place that serves Gascon specialties. The Gascons favor the goose and its by-products. He looks at Candice and she puckers her lips, perhaps ironically. By casting her, one of the hottest young actresses in France, he has laid the ground bait. He is working the trade press both in Europe and the United States. Soon he will talk to local producers about taking a share, but for the moment he is holding them off. The script comes next. He has sent off some ideas to Africa for inclusion in the first draft, which should be ready in about ten days. He knows it will need work.

The manager and waiters treat them to a respectful embalming. He orders ravioli with foie gras and white truffle shavings. The ravioli are huge, like saucers, each one stuffed with the exquisite mixture. Around him, knowing people, people who were born eating this stuff, are conversing in that world-weary but photogenic way. He tries to remember accurately Flaubert, which he was combing on the plane: "Their indifferent glances told him of passion dulled by daily satisfaction." Candice is eating a dish of beans and preserved goose. He will never feel at ease with the French: he will never wear the right clothes; he will never feel healthy on goose and red wine and he no longer wants to try. Yet he admires them. He imagines that his own family might have had this ease in the bourgeois world before they left Europe. But for all his misgivings, here he is with one of the most desirable women in France, eating truffle shavings, and half an hour ago they were lying on a bed together. Still, he feels that the waiters know that he comes from Dearborn and they can see that in his cashmere tweed jacket he is sailing under false colors. He looks at Candice: a tiny globule of goose fat is glistening on her upper lip. He wonders if she has told her husband the *docteur*—he imagines a cheerful Depardieu in a white coat—of the steps she has been obliged to take in order to get the part.

"You like geese liver?" she asks. She pronounces "liver" with a long *i,* so that for a second he thinks she is asking if he likes geese saliva.

"Goose . . . ? Sure, this is the greatest thing I have ever eaten"—he drops his voice—"apart from your pussy."

She looks round in mock horror. She laughs. His tired heart bounds. He thinks—Jesus, he is so suburban—of a tennis ball bouncing off the court.

He looks at her and he can see—in her dark hair, her quite high forehead, her wide, generously made mouth (oiled and glistening), her intensely brown eyes—Claudia. No doubt about it.

30

It is dawn. The first rays of the sun are just touching the summit of the Mountain of God. In a cleft in the escarpment beside a stream is a camp of a few tents. There is also a hut with a thatched roof and beside it a storeroom of split poles. The main tent stands near the stream, away from the others. It has a thatched roof over it. It is open on one side to the view of the mountain across the valley. Seen through the mosquito netting are Tom Fairfax and Claudia Cohn-Casson. She lies asleep on her bed, which is draped in a mosquito net, now tied back. Fairfax leaves the tent and walks over to the fire. He starts to rearrange the still-smoldering logs, fanning them into flame. He places some more logs from a pile nearby onto the fire and pushes an old, blackened kettle into the middle of the newly revived flames. He rubs his hands.

It is still quite dark in the tent. Claudia opens her eyes. They are greeted by the magnificent vista of the plain and the strange but familiar shape of Ol Doinyo Lengai, which is steadily catching fire at its summit as the sun rises. She is naked and makes no attempt to cover any more of herself than people do who are all alone.

Fairfax returns with two enamel mugs and a brown teapot on a tray. He passes her a cup. Outside, the sunlight has raced down the slope of the mountain and has almost reached the floor of the valley.

"I love you," he says, placing her tea beside the bed and sipping his own.

She is lying on her back; her breasts adjust to a new position tardily as though they contain some viscous substance, settling gradually as she raises herself on her elbow.

"Thomas, je t'aime."

"Thomas. You make it sound suave. Thom-as."

They drink tea. They are at ease. Outside cowbells can be heard and in the distance a group of Masai enter the landscape driving their animals; despite the fierce colors of their robes, they are completely at home in this brown and ochre world. Fairfax puts down his tea. They kiss.

In the police cells the Masai warrior, Tepilit, lies on the mud floor. He is roused by the sergeant, accompanied by armed askaris. When he stands up he is handcuffed. The handcuffs are cumbersome, perhaps little used, and it takes an askari a long time to adjust them to Tepilit's thin wrists. Tepilit is led by the askaris out of the small police station to a waiting van, which drives off down the track in a billowing cloud of dust.

Fairfax is driving down the same track in the opposite direction. He arrives at the police station. The sergeant comes out to meet him.

"What's happened?"

"I'm afraid he's been sent off to the railway, sir. We had orders from the DC."

147

"When did he go?"

"He went this morning, sir, just after dawn. To meet the midday train." He looks at his watch. "He'll be on the train by now, sir."

"I see. Did you tell the DC I was here?"

"He knew, sir. He would know. There are not many white people in this district."

"Does the man's family know what's going on?"

"We haven't had a chance to tell them that he's gone for trial yet, sir. To tell the truth, I'm not sure it would make much difference. They don't understand our system at all. We tried to get witnesses for the defense, but they all confirmed that he had killed the DO on purpose. That, as far as they were concerned, was the whole idea. 'Yes, he did kill the DO. How many cows is his family asking?' That's how they saw it, sir. All they've done is sign his death warrant for him."

"Do you think he should be hanged?"

"It's not for me to say, sir. But I think it would be a shame."

They stand for a moment locked by their feelings in an awkward embrace. Around them cicadas are screaming at the sun.

"Do you want a cup of tea, sir?"

"No, thanks, I have to be going."

Claudia has been weeping. She and Fairfax stand beside the stream in front of her tent. He has an arm lightly around her, his hand cupping the point of her shoulder.

"Will they hang him?"

"I will go and see the governor tomorrow. I'll explain the problems with the Masai evidence to him."

"Do you think he will listen to you?"

"I'll do my best. I want you to come as soon as you can."

"It's finished for me here. I can't go on with these people. How can I speak to them? I will come as soon as I can."

"You can stay at my house."

"I would like that. I must write my thesis. Just for a few weeks."

"And then?"

"We will see."

"Claudia, I will move heaven and earth. Please try not to think about it."

"They just want to take him away and hang him. Finish. As quick as possible. That's the truth. You know it."

"Unfortunately, he did kill someone. All the witnesses say the same thing."

"Of course. They think it is an honorable thing. Already that day is famous among the Masai. The day the muzungu was killed. Will you walk with me?"

They walk up the cleft in the hills beside the stream and begin to climb above the valley. Now, across the savannah, they can see the Masai village. They stop beside some huge aloes, spiky plants with red flowers, where sunbirds hover and dart.

"I have lived here for more than four years. I don't want any other home."

"Do you know, almost all of us who have lived out here prefer the bush and a tent? I don't believe we are so far from the nomad as people in Europe believe. Tell me, what have you discovered about the Masai? What is your thesis about?"

"You know the main idea, the academic idea, is to understand where they fit into human society. We must compare with other societies. But the more I know them, the more I ask myself the question, 'What is the purpose?' I find that I am writing a kind of completely sterile account of their life. It is like writing a family biography using anthropology terms. Do you know what I am trying to say?"

"I do. I believe I do."

"Your birthday anniversary would be described as a ritual exchange of gifts designed to cement clan relationships. For a researcher like me, you are not supposed to become involved.

How can you not be involved? If some child is sick. If someone needs some clean water. It's impossible. And now I have been responsible for getting this man hanged. I have been a disaster for these people."

She sits on a rock. Fairfax crouches beside her, African-style.

"You are not responsible and you haven't been a disaster. Your thesis will help them because it will enable people outside to understand their life."

"Thomas, in Europe millions of people are being killed. Nobody cares about a few thousand Masai. Why should they? I am here making recordings of the Masai singing about cows, and meanwhile my father is sitting in Paris pretending to be a man of the world, a savior of his people, while they are being sent off to be killed."

"Hang on. That's a bit exaggerated. Don't be too gloomy. The war will be over in nine or ten months at the most."

"You know, my father thinks he has somehow mastered the situation. He, of all the Jews in Paris, has been able to understand the character of the Nazis. He is the only one who is doing his duty. It's crazy. He must come out before it's too late. And my brother must come out, too. He is only eleven years old. Will you help me arrive to Paris?"

"Just wait a few months and we will go as tourists."

They rise and walk back down the valley. In the distance over the mountain, thunder sounds. The noise is like kindling crackling.

On the landing strip, Fairfax says goodbye to Claudia, who stands, subdued but beautiful, at a short distance from the plane. A few Masai look on. There is lightning in the sky. Fairfax walks to the plane. He removes the chocks and starts the plane by hand. Claudia's face is obscured by the dust that rises. Soon we see the plane bumping along the runway. Fairfax waves. The plane rises unsteadily into the air. Claudia's brown eyes well with tears. She stands for a long moment. A twisted filament of lightning signals a constriction of the atmosphere. It is accompanied by the distant rise of Masai singing. In this landscape she seems, despite the onlookers, completely lost. We fear for her. She turns back toward her camp. We hear the distant—and growing more distant—engine of the plane, a whine underlaid by an occasional choking sob. A small Masai boy, carrying two whittled sticks, joins her and they walk together. The moment is poignant. The sky is full. The singing overwhelms us.

A small colonial town. The main street, which circles round a clocktower, is busy. A broad road, with a park on one side, leads to the small stone law court, a modest Palladian building. In the street outside the court, Indian traders, a few Masai and the occasional European in military or tropical kit pass by.

Inside the courtroom. The Masai, Tepilit, is standing handcuffed between two policemen in the dock as the circuit judge enters. The policemen push down on Tepilit's shoulders as the judge takes his seat to indicate that he, too, should sit. The judge wears a wig. He is short of time.

"Who represents this man?"

"He has pleaded guilty, my lord," says a senior policeman.

"He has no defense?"

"No, my lord. He pleads guilty as charged."

"Ask him if he understands the charge fully."

The court interpreter exchanges words with Tepilit.

"Yes, my lord. He understands the charge. He killed this man."

"All right. I will pass sentence tomorrow when I have seen all the papers. Take him away. Who is next?"

Fairfax waits in an echoing anteroom of the governor's office. He is summoned by a male secretary. The governor is sitting at a broad gilt table. He stands up and extends his hand. He is about sixty, tall, thin and elegant.

151

"Tom, how are you?"

"I'm fine, sir. Fine. Very good of you to see me at such short notice."

"What can I do for you?"

"Well, I wanted to see you two days ago, sir, but my plane was grounded by storms. It's a matter of clemency for a Masai. The facts seem cut-and-dried, but I am afraid there has been a grave misunderstanding. You know the Masai."

"I used to love watching Lord Delamere's chaps going out with the cattle carrying umbrellas. Marvelous sight."

"Yes, sir. I have seen it."

"Wonderful chaps. Can't help thinking that they are on the right track and it's we who are barking up the wrong tree. That's not for publication. So what is the problem?"

"Well, sir, I went down to see Claudia Cohn-Casson, the anthropologist, whom I have known slightly on and off, whenever she came up to town, over the last few years."

"And rather a beauty, incidentally."

"So they say, sir. It seems the Masai man who killed the DO down there was under a misapprehension. He believed the order had been given to kill him by the DO. It was an interpretation problem, sir, with a rather rum Nandi interpreter who has since run away. Anyway, the Masai threw a spear and it struck the DO."

The governor speaks to his secretary.

"I'll just get the papers. How's the army? Looking forward to getting back to your farm, I should think? What's your guess on the invasion of France? January's probably too soon. May, June. Ah, here we are. I see. I'm afraid he was sentenced to death yesterday."

"But it's only four days since I saw him."

"It's policy now to get these things done with all dispatch. There just aren't enough policemen and warders to feed them and so on. I must say, it seems quite clear that he intended to kill the DO. Wretched business. You can enter an appeal for clemency, of course. But don't let your heart rule your head."

152

Fairfax stands up.

"Thank you, sir."

"Goodbye, Tom. This whole awful war will be over soon and we can get back to normal, thank God."

Fairfax turns toward the door.

"Tom. You going to be able to turn out for the polo team?"

"I hope so, sir."

"Good show."

Fairfax speaks in short bursts, like a seal barking, when he touches on difficult matters.

"Claudia came up to town. She had already heard the news. We didn't have dramatic scenes or anything like that, I'm afraid, if that's what you are looking for. The truth is, we rather put it behind us. I did at least. Things moved terribly fast during the war. You were always being sent somewhere. Time was precious. And we were in love. I find it hard to say, because it seems so inadequate to describe what we felt. But, yes, the truth is we were madly in love."

Here we sit. The tin roof of the verandah is home to all sorts of creatures. Newcomers to Africa find this constant primitive motion disturbing. Insects lurch and stagger and scramble.

Lizards dart and pause, treachery in their Iago eyes. Small vertebrates lurk and pounce in the bushes. Giant moths flap into lights. They are like scraps from a tailor's cutting room that have taken clumsy wing. I speculate about the number of hours Fairfax has spent, drink in hand, on insect-bombarded verandahs and stoeps. It's one of those impossible calculations where a few more noughts would make no difference, like the number of light years to Orion, whose belt Fairfax pointed out to me earlier. I have no interest in stellar location.

"Awful, really. Poor blighter was hanged and we were dancing the night away. In her, of course, it was a reaction. I didn't realize then. In fact I didn't realize until years later," he says.

Something lands with a soft thump on the concrete, a small death, but he does not pause.

"We didn't think much during the war. Certainly not out here in the colonies. Although a lot of us were in action in Europe, it still seemed rather remote. The Jewish business also seemed unreal."

"Did she work on her thesis?"

"She would stay up all night writing sometimes. Playing her tapes and writing."

"I've got some of her tapes."

"Good Lord. Is her voice on them?"

"Yes. Do you want to hear them?"

"No. I don't think so. What is she saying?"

"She is translating Masai songs and gossip."

He draws up his chair. It scrapes across the polished cement of the verandah.

"How did you come by her tapes?" he asks, perhaps fearful of unknown fact. (Who isn't?)

"They were in her brother's loft in Montreal. He is retired now, but he had been sent all her possessions sometime after the war from the house in avenue Hoche. I just called him and explained my interest and he sent them to me two days later."

For a moment he is confused. He is rearranging his thoughts like a man trying to move heavy furniture single-handed. He is perplexed by the idea of effortless intercontinental telephoning and overnight shipment of packages. He lives in a world where the simplest transactions, phone calls, postal services, pensions, come in a miasma of suspicion and skepticism. The essence of the capitalist system is the knowledge that these basic services are simple and their outcome sure. This is why Russia will never become a Western democracy. The democracy is the product of a Western mind, not the other way round.

The elderly mercantile brother in Montreal was bluff and cheerful on the phone. His French accent had been through the grinder in the New World, so that he sounded like a gangster in a B movie. He told me that his younger brother, Georges, had died aged just twelve, in Neuengamme, having received fifty different injections of bacilli in medical experiments. He would be proud to have his sister's achievements known. He had himself escaped, but, he said matter-of-factly, he had always felt lousy about the others. That was it. Nothing deeper.

"You've thrown me," says Fairfax. "I didn't know she had two brothers. He would have been my brother-in-law."

Paper-thin circumstance separates us from other lives and alliances.

"Tomorrow I would like you to come with me to see the laibon. He is the son of the previous laibon and the brother of the man who was hanged. He had dreamed that you were coming."

"A nightmare, I should think. Have you finished with me for tonight?"

"Of course. We can carry on tomorrow."

"Good show. I'm tired of the sound of my own voice."

His face is beginning to congeal, the reluctant eyelid is drooping and his words are becoming slurred.

"Would you like to stay here?" he asks. "I've had them make up a bed for you. Shall we set off early? Tea at five?"

• • •

At five the birds are already loud. Tea is brought by a small furtive man in a gray safari suit. The water for my shower is scented with wood-ash. It has been heated outside the room by a log fire under a petrol drum. Fairfax is seated in the dining room beneath the stuffed heads of a cabal of gloomy animals as he eats sausages and eggs. In his world these fixed points must be observed, if only because the servants expect them.

We set off in my Toyota down the now familiar road, past the Police Training Center, where motorcycling policemen were once taught to do multiple handstands on BSA motorcycles, past the Firewood Project, a scheme to plant a fast-growing species of tree, now abandoned, down the long, straight, rutted road lined with workshops, past the ruined dairy farm, past more shacks, which are alive with banana sellers, wood choppers and maize roasters. Soon we are out on the savannah, leaving behind the rain shadow of the mountain.

But rain has fallen here, too, in that arbitrary way that makes life so unpredictable. The brown of the plains has been replaced by an underlying green, like the velvet on a stag's antlers. Fairfax hasn't been this way for twenty years. He tells me that there were once herds of antelope, thousands strong, roaming these plains. Everything he tells me of former times is suffused with loss. The sense of space is an illusion. Every inch of these plains is grazed daily. The bush, the wilderness, was a state of mind, which was banished once boundaries and limits were recognized.

"You told me," I say as we bounce along the ever-dwindling road, "that you thought of marrying Lady De Marr. Have you ever been married?"

"I was actually married when I was with Claudia. My wife was in Devon at her father's. We were divorced in 'forty-seven. And then six or seven years later I married again, but she died in nineteen seventy-three. I haven't been married since."

Although age has made its inroads, I can see that Fairfax has the mark of a man who is attractive to women. He has the assurance conveyed by a lifetime of being admired. This is an embalming process. It reminds me of those handsome bottles of fruit at Fauchon, their shape and color not only preserved but given lustre by the amber syrup they bathe in. Even here in the dusty, bounding Toyota, this old man has a distinctiveness, the clubbable, dependable qualities of what used to be called a gentleman. As we travel, the frozen side of his face is turned from me. I see only the seal profile, the rounded and compressed nose, one brown and masked eye. His skin in this brutal morning light is textured and darkened by a weft of tiny arterial threads, some almost blue. The effect is noble, an honorably acquired patina.

"Back in nineteen forty-four when Claudia was working on her thesis, I understood intellectually"—he says the word with a certain fastidiousness—"what she was saying about the Masai, but as a man who knew the country and the natives, or thought I did, I couldn't really accept it. Their customs seemed to me to be too flimsy. She wanted me to believe that there was a relation to a universal spirit. It seemed a very artificial idea. After I got back to civilian life, I fell back into the habit of admiring the Masai, but regarding them as insubstantial. Now I am not so sure. Did I tell you that I was at Belsen just after it was liberated?"

"No. Good God."

"Two days after. I was looking for Claudia."

"They weren't there."

"No. We didn't know that, but I thought I could find her. I had a mad idea that she would be there. That's where my regiment was sent. When I got there our chaps were burying the bodies with bulldozers. I tried to make some inquiries."

In the pictures of Belsen, the sheer anguish on the faces of the Tommies contrasts starkly with the indifference of the SS recorded in their cheery souvenir albums.

. . .

After a few hours' driving, we stop by a small lake brimming with clear water which has tumbled down from the escarpment through dense forest. Fairfax's steward has packed sandwiches for us and an ancient vacuum flask of tea. Vervet monkeys with their anxious faces come closer to look at us. They chivvy and reproach one another as we eat.

We find the laibon in the late afternoon. He shows no surprise that Fairfax has come to pay his respects after nearly fifty years. They shake hands in an unhurried fashion and exchange the courtesies. The laibon goes off for a moment and returns wearing his cloak as the old lady produces some stools. We sit in the boma, the place de l'Étoile of Masai life. Radiating outward are the paths to the pastures and the frontiers of the Masai world. When I sit here with the laibon and his family I feel envious of their flimsy values.

I am running my tape recorder as they talk. They are too old to be worried about the physical changes that have taken place in them, but I also see that they share a certain self-regard, a comfort that—I hazard a speculation—is robbed from old people in our cities. These old chaps have some substance in the universe. Sure, they are soon going off into the night, their lights flickering and fading, but it will be with dignity. And yet dignity is a synthetic property, invented to stop the ears against the noises of humiliation.

Their conversation starts slowly and in ritual fashion. I am just able to discern the formalities, which are like the horns of ships circling in the fog to dock. Fairfax is in no hurry. His Maa is, as far as I can tell, fluent and unaccented. He seems transformed, as though he is speaking in tongues. He has taken on a personality, like those crackpots who claim to have been reincarnated, from another culture. He inclines his head in a way I have not seen. He issues long, philosophic vowel sounds—*eehh, aaie, eh-eh, hooh*—and clicks of the tongue and palate like plastic cutlery rattling. The laibon now begins to unburden himself. It is his boma and his forum. The koko serves us tea respectfully, although she smiles at me complicitly as she hands me my mug. Her ears are so stretched by ornaments that they flap as she leans toward me. From her rises that familiar scent which I take to be human. These two men and the koko knew Claudia. It seems to me almost inconceivable that they could all have survived Africa. The old lady would have been a lissome girl, like the girls now coming through the main entrance of the boma, carrying large plastic containers of water on their heads, keeping them in place by a casual touch of the hand. (I know these girls; they are the new wives of two of the laibon's elder sons. They have both been to school and like to speak their few words of English when their elders are not looking.)

Fairfax turns to me: "The laibon is telling me about the lion hunt in which his brother was injured."

"Did Claudia tell you the story?"

"I think she did."

The laibon is gesturing. He stands up and mimes throwing a spear. It is a stiff movement (as crabbed as Letterman's second serve) but children gather to watch. I look at Fairfax. He nods frequently and issues his vowel noises in harmony with the narrative. He and the laibon laugh loudly, which causes the laibon to cough. The children, who stand in a small cluster near the goat enclosure, now look at each other and laugh too, but when the laibon swings his impressive, lidded gaze toward them, they freeze. He swats the side of his head with one of his large hands and sits down again.

At least half an hour goes by before the laibon breaks off to welcome the returning cattle. We have heard them for some time; now we see them, red and white on the green of the plains. What a change. They have somehow, in the few days since the rains arrived, become biblically sleek. Their flanks wobble and their eyes are moist and content. The warriors have been with them because lions have been seen in the area where they were grazing.

"He's a nice old boy," says Fairfax as we watch the laibon counting in his cattle. "He has problems with his family, like most old people. He asked me to tell you that the government has not yet sent the compensation. He wonders if you filled in the forms correctly."

He laughs, a short, merry bark.

"Don't expect gratitude from these buggers," he says.

The women and children take charge of the cattle's nighttime arrangements, gently guiding and scolding them. The warriors come to greet us. The laibon gives a short introduction. The warriors gaze steadily and silently at Fairfax. I wonder how much they know about their parents and grandparents. One boy I have not seen before has the perfect Masai physique, tall and slender but muscular, like a high jumper's. His face is arranged in planes and his long hair is oiled and ochred. Fairfax tells me that he is a suitor, eager to lay claim to a girl who is now only eleven. He is keen to exchange the first gifts, but the laibon's family first want to see if he can cut the mustard.

The laibon communes with his cattle and goats. His family is doing all the work, but he is the bishop of this church: the cattle must receive his blessing. Fairfax is happy to watch. He has no need to analyze. He has confided that he once told Claudia that in real life people do not go around analyzing everyday rituals. Claudia had concluded that the rituals of life have a social significance: they are what makes us human. Incontrovertible, but so what? *Arbeit Macht Frei. Hände Waschen, Nicht Vergessen.* These were the social strictures of the lager, which, as an anthropologist, she must have found impossible to understand. They were drawn from a deeper and darker place than this whiskery, milky, dungy communion with the cattle.

160

Victoria had accused me of trying to thrust myself into the action while pretending I want to live a quiet life. She suspects me of a form of vanity in sidling up to the existential questions. Here, with my seal-profile friend Fairfax, in the sight of the Mountain of God, I see that Victoria may have had a point. What business is it of mine, anyway? All I have to do is get a few facts, give them some colorful detail and write the script. Nobody, and least of all S. O. Letterman, expects me to come back with answers to unanswerable questions.

The laibon's cattle are streaming in, in their fullness. They have all come home from their temporary manyattas. Their big eyes are content. Even their horns seem to be full of vitality. They low as they push and shove. One or two try to mount the animal in front. The Masai stand among them. They guide them with the flick of a thin stick or a gentle word. The count takes an hour. Fairfax reckons there are nearly two thousand head. He says the word "head" without self-consciousness. He's been a farmer, a pilot, a director of coffee plantations and an army officer. And he's had a glimpse of hell.

"Do you know what I enjoy about this?" he asks.

"Please tell me."

"I like to think that it is going on all over Masailand in fifty thousand kraals at this moment."

But I am plagued by the thought that we have arrived at a moment in history when this is about to be swept away. Of course the swell has been gathering force for a century or more, since Joseph Thomson first saw "the most peculiar band of men to be found in Africa." Now the wave is about to break. How many Masai will be doing this in twenty years' time? I also wonder how many Fairfaxes will be left in twenty years. I would hate to have to tell him that a new type of gentleman has taken over the clubs and boardrooms, a man who does not consider dishonesty the property of the criminal classes and who, moreover, believes that the notion of the gentleman is negotiable. I see that what Durkheim and his pals feared has come to pass: our century has turned humanity into a commodity.

It is nearly dark. We must go. Our conversation is on hold. The laibon is a descendant of the great Mbatian, the Bismarck of Masailand. He doesn't need to excuse himself for interrupting his narrative. We leave the boma, which is jam-packed, seething with cattle. Fires are bright, each one a reproach to the night. Cows are being milked. Some girls are singing. The young suitor is deputed to escort us to our camp. I wonder if this is a test of bravery. Fairfax speaks to him as we walk across the plain. I trail a pace or two behind. Although the sun has gone, the moon has caught its radiance. It is rising fast—I swear I can see its motion—above the mountains. Even as it rises, it loses the counterfeit warmth of the sun that it has appropriated and becomes glacial, all its pockmarks visible.

I envy Fairfax his fluency in Maa. I can only pick up the linguistic crumbs. Even Professor Uitsmijter's excellent translations involve a filtration of the nuances. When the SS forced naked and freezing prisoners to hop up and down in a swamp making frog noises, they were acknowledging the importance of language in rendering us human. (Perhaps if I knew the language I would not have time for these facile analogies.) I want nothing more than to walk along on the darkened plain, the moon as strong as winter sunlight in London, speaking Maa with this man. He and Fairfax are laughing, but I notice that he looks around constantly, like a city dweller guiding country cousins across Oxford Street, and his heavy spear is ready. If we are eaten, he will not be celebrating his engagement.

He leaves us at our camp under the trees. His tall figure, spear held on his shoulder, strides back across the savannah until the moonlight gives out and he is consumed by the landscape.

Fairfax has a couple of gin-and-tonics ready by the time I have the fire blazing. He has forgotten that I do not drink, or perhaps he thinks I am bluffing.

"Nice chap," he says. "Little nervous. The old laibon has quite a reputation."

"Is that what he was telling you?"

"Yes. He needs to get betrothed fast, and naturally he wants his little heifer to be rich. He's from a few miles away, near Natron. The old boy is giving him hell."

So under the unlikely moon they were talking marital shop. I am disappointed.

"What about the laibon? What did he have to say?"

"He wanted to tell me about the lion hunt Claudia organized. Bloody shambles from start to finish."

"Why does the lion hunt worry him so?"

"I think he traces a lot of his troubles back to that time. For a start, his brother would have been the laibon. What are we eating?"

"I'm not sure. We've got tins of soup, beans and some sort of sausage."

"Do you want me to make something?"

"Please."

He opens three cans deftly with a penknife and pours the lot—mushroom soup, wieners, white beans—into a pot, which he places on the fire while holding a small flashlight in his mouth.

"That looks interesting."

"In the old days we should have thrown a guinea-fowl or a few warthog piglets in, too. The old man wants you to know that the lion hunt for the producer fellow . . ."

"Leavitt."

"Leavitt, was not his doing. Claudia brought Leavitt to see his father to organize it. But Leavitt had already signed up a group of Masai from another district. In the confusion his brother was badly wounded and two men were killed. He thought you may have misunderstood."

"He's already told me the story and I've read Claudia's account."

"He's a troubled man."

"Does he know that you and Claudia were"—I stumble—"in love?"

"He does. Claudia was fast. Even by our quite advanced standards. Maybe the servant told him. You can't keep a secret like that for long."

He laughs. It is an old-fashioned noise, the sort of sound you associate with lounge lizards—liquid and urbane.

"Do you think he resents it? I mean, the fact that his brother was in prison while you were . . . ?"

"Carrying on? No, I don't think so. The Masai are pretty tolerant in these matters in my experience. Shall we eat?"

He ladles out the contents of the pot while I am wondering if the laibon thinks it was a handy way to get rid of a rival.

The stew, if that's what it is, tastes strongly of tin can.

"May I ask you a question?" he says.

"Of course."

My mouth is full of small sausages, which are shedding their rubbery, indigestible skins.

"Fire away."

"I wanted to know why you need all this detail. It's not a documentary film, is it? I don't mind in the least, of course. I'm just curious about what you are going to do with it."

That is the question S. O. Letterman would be asking me too if he were here. I try to answer. I explain something of my personal circumstances. We talk for many hours. In a tree an owlet whistles; it is an irritating, nosy-parker noise.

32

My personal circumstances. Avid as I am for details of Claudia's personal life, I have lost interest in the details of my own. Like Pascal, I wish to live quietly in my room, which I have interpreted as my head. Victoria has slipped from that part of the head where pressing thoughts gather, taking with her a lot of the baggage that was cluttering up the hallways. The sexual longings, the accusations, the lubricious details. All gone, for the moment anyway. As a teenager I was worried by the battle between the sexual thoughts and the more exalted impulses going on in me. I see now that these were just the first skirmishes in a never-ending guerrilla war.

These are not the personal circumstances I recount to Fairfax. I don't tell him why I was so keen to accept a commission that involved six weeks in Africa, from a fading and somewhat ridiculous Hollywood producer. Even as I am recounting the edited version, it occurs to me that Fairfax has probably been doing the same thing. What I tell him is the background to my commission to write the script. I tell him how it all started with an article about French involvement in the transportations from Paris. I tell him that the idea of investigating the life of a beautiful French anthropologist, who, in common with seventy thousand other Jews from France, was gassed (in a crowd, indistinguishable to the SS as the laibon's cattle are to me), was my starting point. My piece on Claudia Cohn-Casson had moved S. O. Letterman, the well-known Hollywood producer, to commission me to write a script. And here I am. Here we are, by a redolent log fire, in a world that has slipped from sight.

I can't tell him how this exercise fits into the human background. I leave out many things that matter. We all dissemble on the subject of our inner life, because it is in such a fluid state. When we talk about it (now all too common in public), we do so as though it had set fast, even for a moment, in some way. But what are my real purposes? I am talking to a man who has seen things I can only imagine. Yet he avoids shows of emotion and personal feeling because he believes they are destructive. Also, if I were to try to explain to him the nature of my personal circumstances, he would be embarrassed. He hasn't bought the widely held idea that a good airing is beneficial for the inner life. There seems, anyway, to be a metaphorical confusion in this idea: if the inner life is in need of air, how come it takes place in the least accessible parts of our being? In my piece about Drancy, I had written, "There are clues here to the nature of humanness." They may be clues, but the mystery is as insoluble as ever.

Why do I need all this detail? Am I expecting to be able to know all there is to know about Claude Cohn-Casson? Am I hoping to understand the nature of the Nazi mind? Of course not. Perhaps Victoria is right. I pretend to believe in living in my room, but it's true that I am trying to thrust myself onstage. The last thing Letterman wants from me is an alternative, goy, version of the human dilemma. What he wants is a confection. (He is, furthermore, doing me a favor: I have no track record in scriptwriting.) He has seen a certain facility in my work for grading and assembling the facts. He probably sees me as having mechanical skills, like a dentist's, which higher types must occasionally employ. I am not so green that I expect to get the sole credit on this movie. I don't really believe it will ever be made; I am just providing the raw material that Letterman and some highly paid specialist screenwriter are going to work up into a proper script. Letterman has already sent many messages. His suggestions, his imperatives, have kept Mr. Shah's fax humming.

I tell Fairfax a great deal more than I had intended, but I believe our confidences are drawing us together. I certainly hope so. He listens, and sometimes he inclines his head sympathetically, as if to get a better purchase on what I am saying. I wonder, however, if he wants any more personal details at his age. There must come a point when you realize that all these confidences are piling up, useless, in the storeroom, like the possessions elderly people sometimes keep for no purpose.

Eventually we retire. Retire is the right term for what he does: it is a ritual demanding a nightcap, a pee on the edge of the firelight, another nightcap, the preparation of a vacuum flask of hot tea for the bedside and a laborious change into old-fashioned pajamas. I have offered to sleep in the back of the Toyota. I hear his *couchée* going on for some time. The tent eventually falls into a deep stillness. I don't sleep immediately. I see the editing together of these elements repeated with new possibilities. Where do you close off the possibilities when you write a script? For example, does the lion hunt become symbolic, bigger than the actual facts warrant? Do I try to see it from the laibon's point of view? How much should Fairfax be seen to know of Claudia's love affair with the laibon's brother, Tepilit? And should I ask Fairfax's permission? All these questions—and there are many more—also suggest to me another, bigger question, the one that Victoria had noted, the extent of my own involvement. As I lie uneasily in the cab, I wonder why it is that I feel propelled to barge in here. What she is saying is that there are hundreds of millions of people out there who can let life go by without trying to relate themselves to the big issues. She thinks the big issues are grist to self-appointed mills. It's a devilish perpetual-motion contraption. Yet I see the mundane matter of the script quite clearly. I see the obvious physical limitations, one hundred minutes, no room for interior monologue, unequivocal scenes of love, grandeur and horror. (All of which are well represented in the story as I am learning it.) What I can't do, however, is close off the script until I know the facts.

In mitigation I could appeal to Proust: "Beneath the signs there lay something of a different kind, which I must try to discover . . ." Sadly, there is a lot about Proust's mission that I will never be able to believe in. My feelings are similar in this regard to what Claudia felt about her father's pretensions. And yet Victoria has accused me of exactly the same sin as I am so lightly attributing elsewhere (incidentally, to people who are more fiction than fact). For all I know, Léon Cohn-Casson might have had substantial reasons for believing in his invulnerability. In the way these things happen, the oppressed are sometimes revealed to have a hold on the oppressors. The survivors are the ones on whom suspicion falls. This is commonly reported by the cursed survivors of Auschwitz.

I lie in the metal box hoping to hear the elephant passing or the lions roaring, but I hear only a distant hyena against the myriad squeaks and screeches of the night. These noises make a tapestry, each one an individual stitch. I owe it to Victoria to lend some retrospective weight to our parting. Yet I can only picture her in the posture of Candice Riberon in *Le Métro* lying on her back, her face caught in an agony of uncertain provenance. Sadly it's not an erotic picture. It's more like a Munch. Recalled sexual longings would at least make me feel we had not wasted our store of human essence needlessly. I feel as if I haven't got that much to spare. Also, I wish to recall Victoria as an entire person. But it doesn't work. I see the rictus and an entirely gratuitous glowing flush on her throat. I remember her claim—which I found exciting—that semen contains Vitamin E and is therefore good for the skin. *Not to be taken internally. For external application only.* But it doesn't summon the erotic circumstance. Gone, gone, gone.

I climb out of the Toyota and go to the fire and push the kettle deep into the ash that now mutes the heat. Underneath, the embers are still vivid. I wonder if more people in the world are still heating their water in this way than on some sort of stove. At first I think that the answer must be no. But then I reconsider: what about China? I can't decide. I place a teabag and some powdered milk in the enamel cup and then pour on the water and stir with a twig. There is a lot of satisfaction in these simple actions. I like the tea with its powdered milk. Excessively milky in the way that artificial banana or strawberry can be excessive in flavor. I drink deeply. Along with the phoney milkiness is the ever-present taste of wood-ash.

The laibon is trying to tell us something. Who knows what he has been dreaming? His famous ancestor, Mbatian, made a prophecy about what would happen after the arrival of the white man. He got his information from God via a dream. You don't need a line to God now to see the way things are going. He has seen that the Masai stories and dreams are not going to be much use in the years to come. I wish I could tell him that we are all in the same boat. I finish my tea and climb back into the Toyota.

The laibon's fingers are like rolled-up tobacco leaves, crudely made cabbage cigars. They are dry. You feel that the skin would crackle if they rubbed together. His hands are always holding the cylinder that contains his stones. He has read what the careworn pebbles say, and he doesn't like it.

I dream about the Masai. Specifically I dream about the old man's parchment hands with their cheroot fingers, endlessly rolling the container in his hand, this movement polishing and burnishing it, an insistent but unexplained movement of the sort that happens in dreams.

33

The grassland waves and undulates in the morning light. It looks like wheat, except that right in the middle of this prairie is a group of small hills rising unexpectedly out of the flat plain. The hills have clumps of rocks precariously balanced on them. The rocks themselves are streaked with gleaming mineral secretions; in the cracks between them grow spiky aloes with bright red florets. Now a line of Masai warriors appears, walking fast. They are in elaborate headdresses and carry shields and spears. They approach the first rocky hill and pause. The color of their cloaks is exactly the color of the aloe flowers, which stipple the rocks like blobs of oil paint.

Some way behind the warriors comes a small caravan of safari vehicles, two open-topped Willys cars and a truck. They pause too, about a hundred yards from where the Masai are fanning out around one of the hills. In the first vehicle are Waindell Leavitt and Claudia Cohn-Casson. Leavitt has binoculars. He looks ahead to see what the Masai have found. In the second vehicle are the cameraman, his assistant and the camera equipment. In the truck are servants and armed guards accompanying the safari goods.

Tepilit signals to the driver of the first safari car to stay where he is. His arms rise and his hands spread out, pushing them back like someone miming the action of pushing against a wall. He walks fast over to the car and talks to Claudia in Maa. He is lightly beaded with sweat.

"The lions are here."

Claudia tells Leavitt.

"Okay, get the equipment out."

The Willys behind them is signaled to move up. The crew begin to rig the camera equipment on a platform. This requires ropes and stays. Leavitt is stout and impatient in his khakis. Under his bush hat he has a thin mustache.

"Let's get moving."

Tepilit is anxious. He speaks quietly to Claudia: "These men from the other side are not brave. They are afraid to kill the lion."

"Be careful."

"A moran must be brave."

Claudia touches his hand. Tepilit goes to talk to the warriors. There is evidently disagreement among them. Tepilit and his brother can be seen arguing with the others. In the tangle of rocks and trees we get a glimpse of the lions, now becoming agitated.

The cameraman is taking light readings and setting his lenses. The camera is bulky, mounted on a wooden tripod. He wants to get closer. They move the car toward the hill. The askaris have their .303 rifles ready. Tepilit comes running back and speaks to Claudia. She translates for Leavitt.

"He says that the lions will not stay any longer. They will either run or attack if they are surrounded."

"Just tell them to wait. Just a few minutes. Come on, load the fucking camera."

The camera assistant drops a cumbersome magazine.

"You dumb-ass motherfucker."

From the hill, which is now completely surrounded by Masai, we hear some growling. The Masai have their spears ready and their shields held high.

"Hold them, for Chrissakes. And tell them we want the action this side of the hill."

Claudia tries to explain to Tepilit. He gestures to her to get back. He says something.

"They can't wait. The lions are going to attack."

"Are you ready yet?"

"Almost ready, sir."

The three vehicles are drawn up in a semicircle. In front of them is the kopje, surrounded by Masai. The snarling and growling are very audible as the lions move about, looking for a way out. The camera assistant is having trouble getting the magazine onto the camera.

At this moment a lion bursts out of the long grass and bush and leaps on a warrior. Tepilit throws his spear, which strikes the lion just behind its shoulder. The lion mauls the warrior, who is desperately trying to fend him off with his knees and shield. Tepilit runs up to the lion, grabs the tail for an instant, draws his long knife from its sheath and sticks it into the lion's throat. The lion immediately jumps on him and forces him to the ground. At this moment another lion bursts out of the bush and attacks a second warrior. Some of the warriors run. Others hurl their spears blindly. At least six lions and lionesses make their escape, but a third black-maned lion stands menacingly ready to attack. One of the spears strikes a warrior in the chest.

Claudia shouts at Leavitt: "Shoot, shoot. They are being killed."

"Turn over. Is the camera running? Roll the camera."

Claudia is horrified. We see her face, paralyzed for a moment. Tepilit has pulled his sword out of the lion's neck and plunges it under its throat again. The lion leaves him and staggers away before falling. Tepilit's head is covered in blood and his shoulders and arms are ripped open. Claudia runs to the askaris and tries to seize a gun.

"Run that camera. On your right. Get that."

The first Masai is dead. Tepilit, however, rises to his feet. Claudia seizes the askari's gun and fires at the waiting lion. It turns and disappears. The Masai wounded by a spear is lying on the ground too.

"Get out of the fucking way. Keep turning. Claudia, get in the car."

The black-maned lion now charges out of the bush in the direction of the cars. The askaris open fire and it drops. Now the Masai are gathering, arguing and shouting. A fight breaks out and one man is struck on the head by a stick. Tepilit, streaming blood, goes over to them. He speaks to them and they separate into two groups, trembling. One man is foaming at the mouth and moaning. Claudia runs over to Tepilit.

"Get out of the way. They are going to go at it again. Keep turning."

"Salaud. Salaud. Salaud."

Claudia is hysterical. The askaris are now gathered around the vehicles, perhaps fearing that the Masai will attack them.

"Get out of the way, for Chrissakes."

Claudia is weeping. The two groups of Masai, who are still highly agitated, back away from each other. One warrior is having a fit. We now see a view of the battlefield: two lions dead, two Masai dead and Tepilit, although standing, severely mauled.

"Okay. Cut. Cut. Fantastic."

Claudia and the askaris move Tepilit to the shade. Claudia goes to get the first aid kit. Leavitt intercepts her. "I'm real sorry I shouted at you. We got a bit excited there for a minute."

"You are a murderer. You don't care about these people."

"I make movies, sweetheart. That's my job."

"Movies. You don't make movies. You are making a mockery. Look at them. Two men dead and another badly wounded."

"I thought they knew their business. Jesus, I have never seen such a shambles. Let me tell you, these guys don't have our feelings about death or pain. Life is cheap. That's how they live."

"You think that? You think going out and killing oneself for a few shillings is normal to a Masai? You are crazy."

Leavitt walks with Claudia back to where Tepilit is lying. Tepilit looks up and sees Leavitt. Claudia starts to clean his wounds with Mercurochrome, but Tepilit stops her. He speaks with difficulty.

"What is he saying?"

"He says you should leave Masailand now. He says you have caused a lot of trouble."

"Shit. You tell your lover boy next time he goes lion hunting he should get himself just a little better organized. You tell him that. Dumb fuck."

34

The laibon has had plenty of time to think about this ugly incident. I hesitate to pronounce on the degree of tranquillity in his life, but since 1943 he has not been farther than sixty miles from this spot. Compared with the removals, job changes and constant travel that have affected my life, his has been tranquil. Of course, death and bereavement have come thicker and faster here. That may not be as important, being so frequent, in his estimation. *Life is cheap.* But in all these years he has certainly been spared those other, uninvited, distractions that sweep over our lives, a snowstorm of diversion and entertainment and half-understood knowledge. What we seek to see in this blizzard is the spectral shape approaching of what was once called—with a straight face—meaning. We know now that the world was not designed for us, but we haven't come round to acting on this knowledge. Explanations are plentiful: absurd, irrational, unscientific explanations, alongside absurd, rational, scientific ones. Although there is no overall meaning, everything can be explained on one measure or another.

The laibon believes that he can pinpoint the beginning of his troubles to this lion hunt. He is sitting at our camp now, holding a mug of our tea, relaxing on a canvas chair. He sees that Leavitt's film introduced a new element into the life of his people. For the first time the hunting of lions was treated as picturesque. It had no other meaning. It was as weightless as tribal dances performed for tourists. It has taken him all these years to understand the implications. At a turn of the clockwork motor of the bulky camera, Leavitt had proclaimed that this submission to the seasons, to the rains, to the predations of lions, to the pasturing of cattle and all the placatory rituals that went with it, was unnecessary. It was flimflam, folklore, credulity. Its only value was as entertainment in movie houses.

Claudia's study, while more high-minded than Leavitt's movies, had the same general effect. The laibon does not strictly say this. His complaint is a more general one about the lack of respect for custom and the gradual constriction of his world that has taken place in fifty years. But the connection is clear enough. The inner coherence of Masai life was destroyed by the implied contempt.

Fairfax listens patiently to the laibon. As always the laibon holds his snuff container. He holds it the way elderly Greeks hold worry beads, a certain anxiety about the dwindling supplies of life remaining, kept at bay by this endless fiddling. There are long monologues before the laibon pauses. Fairfax then summarizes thoughtfully what the laibon has been saying.

The laibon sees this moment as the beginning of the end of innocence. Leavitt may be the serpent, but Claudia is Eve. Gradually the consequences of that day, the wising-up, have become apparent. Of course, the laibon does not phrase it as I have. He simply sees a connection between the sham lion hunt and the all-too-real execution of his brother. Because of his brother's hanging, he assumed the mantle of laibon. He is wearing the mantle now, made from the skins of the hyrax, a flea-ridden animal that looks like a giant guinea pig. Perhaps he has no calling and has been unhappy in the family business for years. The mistake Claudia made was to become part of the total social fact herself. Yet the laibon seems to be suggesting complicity by his own family in what Fairfax calls "the balls-up." They should never have taken part in something so unnatural. They never would have, but for Claudia's influence on his brother.

It also occurs to me, as I watch the laibon direct a stream of sugar into his second cup of tea, that there may have been something degrading about being delivered this cultural snub. The idea that hunting lions was just another native custom, albeit risky and magnificent, must have been deeply wounding. The laibon wants it understood that it has taken him some time to trace the trouble back to this incident.

"Ask him, if you don't mind, if he blames Claudia."

Fairfax asks him and I hear the choppy pronunciation of her name a number of times.

"Unfortunately," says Fairfax, "he does believe she was the cause of the problem. But as she was a woman he doesn't want to give her too much credit. He doesn't think that women should be allowed so much freedom of movement, although he understands that this is regrettably the custom, to this day, among white women."

I look carefully at Fairfax's moist, fatigued eyes, which have seen so much, for signs of irony.

"Is that your little joke?"

"I may possibly have added a word or two."

"What about Claudia looking after his brother?"

"He liked Claudia. In a way, that was the problem. Women should not be able to surpass men in understanding. It is not an advantage to a woman, and fatal to society, if women are allowed to take too important a role. It just causes trouble."

"Does he have any idea what happened to her?"

Fairfax does not answer my question. After a pause, which is, of course, shredded by the cries and protests of birds and insects, he says, "I don't think any of us does."

The laibon takes us to the spot beneath the escarpment, looking down through two rock walls onto the plain, where Claudia built her little house. The plains are movable, subject to wind, water and grazing. The watercourses wander, breaking and re-forming with the seasons. But the escarpments are fixed, and here, where a stream tumbles down onto the plain, is the site of Claudia's camp. This is where she and Fairfax made love.

To a Masai it is not a good site. It is close to high cliffs where leopards live, and it is surrounded by trees, which make cattle ambush easy. This is the pastoralist's view of topography. For a Masai a broad, grassy plain with barely a tree in sight is prefer-able. But to my eye it is beautiful.

I watch Fairfax carefully as he talks to the laibon. They are discussing the layout of the camp. There is nothing to be seen, but the reconstruction in the imagination is tangible. Here stood the little house looking down through a frame of brown granite to the plain below. There were two tents, thatched over against the sun, and here was the storeroom. Claudia's sleeping tent stood just here, with a view all the way to Ol Doinyo Lengai. Fairfax and the laibon stand on the spot. They remind me of a builder and a client discussing the positioning of proposed works. They agree on something and smile. It is camaraderie on the most ordinary level.

A few hundred yards away, behind the site, is a cliff face, down which a stream tumbles. I know from Claudia's notes that this was a seasonal stream. Sometimes she had to have water fetched from miles up in the mountain. Like all researchers and scientists in remote places, she found the arrangements, the logistics, more demanding than the work itself. She wrote a long letter to her older brother about these problems. She worried about the amount of supplies she needed. She contrasted this unfavorably with the simple needs of the Masai and tried for a while to live on their diet of milk and maize meal. It didn't last: "Mais enfin," she wrote, "je suis française." She bought a small shotgun, and it was a simple business shooting spotted guinea fowl or the umber-colored francolin, which she stewed slowly on the fire. Later she tried to make an oven out of an iron safe, but it did not work.

The old men talk. Fairfax is no longer breaking off to translate. Against the cliff they are figures in a landscape painted in watercolor by some Victorian with grandiose ideas about nature and the sublime. It pulls at the heart. Here they are, shooting the breeze, Fairfax in his outmoded but perfectly cut clothes, the laibon in a dark blue shift and a cape of fur, with ear lobes that contain three or four little bead earrings and a silver wire holding a small copper bell. As he gestures, his robe slips and I can see his penis, which is inky black and purplish toward the (circumcized) tip. It is very long.

The century is closing. Everywhere I hear about the malaise and uncertainty this is producing. But I am looking at something from the previous century. Behind them the rock face is bound together by the rope roots of the fig tree, and on the hillside above them are ravines thick with flowering Cape chestnuts; above that level there are hillsides of succulents and, even higher, alpine pastures and more cliffs.

These two old chaps both knew Claudia. It's miraculous.

S. O. Letterman is trying to get to know Claudia, in the person of Candice Riberon. In the depths of his Dearborn soul he is shocked by Candice. He has never before had the feeling of being used so blatantly. He thinks his hairy, carefully nurtured and manicured body excites and disgusts her. She uses it for purposes that he can't figure out. It excites him in turn to see her perfect back which, after the opening formalities, is what he sees most of during their lovemaking. Her back is expressive. After it is over, as they are having lunch, he watches her treacherous mouth eating the regional ingredients they seek out each day. Today they are eating seafood from Brittany. Yesterday it was *choucroute* from Alsace. The day before . . . he has forgotten. Her mouth, which has a confident but inexpert command of English and also a very Gallic command of sexual practice. Her mouth, which is an obstacle to the closer understanding that he desires.

As he eats he feels a ball of melancholy in his vitals. It lodges there indigestible, as if he had eaten it with the *fines belons*. He feels an urge to shove all the idiotic *crustaces* off the table. Jesus, the little crawly things the French love to eat. Now she is probing a periwinkle with a pin; now she is sucking the leg of a *langouste,* the bony, knobbly carapace of its knee joint resting right where his cock had been twenty, thirty minutes before. She gives it a final appreciative tug with her famous lips and he experiences a fellow feeling for this humble, stunted lobster. He wonders what they would do if they ever got their hands—or their mouths—on some decent-size seafood instead of these dwarfs which (God, how he is enjoying this moment of contempt) come from the diesel-scented Mediterranean. These people would eat anything: snails, blackbirds, skylarks, dry rot, even adders.

Candice's renowned lips are now, briefly, smeared with parsley butter.

"If you had anal sex you would use *sauce ravigote,*" he says bitterly, but she does not understand him.

"It's good, *ravigote,* super."

"Soopair," he says, "up the ass."

"What's the matter with you today? You don't look happy."

"I am happy. Paramount is jerking me around. My writer's gone walkabout in Africa. I sent him some notes five days ago and I haven't heard a word. But in every other respect, yes, I am happy."

The truth is that Paramount doesn't think Candice can open the picture. They want him to use an American star. They have cited the case of *Out of Africa,* where Robert Redford played an Englishman and Meryl Streep a Dane. He has tried to explain that this is not some sentimental love story but a major and symbolic movie to close this troubled century. But he knows already that it is the romantic element that is going to drag them into the movie houses. He hasn't even hinted to Candice that she may not be acceptable. He is proposing to take her to Hollywood to let them tell her.

Now when he looks at her he sees Claudia. He sees her in the cattle car, the dreamlike, unending, unbearable journey. He sees her out in Africa among the Masai, speaking Masai; he sees her doomed attempt to persuade her father to leave the house on avenue Hoche. He sees her making love to a Masai warrior out there, all white linen shirts and those high boots, and he sees Fairfax, the love of her life, with his small plane, his Fairbanks mustache and his no-nonsense colonial (read "frontier") manner. It's such a human drama, the pull of family, the counterweight of love, played against the dreadful knowledge of the death camps. Which some French, as is now well known, were all in favor of. She was turned in by a colleague from the university; but Letterman thinks this should be left ambiguous. In the first roundup, *la grande rafle,* gendarmes had done the actual rounding up, but Letterman is not sure they will get much cooperation from the French if he makes this scene—when Claudia returns to Paris to see her deluded father—appear anti-French. Anyway, Claudia and her family were picked up by the SS themselves on the direct orders of Alois Brunner. This morning it was reported from Syria that Brunner had died. The part of Brunner would be easy to cast: Max von Sydow. A Swede who has made a corner in Krauts. Unless he is too old.

Opposite him Candice/Claudia is now eating a *salade composée.* His melancholy is quickly banished when she reaches under the table and squeezes the front of his trousers.

"I love your zizi," she says, leaning forward and using her napkin in her spare hand to wipe his mouth.

"And me?"

"Ça, c'est autre chose. When is your writer coming? I want to meet him."

"I'm meeting him in London at the end of next week. Do you want to come?"

"I want. But it would be difficult."

"Do you love your husband?"

"You know, you Americans, you ask some funny questions."

"What do you mean, funny? It's a perfectly goddamn sensible question under the circumstances. And not a particularly American question. It's not like I'm saying, do you love baseball or root beer? I'm asking if you love your husband."

"If I answer that I will already be rising the question onto a *niveau*—"

"Level."

"Level which is not the dignified level."

"Dignified?"

There seems to be some semantic confusion here. It is tiring conveying intense and complex emotions in pidgin. She lights a cigarette.

"You don't want to talk about it?"

She exhales, a breathy tremor passing through the lips, slight but expressive. He is clearly not on the right *niveau* here. It troubles him. In his career he has fucked many young actresses. Sometimes he has felt that they were not one hundred percent willing. Sometimes he has felt that they were doing what was required with an excess of gusto. Quite often they fell in love with him. To an outsider it might look as if he was using his patronage, or at least the promise of it. But nothing is this straightforward. With his intuitive qualities—at the moment failing him badly—he knows that the compact between young women and powerful men is well understood on both sides. The people looking in the window of the limo may see an incongruity cuddling on the backseat, but the two inside know the score.

But Candice is truly *autre chose*. He fears she is bringing more to the party than he is, but he cannot quite understand what it is. Also, the language problem cramps their understanding somewhat. Her vocabulary—slangy and comically inaccurate—leads along byways that are closed to him. This does not worry her.

On the contrary, she ducks behind the language barrier whenever it suits her.

The waiters know her. They know her in every place where they have eaten or nibbled *amuse-gueules* with her filmic friends. They are solicitous but discreet. Being French, they naturally regard him as the less important half of the duo taking the culinary communion. It is beginning to annoy him. In Hollywood, and in many other places, his name is enough to ensure a good table and the right amount—that little extra amount—of solicitude. Here he might as well be wearing plaid Bermudas and a Lakers sweatshirt; they have him down as one of the anonymous, and strangely impertinent, American lumpenproletariat. His relationship to the lovely Candice Riberon, they imply by their grave faces and approving nods when she makes known her choice, is her business. He thinks that while most of them can imagine themselves in bed with this gorgeous creature, none of them can imagine him in bed with her. So when her hand reaches so deftly under the table, it is to him a wonderful release from his doubts, even though their waiter is too far away to get the message, just gliding behind some heavy, velvet-trimmed curtains. These curtains enclose a hallway decorated with a copper jam cauldron full of poinsettias. It is a meeting point for the customers and the *patron*. Many French restaurants, he has noticed, advertise their seriousness by expensive curtains.

The language hurdle—her misplaced confidence, his film-business phraseology—has also prevented a proper discussion of the character of Claudia. He finds that all his inquiries lead to a dead end. To Candice and her friends it is perfectly okay to talk of betrayal and transportation and the moral issues involved as though they had some dialectic or aesthetic, independent of the facts and, of course, independent of life as it is lived in Paris, which is—he is becoming bitter again—the masterwork of Western civilization. Claudia Cohn-Casson has become a symbol in the popular culture on a level—oh, yes—that in his youth was reserved for Arthur

Miller or Earl Morrall, people whose real life bore no relation whatever to their existence in the popular imagination.

Candice is now moving, sliding, her two long and firm legs under her, out of the booth. (If he has a criticism of her, it is that she spends quite a lot of time in the can.) He is alone. He thinks of Earl Morrall before the days of the Silverdome, the fog and snow coming in off the lake, not so much rolling as avalanching across the water from Canada, bringing in its billowing, impenetrable folds a frozen ticker-tape blizzard, which struck Morrall, shrouded in a cape, his head bowed, in a personal and elemental fashion. It didn't matter to Letterman that the other guys, the big crude guys, got snowed on, but it was essential that Morrall should not be disturbed. Soon the whole stadium was slipping under an anesthetic, the other side of the field flickering with life only intermittently. Yet Letterman, the chunky fan, already, at thirteen, inches beyond his immigrant Plimsoll line, knew that Morrall would find his way around this winter wonderland as surely as a bat in a cave.

The French know nothing of all this. He had read somewhere that the French have, essentially, a Deux Chevaux mentality. Fuck them. Through the velvet curtains comes Candice. She has no idea of these things. If he tried to explain to her his irrational love of Earl Morrall or his trembling anxiety as the northern winter bombarded his hero with hard pellets of snow—a winter, by the way, that would freeze the balls off Parisians in their clown-suits—she would smile indulgently as if he were describing the attractions of Thunder Mountain at Disneyland. They couldn't even pronounce the fucking word: "Deez-neigh," they sneered, like a horse in a Western. She sits down. It is a very erotic action; all her movements are choreographed by an erotomaniac. He doesn't want to surrender this erotic treasure trove just yet.

"You know," he says, "I was just thinking. I was wondering if we should go to Africa. We could meet the writer. You could get some idea of the locations and so on."

"You want to go to Africa?"

"Sure. We can have our meetings there. And we can do some scouting."

He really wants to get her away from Paris and delay telling her that she will never play Claudia Cohn-Casson. Also, in Paris she has home-team advantage.

"Okay. Sure," she says.

"What about your husband?"

"No problem. It's the work. He understands."

When he gets back to the club, he discovers his satrap, Farwaggi, deep in faxes from Hollywood. He also has one from a Mr. Shah of the Clocktower Hotel who fears that Mr. Curtiz may be lost. Farwaggi is glad to see him. With the responsibility, his eyes have become feverish; they burn like the chestnut braziers outside.

"Have you got a chill?" asks Letterman.

"Chill? No, no. Not at all."

He is one of those people who take on in their corporeal person their mental state. The time zones are keeping him in a state of anxiety. He wears three Swatches.

Letterman reads the message from Mr. Shah, which Farwaggi presses on him.

"You better check out the flights to Nairobi. We'll need three tickets."

"Who should be going, Mr. Letterman?"

"You and me and Miss Riberon."

The feverish eyes glow damply, like headlights on a wet pavement. It is only four in the afternoon but his jaw is darkly stained. So is Letterman's. It has led him to speculate about their common ancestry in the Mediterranean basin some centuries before Detroit and Earl Morrall.

"May I speak with you, sir?"

"Sure, go ahead."

"It is a delicate matter."

Letterman likes the word. It has a Proustian ring. The St. James's club has been got up for Christmas; the decorations are wonderfully rich. The French have an eye for these *haut bourgeois* knickknacks. He can imagine Proust standing under just such an arrangement of walnuts and tangerines hung in a silk tree, worrying about his lover's movements at Christmas. A delicate matter.

"Shoot."

Farwaggi finds it hard to speak.

"Go on. Let's have it."

"Miss Riberon is a transsexual."

He pronounces it in the French way, with emphasis on the last, feminine, syllable.

"I am sorry, sir, but I thought you have the right to know."

Letterman's first thought, bizarrely, is of Earl Morrall in a snowstorm. He wonders what the great man would have made of it if he had known that thirty years later one of his fans—his greatest fan—would have been making love to a transsexual in Paris.

"At least I now know why she faces toward the window."

"Excuse me?"

"Never mind. Plus ça change."

But later, questions begin to assault him. He makes inquiries and finds out that her husband is a plastic surgeon. He performed the operation when she was fifteen. Candice was the son of a nightclub singer who did an imitation of Edith Piaf for tourists. Her little zizi was simply an oversight of nature.

36

We are in no hurry to go back to town. We have moved our camp to Claudia's old homestead. Fairfax has a comfortable routine. He wakes early, takes a shower sluiced from a bucket slung over a tree, makes tea and then shaves carefully. Slyly, pretending to be asleep, I watch him. His body is barrel-like, quite hairy, but his arms and legs do not match this robustness. They have dwindled. Eventually he says, "I've made tea. Would you like some?" I unzip my sleeping bag and then the flyscreen on my mossy tent.

"What do you want to talk about today?" he asks me as we drink our tea.

Like a good soldier, he wants to do the job properly.

"Well," I say, "could you tell me about your months with Claudia?"

"Weeks. Six weeks."

"Your weeks with Claudia before she left for France?"

He sips his tea, as if in difficulty with retrieving these memories. He sometimes talks about people from his past as if I knew them. Although he is modest, he is an old-fashioned hero of the sort you find in Hemingway novels or miniseries on television, a man who is always the central figure in any drama. Women are there to pay court and to admire. No matter how tragic or how broken down, these heroes remain central to the other characters' lives. This was what the purpose of a gentleman was. Gentlemen had a dispensation, even a vocation, to be free of the common anxieties and vulgarities. Of course, Fairfax knows that the world no longer recognizes the archetype. He also holds the view that the lesser evolutionary archetypes are breathing their unsavory breath down the collars of the few remaining gentlemen. I detect a general fear both in New York and London that this is happening, although it's no longer phrased in Darwinian terms. No good comes from explaining that this sort of fear has been around since man began to wander about and encounter his neighbors.

"The truth is, I don't think the people of the world were supposed to meet," he had said.

Only the more evolved types can travel, to the benefit of the people they meet.

"I am not sure," I say, "about what exactly prompted Claudia to go back to France when the Germans were still in Paris, particularly as it must have been obvious that they would soon be pushed out."

"That was her worry. She thought that the Germans would take the family with them or kill them in Paris."

"Did you try to stop her?"

"Of course I did. I loved her. I wanted to marry her. But she wouldn't stay. When the news came through of the hanging, she didn't say much, but it obviously preyed on her mind. I would sometimes find her weeping down near the dam, just sitting there crying."

"Did she talk about it?"

"No. She felt we had let him down, which of course we had, but I am afraid most of the time I simply forgot about it. We seemed to be out every night and riding every moment when I was free. But eventually I said something very foolish. I accused her of having an affair with the moran."

"What did she say?"

"I can't remember exactly. I have probably tried to forget it. It's one of those things one is always ashamed of."

I now feel guilty. It has been clear to me for weeks that she made love with this Masai. Why not? What do I care? For the purposes of the movie it is almost essential. I have written the scene. Yet what if he doesn't know the truth, or if he deliberately did not want to know, as he suggests? He was a young man, married, but hopelessly in love. I can imagine the shock of discovering that the woman you love had been conducting an affair with a Masai warrior.

"You had an altercation?"

Even my language is stilted.

He looks at me. He takes the tea from his lips. He wipes his waterproof mustache.

"It was more than an altercation. I accused her of having syphilis. Like Blixen. Of course I didn't mean it."

I hold my enamel cup tightly.

"And she accused me of not caring about the moran being hanged. She almost said I had encouraged the governor."

The insects abhor an auditory vacuum. Some birds also take up the challenge with sibilant, jeering whistling.

"The truth is that I didn't care about him enough. After all, he had stuck a spear right through the poor bloody DO, an inoffensive chap by all accounts."

"The laibon says he was hard on Tepilit because of his closeness" (God forgive me) "to Claudia."

" 'Closeness.' Funny word to use, don't you think? Are you trying to be diplomatic?"

"I am just trying to get at the facts without offending too many people."

189

"Do you really need the facts? It's not as though they are very clear, anyway."

"I would feel better knowing as many as I can before I start making things up. Because of—well, because of where she ended up."

"Thanks to me."

"Thanks to you?"

My voice is strangled. I have become pious, without meaning to. I know that the world is made up of stories of wretched betrayals and wrong turnings and destructive love affairs, but the evidence always comes as a shock.

"Yes, if I hadn't accused her of—of doing every damn thing under the sun, she wouldn't have gone on her very foolish journey."

"Do you mind if I get this down in order?"

"If you think it will help."

We start at Fairfax's farm, near the Masai village of Ngong.

Tom Fairfax and Claudia Cohn-Casson are riding. Below them is the Rift Valley and behind them the knuckles of the Ngong hills. We follow them at a distance as they canter along the skyline.

The horses pull up. They are blowing. The sun is setting behind the hills.

Fairfax leans across to kiss Claudia. They canter off again. They pass two Masai walking—they are always walking—and call out to them. The Masai wave negligently.

The horses are being led away to the stables. Fairfax and Claudia walk toward the house, which is a pleasant low stone house with a tin roof, surrounded by a wide verandah. The interior of the house is simple but spacious. Above the stone fireplace is a large fox-hunting oil. The chairs are cane or wood and hide. On a table is a huge bowl of flowers, picked from the flame trees and bougainvilleas that surround the house. The heads of waterbuck and kudu hang on the walls. An old phonograph of the wind-up variety is playing a Chopin prelude. A servant in a white robe and a fez brings a tray of drinks as night falls sharply outside. Fairfax pours two drinks and wields the soda siphon.

"Do you believe there is a war going on?"

"It is difficult to believe. You know what seems crazy is that from here it looks like a war of the mad people. My father is still there trying to uphold the honor of the family. Why? For what? He could be here with us."

"Ice?"

"Yes, please. Do you know why?"

"No, although I would guess at something to do with *la gloire*."

"Because he wants to be recognized as a Frenchman first and a Jew second. That's why. It's for that he has not left Paris. Even the Rothschilds decided a long time ago that discretion was better than valor. But, no, my papa has to stay right to the end. The absolute end."

"Maybe he will be justified."

"Do you think the SS will leave him alone? Goodbye, well done, thank you very much for everything. We will be back next year as tourists. And, *entre nous,* let's not say anything about what happened. *Wiedersehen.* You know it's a kind of obsession with him that he must prove that he has more sense of duty than the Nazis. In a strange way he admires the Nazis because they know their own minds. They have a purpose. He wrote that to me. He thinks we French don't have sufficient purpose."

"I wonder about that. What I find is that it is the people with a purpose who cause all the trouble. These Masai may not have much idea what's happening over the next hill, but they are never going to cause any problems for the world."

"Tom, may I ask you a question?"

"Of course, my darling."

"Do you still love your wife?"

"I don't believe I do love her anymore. I haven't seen her for nearly a year and I don't think about her at all. Never. She has gone from my mind. What else is love if it's not an invasion of your mind, a complete occupation of your mind and senses?"

"You know, for an Englishman you are quite romantic."

"Can I ask you something?"

"If you wish."

"Did you love the Masai, Tepilit?"

"I never loved him. I treated him like my own family. No more."

A silence falls over them. Claudia stands up and walks out onto the darkened verandah, lit by hurricane lamps, which are burning very yellow, a mineral color, against the immense star-washed sky outside. Fairfax follows her.

"I don't want to make you sad."

She turns to him.

"I have never been happier in my life. My senses are occupied."

"And your mind?"

"That also."

In the bedroom a roof fan stirs the mosquito net that hangs over the bed. The net is draped from a wooden frame. It is not completely closed. By the light of an oil lamp Claudia lies naked but awake beside the sleeping Fairfax.

We see the old Portuguese fort, which serves as a prison. Dawn is breaking. We hear, but do not see, the escort marching. Suddenly in close-up we see the completely unmoved, perhaps already in some sense dead, face of Tepilit. Without warning the face drops from view and the rope becomes visible. There is a sharp, breaking sound (a horribly magnified effect of snapping a chicken drumstick off a carcass) and immediately the sound of voiding the bowels.

Fairfax and Claudia are lunching on the verandah. The phone, a party line, rings. Fairfax stands up.

"Two longs and a short."

Claudia watches him go. She can hear his voice.

"I see. But what about the appeal? That was supposed to be next week. I don't care. You said there would be an appeal. You promised. Why wasn't I notified?"

Claudia understands exactly the significance of the conversation. Her face turns away from the house and out to the hills, where two Masai in their red robes, small figures, can be seen. Her face is undermined by grief. It appears to collapse, as though the muscles that hold it together—all those muscles children believe are necessary to make a smile—have lost their torque.

Fairfax appears behind her on the verandah.

"They have hanged him."

"I know. I know."

"I'm so sorry, darling."

"When did they hang him?"

"Early on Saturday morning."

"He was so beautiful."

Fairfax stands behind her. Her eyes are full of tears.

"You slept with him."

"The man is dead. He has just been hanged and all you concern yourself with is if I sleep with him."

"Not just that."

"What? What?"

"I don't want syphilis."

A ship is leaving the harbor. On deck, standing alone in white, is Claudia Cohn-Casson. She gazes back at the port. She sees the fort where Tepilit was hanged. The ship's horn sounds. The shore recedes.

There is a spot where I sit and look down at the plain. When I was a child my mother was always saying, "What a view," or "What a lovely drive" or "Just look at that." She saw something inspiring in nature, just like Wordsworth and his chums. Now, as I get older, I find the early conditioning has worked. Unlike my mother, however, I don't see any evidence of the Grand Universal Design. In fact, I know there isn't one, that the natural world is completely mindless and aimless. (Although some have argued that it is in its very randomness that we may detect the cunning of the design.)

Here, the enjoyment of the view is underscored by a relentless scuttling and creeping, particularly lively down on the insect level. Fairfax is asleep in his tent. He takes his afternoon nap seriously, undressing and covering himself with a light fringed Somali cloth. He sleeps for forty-five minutes, after which he wakes and has some tea. Tomorrow we must go back to town. We have been out here for days. I like to think that we have become friends. He has been frank with me, even if he is not sure of the ultimate destination of the information. I can't tell him that I am not too sure myself. I parade my limited vocabulary of movies—distribution, casting, studio, locations and so on—to hide this fact from him. He thinks that someone like Stewart Granger would play him very well, although of course he knows that Stewart Granger is as old as he is—if not actually dead—and that we are talking about a time when he was just thirty years old. He remembers Stewart Granger in *King Solomon's Mines* in the fifties.

"But there aren't many English actors nowadays, are there, who aren't pansies or rather peculiar? I saw Kevin Costner in the Red Indian film, which I liked very much. They ran it at the club. What about him?"

I wonder how S. O. Letterman is getting on in Paris with his casting. I imagine his casting is like his tennis: it has a biographical significance reaching far beyond the act. Hollywood insiders like Letterman are always looking for the magical fission caused by great screen actresses. They are seeking to renew themselves by their association with this magic, particularly if they can claim some part in its creation. When Letterman has cast his Claudia, I wonder, will I be able to see her more clearly? A friend at university used to say that he could not know a girl until he had slept with her. It was a ploy that occasionally worked. In the tent, under his Somali cloth, which looks like a purchase from a crafts fair, is a man who has made love to Claudia. He has known her. I want to ask him some impertinent questions: how was it, chum,

195

did she squeal, did she bounce about, did you think she was comparing yours to his, did she do like an intellectual, is it true about
the soap-scented fanny, did she speak a lot or become *triste* after
sex, did she lie to you, did you know about multiple orgasm, had
she had sex with Marcel Mauss, did she wear a silk camisole, did
she look very Jewish undressed, did she have breasts that were
widely spaced or cosily nesting, did she have irritating little
habits, did she have a crease at the top of her thighs?

I am not going to ask any of these questions. He has lain on
top of her (or underneath her); he has been privy to her most
intimate secrets, the little folds and tucks and ways of sleeping,
the night noises and possibly endearing odors. He should be able
to tell me about her, but we do not have the language. The generations have cut us from each other. Time has put a layer of ash,
like the ash that lies on the shoulders of Ol Doinyo Lengai, over
their love affair.

Fairfax wakes. I have the tea ready. His face, infantile from sleep,
is puzzled for a moment.

"What do you want to know?" he asks, smiling as he recognizes me.

"I want to know if you had plenty of laughs or if it was all
Sturm und Drang. What was she really like?"

He sips his tea. I sit on the end of his camp bed.

"All right?"

"Perfect. Nothing like bush tea. It's the condensed milk. What
was she like? She was quite serious. But, yes, we had a marvelous
time. She had a wonderful sense of humor, although it probably
sounds ghoulish now."

This trip has become an excursion into unknowable places:
perfumes, jokes, popular music, clothes, pubic hairs, safari cars
and *l'âme universelle*. They are all buried together in a mass grave
now. Young Claudia and young Tom riding across the golden
savannah, the Rift Valley untouched by this century, the phono-

graph record revolving giddily, the celluloid overheating, the biplane tossing in the thermals, the red-ochred Masai always walking. They are all saturated in death. Yet here is Fairfax, sleep-flushed and amiable and still alive. As I top up his tea from the brown pot, I find myself wondering if there is any point in trying to get a fix on these things. But of course I try.

"Did she know what was going on in the extermination camps?"

"I am sure she knew and yet I don't think she could have comprehended the extent. None of us did. Also, I can't remember a single conversation about them. Of course, she spoke about deportation and transports, but we never discussed the destination. Now I am not sure if we really knew, although it was obviously rumored. She wanted to get her father and her brother Georges out. He was only eleven."

"Do you know what happened to Georges?"

"The same, I am afraid. Do you know?"

"I believe he was experimented on, first in Birkenau and then at a place called Neuengamme."

I see in the distance the laibon followed by his son, coming over for a chat.

"Poor Georges. She so wanted to save him."

"Did you hear from her when she got to France?"

"Yes. She wrote to me via the Red Cross. There were a surprisingly large number of ways."

"Did she want to see you again?"

"She said she would come back after the war."

"Did you have any contact with her after that?"

"She wrote to me five times. I have the letters at home. One of them was posted from the cattle car."

"You haven't mentioned them before."

"I know. To be honest I wanted to see what sort of chap you were."

I take this as a compliment. I am strangely eager for his approval.

The laibon arrives. He shakes my hand wearily and I give him and his son tea as we wait for Fairfax. The laibon is grave today. His eyes are cloudy and yellow. He drinks his tea but he does not look at me. When Fairfax emerges from the tent (actually he has been visible for some minutes, wraithlike, through the fly screen, preparing himself), the laibon begins to talk. His son puts down his mug without a word and wanders off, following the stream up to the cliffs, where he has heard women at work, chopping at the trees with their long knives, talking and laughing. The women always laugh when they are together. They laugh at men to whom Ngai did not give a full deck. The laibon is unwrapping a cloth. In it is a small leather container, and seven shiny pebbles.

"He is going to tell us our fate," says Fairfax with a smile. I am not sure if he is joking.

The old man now places the pebbles in the container, which is a smaller version of the cylinder in which he keeps his snuff.

He leaves his chair and crouches on his haunches in a position I would have thought impossible for an old man. I feel something in my chest surge and bound, a large fish in a creel. I don't know what I am expecting.

He gives the container a good shake. The pebbles in there clash like children's marbles. Fairfax watches, smiling gently. The laibon throws the pebbles with a casual flick of the wrist. He bends his melon head and his large floppy ears toward the stones. He rises and genuflects, from his hands onto one knee. What I see is not a deluded old savage, but a scientist. *Stone and steel are both well made.* The laibon looks at the stones where they have fallen. A large red ant is already exploring one of them. They are polished from years of use. They have been handed down, and the hands have worn them, giving them a human patina. In fact they are about the only thing in the Masai's possession that will last. Under the sea in Turkey I have seen giant carved blocks that once formed a harbor wall, five hundred years B.C. Unmistakable, as the fish and the flipper-clad visitors swam around them, was the human agency involved. These little stones are equally charged.

The laibon speaks. He points out to Fairfax the position of the stones. He explains patiently their meaning. Fairfax has told me that in the past he was prone to undervaluing the preoccupations of these people. He would have agreed with early French academics in their division into the logical and pre-logical minds. But what Lévi-Strauss sees is that there is no such distinction: myth and science flow from the same impulses in the brain and require just as much savvy. His stones are just as well-made as any product of industry. *Cuit et cru.*

So when Fairfax tells us that the laibon is giving us a prognostication for our futures, a free consultation, I am not inclined to sneer. In fact I feel nervous with the anticipation. The laibon spits on the ground. He shakes his head. He moves a stone. Then he turns to Fairfax again and sums up.

"What's the verdict?"

"Red Ngai will prevail over black Ngai."

"What does that mean?"

"It's not good," says Fairfax, but he doesn't look too concerned.

The laibon gathers up his pebbles. He shakes his head, causing the ornaments in his ears to dance. The slippery thing in my chest is still twitching. The laibon's son, his escort, reappears from the trees just as the old man stands up. I see the buffalo scar on his haunch again in the process. The laibon looks at me and says, "Stay in peace. Ole sere." He turns to Fairfax and says a few more words. I hear my name: *Teem.* He and the moran walk down through the rock portals onto the plain.

"What did he say?"

"You remind him of Turnbull, the district officer."

"From what's known of him, he was a decent sort of fellow. Your words."

"Yes, and look what happened to him."

Fairfax laughs. He laughs loudly enough to frighten some rock pigeons into an explosion of flight. I am startled, too.

S. O. Letterman is walking in the Luxembourg Gardens. The gardens, while beautiful, are coldly formal. The urns on plinths confirm this *froideur*. Mist hangs over the children's playground and over the palace. Out of the mist joggers appear, chicly clad. The French have turned themselves from little, unathletic people into medium-size, fit people. They have an appetite for adventure and activity. Although they eat a diet of cheese and cream and things made from pigs and horses, you never see the obese, crazy creatures who inhabit every street in America. These people are like chickens that have had too much hormone-spiked food. They have become unspeakable monsters in their giant sweatshirts and bulging shorts, great mutant pullets and capons. He has seen two of them only a few minutes before, alighting, with difficulty, from a tour bus outside the Sorbonne to look at a statue of—he believes—Descartes, anyway someone in a wig. They are two huge girls, wearing bright, funster clothes, sneakers with stars on them and capacious—this hurts him—Lions sweatshirts and Lions caps and immense designer jeans. Designer jeans, Jesus Christ. He had to avert his gaze in case some French person should associate him with these objects of his disgust. At the statue they brought out their Instamatics and snapped away, the winking flashlights sending an unmistakable message: *Attention, citoyens, Amerloques.*

He hasn't seen Candice since Farwaggi's news. Substantially, Farwaggi was correct. Candice's vulva is the creation of her husband, the plastic surgeon. In order to achieve orgasm, she must obviously practice some manipulation, which he does not want to know any more about. Yet in every other respect she is a woman. In the business, her *petite opération,* as he now knows it is called, is taken lightly. She is regarded as exotic. Letterman, however, does not wish this kind of exoticism to rub off on him. He does not want it known that he has had sex with someone who was once a boy. Strangely enough, if he had had sex with her knowing about her little operation in advance, that would have been acceptable. Now he worries that he will look like a hick, a rube, a provincial. How could he go to meetings in Hollywood after he has announced that he has signed a transsexual actress to play Claudia Cohn-Casson?

A middle-aged couple in matching gray tracksuits with elegant red piping down the legs and arms jog by, moving more slowly than if they were walking. Her face is so intensely French, framed by short well-cut bleached hair, the color of an Afghan hound's coat, eyes round and bright, mouth still sexually avid, lips pursed, high cheekbones. The man is gone into the mist before he has time to turn his gaze on him. Now, following them, he sees an extremely small dog, a sort of hairy dachshund, trotting with even less enthusiasm than its owners. Letterman passes a glass pillbox housing a gendarme in a winter cape. He is carrying an automatic weapon. The palace, which he is guarding, is now the home of the senate.

Letterman sees a little wooden *Hansel und Gretel* house under the trees. It is a simple restaurant, each table holding a basket of primulas, yellow and white. He sits near a window and orders a large coffee and a cheese sandwich. At another table a couple of students are writing essays or notes and conserving their bowls of hot chocolate. Letterman had Farwaggi cancel his lunchtime meetings with Candice. He has left no explanation. He has not told her that she is out of the running, although in truth she was never in the running. Sooner or later, he will tell her that the studio would not consider the idea of a minor French actress playing the part. The unspoken assumption in Hollywood is that any movie is far more important than the historical facts on which it may be based. Movies have a reality all their own. A great movie owes nothing to its origins; it is its own truth. The problem he faces is really just timing. He must not lose credibility at this stage. They will use anything to tip the balance: Letterman pushing for a transsexual French hooker to play a great Jewish heroine is how they will make it look, if they want to, or if there is a change of heart at Paramount.

But there is a complication: he wants to have sex with Candice (*née* Candide) armed with his new knowledge. He pays and leaves the restaurant. He is too restless to linger. He wants to have sex with Candice urgently. He gets a hard-on as he walks now past a row of weather-beaten busts of classical figures, who have posthumously taken French citizenship. His feminine side, which he knows has been an asset in many of the creative decisions he has had to make, has perhaps responded at some cellular level to Candice. But Letterman is confident that his feminine side is simply a heightened understanding of women. It has served him well, both professionally and sexually. He passes some more urns on plinths and a strange statue of a lion eating an ostrich, and then he finds himself in an avenue of severely pollarded lime trees that look like an advertisement for man's dominion over all natural things, and he longs to see her back and its finely tuned, juvenile muscles conveying by their strumming the mysterious activity of her plastic parts. While she was attending to her needs, she would have extraordinary contractions and pulsations of her man-made interior which drove and goaded him, and his Dearborn *schlong,* to exquisite, almost dangerous levels (*niveaux*) of sensation.

He passes a group of figures, modern sculptures in the ovoid style, which loom out of the cold mist like doughnuts and bagels, and he feels keenly the reproach that the sculptor is signaling to him. These round, fecund shapes are real women. Real, worthwhile women like Claudia Cohn-Casson. And still he wants to lie down with Candice in his little apartment up the road more than with any other woman he can recall. French films are often about sexual obsessions. They rarely touch on large themes like Claudia's story. When they do, they are approached by the leafy avenues of adolescence, and the winding byways of nostalgia. What they seem to recognize, and what he has discovered, to his extreme discomfort, is that sex is a distorting mirror of rational life. All the high-minded principles—all the Oscar-winning stuff—and all the ironies and tragedies of history can be put through the sexual wringer at a moment's notice.

When he was growing up his parents and grandparents and their friends used to discuss at length Spinoza's critique of Judaism, Hermann Cohen on atonement, Franz Rosenzweig's open letter to Martin Buber and so on. It meant nothing to him; although he appreciated the seriousness of the discussions, he found them embarrassing. They were trying to understand how it had happened. It seemed to have no relevance to their life in bustling Detroit. The longest production lines the world had ever seen—now there was a fact. The Jews had been too defensive. They had been too prominent. They had taken a crazy Christian idea about Eden and Gehenna. His relatives could never stop. They were replaying the thirties, all these grave Germans, while he was replaying Earl Morrall's every rush and pass. But if some of it had sunk in, then it could only have been by osmotic action. ("Osmosis" was a word he used a lot in high school.) His parents, he realizes, were intensely European. Europe is a place where the eternal verities are taken more seriously than at home. At home they are decoration, like a high school diploma. Here in Europe history still breathed on the back of your neck. This was because history has dangerous resonances entirely absent at home.

At the moment, as he circles the hibernating fountains, his Timberland boots crunching on the cold gravel, he feels that he has been given a kick in the *cojones* by this tricky European world. Despite the cold, some men are playing chess under the bare bones of an arbor. He stops just outside the gate that opens onto rue Guynemer. The phone booth, which is all polished steel and handsome glass, would last about three hours in South Central LA he thinks, with pride.

"André. Yes. Fine. I got called out. Listen, send this fax to Karel Woodin at your studio. Ready? 'Karel, after my casting here, I share your opinion that no French actresses currently can carry this picture. Suggest we think about big names. I will contact you from London next week. Speak to Lynn if you get a chance about casting.' "

It was an act of atonement.

"And, André, make sure Tim Curtiz gets to London as planned. Any news from him? Okay, I'll be back in an hour. No, tell her I'll call her in the morning. And, André, I don't want the whole of Paris knowing this. Okay? No, we are not going to Africa."

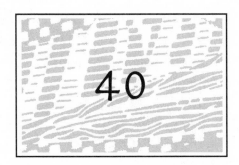

40

"Did she ever speak to you about Marcel Mauss?"

"Yes, I think she did."

"He was her tutor. He said that once you free magic from the idea that it's absurd and irrational, you realize that it is a sort of idealism."

"Too deep for me, I am afraid," says Fairfax. His webbed, frosted side is turned away from me. I realize that he does this deliberately.

"What Mauss meant, I think, was that magic or prophecy are not nonsense. They just fill the role of other explanations, the ones we accept without thinking. They have the same role as science."

We have been talking about the laibon and his polished stones. I go on: "When Hitler used science to exterminate people, that was a kind of magic, the redemption of the world from all its troubles by means of the gas chambers. I don't suppose Hitler thought of what he was doing as magic, more like applied science, evolutionary or genetic science. I think it was this zeal for solutions that made people like Heidegger Nazis."

"Is Mauss still alive?"

"I'm afraid not. He killed himself."

We are bumping along a track that leads up a scree of small, flat stones and shale. The wheel of the Toyota fights for its freedom. Way above us, where I walked only a few weeks ago, I can see a stream diving over the edge of a cliff in a tinsel waterfall. As we jolt and hop and leap about, the mountains look like back-projection in an old film.

Fairfax is a sensitive man. He avoids displays of emotion and skirts serious discussions. I am familiar with the type from my own father: emotions are treacherous, intellectual discussions are pretentious. But the laibon has demonstrated the connection between the rational and the irrational: there is no difference in the impulse, only in the expression. Now I see clearly how the German people were able to allow themselves to be so deluded: the irrational and the rational were simply relabeled. The killing of Jews became a scientific imperative. Human beings became animals. Prisoners became frogs. This is probably a lot easier to achieve than we, and certainly poor Mauss, could imagine.

"Too deep for me."

I don't believe he means it. What he means is that humility is in shorter supply in this world than self-important theorizing.

Still, I can't let go. I see that the laibon is performing a rational act with his pebbles. He could be the president of the Bank of France fixing the interest rate; it's no more absurd. And I believe I see now what Claudia was looking for, the humanness that is trying to secure itself in an incomprehensible, unmanageable world. It is common to all people. And also, I see why the laibon is anxious: ever since Claudia arrived, and perhaps for some time before that, the message has been getting through that there are other explanations. Red Ngai is the god of uncertainty. Black Ngai is the god of order and continuity. I am with the laibon on this: the red god is on the march as our century closes.

I can't picture myself in the next century. Fairfax is not going to make it into the next century. He is a product of the previous century more than of this one, anyway. If I could explain it to the laibon, I would try to tell him that at the end of the day all you can do is apply your own home remedy to your soul. Understanding genetics or biochemistry or even the art of making money does not help you with this problem.

We are moving down a sandy track now, smooth and easy, the tires humming, down toward the improbably blue lake, which lies there like a fragment of the Aegean that has got lost.

"Are you going to need me much longer?"

Fairfax is turned toward me now, his peach-bloom cheek and his slightly reluctant eye a surprise after a few hours of seeing only his good profile. My easily diverted heart is squeezed.

"How long can you stay?" I ask. "A few more days?"

"I have things to do, but they are not important. I could say that at my age nothing is important. You can't take it with you."

But he is a man who has built up a store of supplies of self-esteem and affection. Perhaps that's what death is, a sort of hibernation into which we go, if we are lucky, like a marmot that has feasted during the brief alpine summer on berries and roots to build up its body fat. We should go carrying a hamper of good feeling. Fairfax has ample supplies. Women have loved him. Also, he is sustained by the idea that he has lost the great love of his life. It has a certain nobility, because it is a story that never ends. In truth, nothing is more disappointing than love that turns to contempt or to indifference, because it confirms our worst fears about our real position in the physical world. So Claudia and her tragic story have an uplifting quality. My own love life (what a cut-price phrase) has no comparable nobility. Victoria's having a one-night stand (are we sure?) and my absurd behavior seem to have caused my human essences to drain down a sump hole. Here, in Africa, I feel them being replenished.

Popular movies, like popular music, rely completely on romantic versions of the human condition. Letterman was probably right when he dismissed some of my early thoughts as being sub-Bergman. He is Bergman's number-one fan, but you can't make movies like that anymore. The world has moved on. What does a Puerto Rican in the Bronx, or even in Puerto Rico, or a Cockney in West Ham, or a Chinese in Singapore care about Bergman's presentiments of death? These are the examples vouchsafed to me over a mineral-replenishing drink at Letterman's tennis club. (It is important to replenish the minerals after a hard game of tennis for a number of sound reasons, which I have forgotten.) No, what these people—and, let's face it, they are the lumpenproletariat—want, is some escape from their lives. So Claudia being taken off to the ovens must be an uplifting story that flatters them by suggesting they would have been on the right side. "Which," says Letterman, "I doubt."

In my pleasantly agitated state I see no conflict now. This is a noble story. It has resonances in the deepest caverns of the human mind, caverns that don't require a degree in Old Norse (or even Old Swede, if they differ) as the price of admission. The laibon and his pebbles tell me that.

We stop by the lake for lunch. It is a fraudulent lake, Fairfax explains, with some freshwater channels near the escarpment where hippos and pelicans live, but farther out, where a thousand flamingos teeter on high heels, its inviting azure surface is deceptive; the waters are caustic. There are crabs and shrimps that live there, but the water stings the eyes, like a swimming pool that has been overdosed with chemicals. Flamingos, frail though their legs appear, are immune.

He and Claudia stopped here, too, on their way to see the district commissioner to plead for Tepilit. The flamingos make a curious noise as they feed, a chattering like a legion of electric lawnmowers.

"We talked about building a house here. In those days we thought we could live anywhere. She wanted to live here after the war. We walked up the hills behind to see where we would build. It never occurred to us that the locals might object."

He laughs. It is a self-deprecating little snort.

"Was she planning to continue her work?"

"I don't think so. It may have been the war, but we had an urge to live for ourselves, at first hand, if you follow me."

I follow. I have been trying in various ways to do just that for years, with limited success. *Vivre pour vivre.* It's not so easy. The world isn't arranged that way, as the laibon has been discovering.

We arrive in town as the clouds are being siphoned off the mountain to leave it rising untouched from out of the shanties, bomas, workshops and missions. The open drains beside the roads are running strongly, taking some of the rubbish and mysterious off-cuts of urban activity with them in a greasy, sudsy torrent.

At the coffee plantation everything is ready for the return of the bwana, although we are two or three days late. Fairfax climbs stiffly from the high cab, refusing my help gently. Soon we are sitting on the verandah again as though we had never been away. I am dreading going back to the hotel, in the knowledge of the papers from S. O. Letterman that Mr. Shah will hand to me joyfully. We agree to discuss Paris tomorrow and, reluctantly, I leave him sitting alone with his drink in a large cane chair. There is a gap in our story, Claudia's few weeks in Paris before she was picked up, but I do have some information. I have the records of the last transports published by Serge Klarsfeld's organization in Paris. And we know when Claudia arrived in Paris, because she wrote to Fairfax to tell him. A member of the Resistance, now dead, has also left a brief account of how he helped Claudia in Paris.

"I've kept some dinner for you. I heard you had got back to town," says Mr. Shah with a hint of a reproach. "I've got a lot of faxes for you, from Paris, especially. I have had a lot of trouble with the machine. It's the bloody lines. Every time it rains they go down. Useless."

"Thank you. I'm sorry I was away longer than I intended. And thank you for taking care of all the paperwork. I hope it hasn't been too much of a nuisance."

I have picked up some old-fashioned manners in the last few days.

"No problem. Really. I am very delighted that you are back safely. I sent a message to Mr. Letterman to say I had lost touch with you temporarily. We have chicken if you want it."

"I would love it."

We pass the bar, where Edson, the steward, is polishing glasses with what looks like a handkerchief.

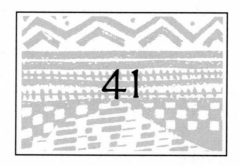

Paris. Hôpital Israélite. The hospital stands in a small park, not far from the Gare de Lyon in the 12th arrondissement. There is barbed wire on the top of walls and a guard at the gate, giving the impression, correctly, that it is as much prison as hospital.

A chauffeur-driven car arrives carrying the director, Léon Cohn-Casson, as it does every morning at 8:30. Cohn-Casson steps out of the car and makes his way up the grand staircase to his office. He is wearing a six-pointed yellow star on his coat. *Juif*. His secretary meets him at the top of the first flight and they walk together to his office, which is huge, with heavy curtains tied back by hawsers of gold thread, and sparsely furnished with a large Empire desk and some gilt chairs. He sits at his desk and his secretary places in front of him a large brown file.

"Anything pressing?"

"The children from Dijon have arrived. Hauptsturmführer Brunner would like to speak to you, sir."

"Thank you."

Cohn-Casson takes a pen from the array in his jacket pocket and begins to go through the file meticulously.

A tall, substantial house overlooking the Parc Monceau in the 8th arrondissement of Paris. At the far end of the avenue Hoche, some way away, is the Étoile, which is patrolled by German soldiers. A bus stops some way from the house. A woman in a shapeless coat and headscarf steps down. It is Claudia Cohn-Casson. She stands opposite the house. Then she walks to the nearby park. She enters by a gate that bears the sign, blue lettering on white ground, INTERDIT AUX JUIFS. There is a children's playground, complete with a carousel of horses, locomotives and camels. Old men, some war-wounded, are playing *boules* nearby. Claudia scans the children playing. She walks over to a kiosk where an elderly lady is selling baked potatoes and chestnuts. Claudia points at the chestnuts. With a small scoop the woman tips a portion of chestnuts into a piece of newspaper. She looks up and stops. She speaks with a strangled, peasant accent.

"Claude, c'est toi?"

"Oui."

"Mon enfant. Comme tu es belle."

"Merci. Je voudrais le voir."

"C'est interdit aux Juifs. Il ne vient plus."

The old woman touches Claudia's hand briefly. There are tears in her eyes. Claudia does not linger. She attaches herself loosely to a group of mothers looking after children. The children, blithely, ride the little locomotives and animals. We see on one of these a blond child of about six or seven, going round and round. From another part of the park comes the noise of a barrel organ.

"Schatzi. Komm jetzt. Komm du."

The blond child is reluctant to get off the horse.

"Jetzt komm, Schatz."

Outside the house in the avenue Hoche, Léon Cohn-Casson's car pulls up. He gets out and the front door of the house is opened for him from within. From across the road, Claudia watches. She glances around quickly and crosses the road. She pushes the doorbell, which releases a cascade of bells far away. She smiles. A woman in black opens the door. Cohn-Casson's voice, from within, calls irritably.

"Who's there?"

The woman's face is rapt, as if she has seen a vision.

"It's Mademoiselle Claude, monsieur," she whispers, but not loud enough for Cohn-Casson to hear.

Quickly, her fingers struggling with the chain on the door, the maid opens it and lets Claudia in.

In the hallway her father appears. He does not recognize her at a distance.

"Who is it, Fabrice?"

"It's Mademoiselle Claude, monsieur."

"Claude."

He is bewildered.

"Claude?"

"It is me, Papa."

"You have come back."

"Evidently. Shall I kiss you?"

"Of course."

They embrace, but her father is upset.

"It's not a good time. You cannot stay here."

"I know. I have somewhere to stay. But I want to see Georges before I go, and also, we must talk about the future."

"I don't think you should see Georges. I think it would upset him too much. He shouldn't know that you are here."

"Perhaps I can see him when he is asleep."

"He is not such a baby anymore, you know. He is eleven years old. Fabrice, prepare some coffee, or tea, which do you prefer?"

"Coffee."

"It's not good coffee."

They go through a large reception room, which is shrouded with dust sheets, through to a smaller room, the study. It is decorated with Cohn-Casson's Braques and Chagalls and filled with books and papers.

Claudia takes his hand.

"We have to leave Paris. That's why I have come back. It's dangerous."

"You have come all the way from Africa to give me your opinion on the situation in Paris?"

"Don't be angry, Papa."

"Claude, it is nearly over. It won't be long now before they go. And I will have done my duty, as I saw it."

Fabrice enters with the coffee on a silver tray. She and Claudia exchange tender glances. Claudia pours the coffee.

"What duty are you referring to? To whom?"

"My duty to the hospital, and to our people."

"Do you imagine someone is going to give you a medal?"

"There are probably thirty thousand Jews still in Paris. Maybe more. Frenchmen first, Jews second. If nobody does his duty, what respect will they have when this is over? They will say we all ran like rats."

"Thirty thousand. And how many tens of thousands have been transported?"

"Not so many of our people. Mainly immigrants. My duty is to try to save our people. French people, after all, to provide them with some help and organization. It's not possible to stop the Germans, but I slow them down, I make exceptions. I provide some support and hope."

"And when they leave, they are going to kiss you goodbye?"

"They respect what I have done. They are logical people."

The doorbell rings. Cohn-Casson stands up. They hear Fabrice's voice whispering in the hall. Georges bursts in. He is wearing shorts and a little tweed jacket with a yellow star. *Juif.*

"Claude. Claude."

Claudia embraces him and she weeps.

"You are big. Enormous. My boy, my darling boy."

"Adults always say, 'How big you have grown.' "

They hold hands. He is overjoyed to see her. Cohn-Casson watches them, preoccupied.

"Are you home from Africa now?"

"Yes. But I'm not sure I can stay in the house until the Germans go."

"They are going soon. Everybody says so. How are the cannibals in Africa? Are they nice?"

"Very nice. Look, they have eaten my hand."

She holds out her arm, with one hand tucked back into her coat. Georges laughs and retrieves her hand.

Outside the house a Mercedes pauses briefly. We cannot see the occupants, but their outlines, hats, leather coats, do not bode well.

42

S. O. Letterman has sent me his thoughts, twenty-six pages, which have passed through Mr. Shah's fax in halting relays. Thanks to our different schedules and the difficulties of telecommunication, Letterman and I are completely out of phase. I no longer know if his worries ("major concerns") refer to the most recent of my dispatches. Our stories have separated, like mayonnaise into which too much oil has been poured too fast. The constituents have gone their own way, refusing to consummate their marriage.

He begins (at least I think so, as I try to arrange his communications in sequence on the tired but clean bedspread) with some minor—his word—criticisms of what I have written so far. They are, of course, major complaints. His general complaint is that I am failing to engage the audience. Do I think they will respond well to the scene involving a lion hunt that goes wrong unless there is some setting up of the characters? By the time Kevin Costner comes to meet the Native Americans, we know, for example, the sort of person we are dealing with. In the case of Claudia, perhaps we need some scenes before she goes to

Africa or while she is en route to Africa to establish her motivation. What about a scene in La Sorbonne with her professor? He has had a look around, and the central courtyard, which has some great statues, would be just perfect. I think, therefore I am. Great evening light with the gas lamps and the wigged ones peering down on them. I am having a hard time with chronology, but in what looks like an earlier fax, Letterman implies that I should forget about the scripting, the craft: that is simple stuff. I must just send him chunks of narrative, which he, like a master butcher, will hack into shape. ("Use your journalistic nose. That's what I need from you.") He also wants me to make sure that Fairfax will sign some sort of "release" form. Long experience has taught him that even Inuit Eskimos and Unitarian ministers start looking for an agent if you leave the release form too late. He has sent me a draft release.

I see myself in the same canoe as Fairfax now. I find the idea of getting him to sign a form exonerating Letterman from all claims offensive. (I am reacting just the way Letterman warns me is common among the cinematically unsophisticated: I am becoming resentful.) I imagine that Letterman has been passing along too many little *rues* with exquisite *boucheries* and *traiteurs,* hence the metaphors, where bits of meat and other foodstuffs are treated like elements in a still life (*nature morte,* as the French say), while we, the old gentleman and I, have been crashing down the byways of Claudia's life. He and I have spent long hours into the bargain talking to the laibon about the state of the world, while Letterman has been having "some problems with casting locally." His difficulties, I feel sure, have been of a sexual nature. A Mr. Farwaggi has sent me a fax confirming my reservations and script conferences in London, prior to sending a first-draft script to the studio.

How about a scene in the Sorbonne? Perhaps he has forgotten his earlier reaction to my suggestion of just such a scene, with the French Nazis rampaging outside. What he said then was "To you and me La Sorbonne stands for something, but to most of the people looking at this picture it will be Disneyland without the rides."

But I know what Letterman is driving at. He has stripped away all the old chummy notions, based on a modest classical type of education, of how the world operates. In matters of taste, particularly, it is no longer subject to the old rules. I understand his anxieties about my attempts at a script, too. I am assuming too much. Not even the French know the whole story, with all its ambiguities. And they probably don't want to hear it. The wider audience wants this story to flatter them, by presenting them with a simple conflict of love and duty, good and evil. They don't want some morbid exploration of the inexplicable. But if I write a scene with Mauss and Claudia, what will they talk about? They will walk across the courtyard past the bust of Descartes as the night falls and the students drag on the *tabac noir* and kiss like tropical fish, or debate Mussolini's invasion of Ethiopia or Jean Cocteau's latest outrage, or perhaps just cogitate, sitting in the many handy nooks under the busts and statues of the *immortels,* as the noise of an accordion wafts from the cafés (more commonly associated with Montmartre, it is true, but we are painting with broad brushstrokes), and perhaps just a hint of trouble to come from a few risible brownshirts passing noisily on the rue des Écoles. Marcel Mauss (pronounced "Morse," not like Mickey up the road at EuroDisney) will discuss the human spirit, which we will transmogrify into a version of the American dream, itself a protean concept, and Mauss, who will look Jewish and shrewd, but with a sense of humor, as if he were a professor of law at Harvard, will tell Claudia how important her work is to the future of mankind (every little helps) as the forces of darkness are gathering, and at the same time the Solidarité brownshirts will gallop down the rue des Écoles, derided for being *plucs* and peasants, but the audience will know better, even as an empty bottle flies over the wall and smashes right at

217

Descartes's feet, or more accurately plinth. Then we can find her on the ship, leaving Marseilles, quite useful because it can double as Africa when she comes back in a later scene. We know that she traveled on the Ligne Maritime-Orientale, lovely old ships, if you like ships, on their funnel the famous symbol of a French *coq* with slightly Oriental eyes against a field of blue. Any amount of scene-setting, character-establishing and even romance is possible on board. I remember a novel by Jean-Paul Sartre in which the elderly captain, who has hairless alabaster thighs, makes love to a young, impassive passenger.

When I read Letterman's faxes, probably out of order, I accept the reproach for including things that no camera can film, such as inner thoughts. But he has also noticed my reluctance, my inability, to get a fix on Claudia's character. After all this time with Fairfax, I feel less confident about putting words in her mouth than I did before I knew him. Claudia, as any lover can confirm, has more than one self. We all do, of course.

I want to discuss this slippery perspective with Fairfax, but I know that it will give him the impression that I have not got this scriptwriting business under control. When I do ask him about Claudia, on the more personal level, he fends me off politely with little generalizations: *remarkable sense of humor; wonderful dark eyes; jolly good fun; quite temperamental, of course, but what do you expect from a Frenchwoman.* Since the night at the club, only a couple of weeks back, although it seems to me that time has become equally slippery, he has avoided all personal expressions of love or guilt or sexual obsession; he has mostly talked about her in a detached fashion, as if she belonged in a much-read novel. He has his reasons.

One had to forget. The gentle heart beating under one's lips in the dusk of the past. Claudia's heart, beating, pulsing in the dusk that descends on Ol Doinyo Lengai. Claudia's heart, perhaps beating more wildly as they made love. Claudia's heart, tormented by the cruelties of the selection process at Auschwitz;

Claudia's gentle heart, perhaps gratefully giving a last feeble contraction. (I think of a hand gently squeezing the moisture out of a sponge rather than the last convulsion of the ugly little meaty pump that lives in us.)

I am no detached expert in these matters, as my own affairs amply testify, as Victoria is no doubt still testifying. I remember Victoria saying to me, "You care more about this fucking French woman who has been dead for fifty years than about me. And I'm lying right next to you." This is the sort of thing reasonable people say in these circumstances, and worse. What I could not say to Victoria—perhaps I didn't realize it—as I thrashed about in the lowlands of our love, was that we are all in thrall to the idea of nobility in our lives. This is where the religious folk have got it wrong: they imagine we are actually seeking God's image, when in fact we have created God in the image of this longed-for nobility.

This is what I am thinking, anyway, as I ponder the fracture that is opening up, not between S. O. Letterman and me, but between the task he has set me and my own expectations of Claudia's life. I see Letterman and the story as ice floes in a nature documentary: the floes, carrying polar bears and seals and sometimes stranded elk, floating past each other on mysterious currents. In one respect I have to admit Victoria was right: I have a preference for the unknown (or even unknowable) over the familiar. You could paraphrase Proust: "Les vrais paradis sont les paradis inconnus." These types of thought seem to be occupying my mind more and more out here. I don't resist them.

The gentle heart beating under one's lips. This is what I am trying to capture, but Letterman tells me that I have failed to engage the audience. He wants me to engage them by offering them emotions and situations that will be familiar to them, but with a side-order of Oscar-winning significance. And he suggests I stop trying to plumb the unplumbable. He asks me, for example, how the audience is to know, as I have suggested, that

Tepilit's face is "already in some sense dead" before he is hanged. He wants to know how the audience is to visualize "the dark soil always thirsty, drinking the district officer's blood." (He has misquoted me.) He wants to know why Leavitt is painted as a sort of joke Ugly American. He has many little quibbles, but his main beef is what he sees as a failure to understand the nature of the audience. You have to flatter them by suggesting that they have a higher nature. So it follows that audiences have an orthodox eschatology: none of them could have been Nazis or Kapos or collaborators. (Although elderly people don't go to the movies very often, I wonder what someone who had been a Kapo or a collaborator would make of this cinematic conceit.) Letterman urges me to finish the first draft by the time I get to London. He is working on it himself. This information does not have the intended effect of reassuring me.

I am driving out to the coffee plantation for what will almost certainly be our last session. I pass a couple of plains Masai in their red cloaks; one is leading a small child by the hand. The child is reddish from the dust of the journey from the savannah; he appears to have been sprinkled with paprika. As they stride along the busy street past the former park, the two men have on their faces a determined detachment, like people in a crowded lift who nonetheless know their ordeal is finite. There is plenty of evidence here of the great variety of human activity—people selling maize (mealies) and soap and razors and regrinding crankshafts and cutting logs in crude sawmills, and others washing their cars in the river—to give the Masai pause for thought, but they don't want to think about these things. They stride disdainfully past this low-level industrial activity as if it were beneath consideration. They don't want to be impressed. Their world is perfect. This is what I imagine they are thinking, but I can't be sure. But they pass the dilapidated cinema without a glance, lending weight to my surmises. I see the pudgy Anglican vicar crossing the road on one of his missions; he waves and I wave back cheerfully but I do not stop. In my mirror I get a glimpse of him and his fat sausage legs disappearing into the post office. He's a lonely man. He's trying to get himself invited to a conference in Sydney on Third World spiritual problems, but his own spiritual problems are uppermost in his mind.

Fairfax is ready for me, but he looks strangely trussed up as he sits in his chair on the verandah.

"Hello. How are you, Tom?" I ask.

"Had a bit of a turn last night. Thought I was having another stroke to be honest, but it must have been something I ate."

"I'm glad you're okay. Are you up to some more grilling?"

"Of course I am."

But he is sitting awkwardly and his face, which I have inspected daily more closely and affectionately than he could know, is furled, as though something astringent had been applied from the inside.

"Tom, are you sure you're up to this?"

"Of course I am. What do you want to know today?"

His voice is slurred as it is when he is very tired. His tongue is dragging a ball and chain.

"I have been thinking about Claudia's story and how the audience will react."

"Shouldn't you have thought about that a bit earlier?" he asks, without malice.

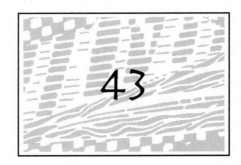

43

Claudia Cohn-Casson crosses one of the courtyards of the Sorbonne. She is carrying a large parcel. She goes up a stairway, past dark, heavy doors. She stops outside one and knocks.

"Entrez."

A middle-aged woman, her hair tightly drawn, her clothes utilitarian, looks up as Claudia enters.

"I have come to lodge my thesis, Madame Penousha."

"Mademoiselle Cohn-Casson?" she says without hesitation.

"Yes. Do you remember me?"

"Of course. And, anyway, the professor spoke of you often, very often."

"I am touched."

"His death is so sad."

"Tragic."

"Your examination cannot take place until after the restrictions have been lifted, I am afraid. It's still forbidden for Jewish candidates. But we don't expect it to be too long now. We need six copies. Have you brought them?"

"Yes, madame. Here they are."

She glances at the copies, bound in linen covers.

"The Masai. Wonderful people. Did you enjoy your stay among them?"

"Very much."

"Was it wise to come back here, now?"

"Probably not."

"Be careful, my child. It's not going to be long now. Don't be impatient. I will keep these safe. I don't believe it would be prudent to have any correspondence until our visitors have gone. Do you agree?"

"Absolutely."

"The professor said you were one of his brightest stars. He was so looking forward to reading your thesis. I am very, very sorry he did not have the opportunity. You should go now. Although they have stopped bullying us as they used to, it's still not safe around here. You must go."

"Why did he kill himself?"

"Who really knows anything about that? Certainly not me, and I worked for him for thirty-two years. But I think—I am only speculating—that he believed he had failed his students. He felt that he had put too much faith in the rational mind. In my opinion, that's what drove him to it."

She stands up and shakes Claudia's hand. Claudia leaves the room. She walks down the stairs and out into the courtyard.

Up above, in her office, the secretary looks down as Claudia crosses the courtyard. She turns away from the window.

Claudia is now on the Métro. There is a large sign reading INTERDIT AUX JUIFS in every carriage. The Métro lurches down the track. It stops at Sèvres-Babylone and some Germans in uniform get on. They look at her but say nothing.

Claudia emerges near the Étoile and walks down toward the park. In the park she watches carefully before approaching a back door of the house.

Inside the house she is talking to her father. He is sitting at his desk, she in an armchair.

"I have arranged for us to go to the house in the forest. We must go tomorrow. I have passes."

"You have forged passes from the Resistance. Do you think we can do that? Do you think I can desert my post now and escape with a pass? Look, I have my own pass. I am completely exempt from all restrictions. That's because I am doing vital work."

"Can I take Georges? It's just for a few weeks. We will keep ourselves out of the way."

"You may not take Georges. Just by being here you are putting Georges at risk and my work in jeopardy. It's not possible and I forbid it."

"Papa, the people I have been talking to say that it is more dangerous than ever."

"People? Bolsheviks? Poles? People have said all sorts of things since nineteen forty. And here I am. We are French. We have a right to be here. We are not immigrants or gypsies."

"They don't distinguish between good Jews and bad Jews."

"That is true. But they do distinguish, being logical, between people who are essential and people who are not."

"Are you essential? Have you been doing essential work?"

"Claude, I hate and detest them. With all my heart I loathe their arrogance and cruelty, but because I believe I am a superior human being, I refuse to allow myself to be made inferior by running away from what is ours by right. Our people must show that they are here by right. That is why I have made myself indispensable."

"I don't understand your logic. If they transport you because they are losing the war and decide to teach you a lesson, what sort of victory will you be claiming? Do you know what people call you? They call you 'death wish.' Even the Rothschilds left years ago."

"Claude, be sensible. They are not going to transport us. There are hardly enough trains left to get the troops out. I happen to know that the SS and the army are already in conflict on this subject. Who is going to ship out a few thousand Jews? That's all that's left. My duty is to look after the people in the hospital until they have gone. The day General de Gaulle marches down the Champs-Élysées, that is the day I can leave the hospital."

"And Georges?"

"What about Georges? He is at school. Nobody bothers him. He is doing well. At least I can offer him protection."

"Do you think your piece of paper saying you are exempt is going to be a protection? Of course it won't be. They may just come in and shoot you and all the patients the day before they leave."

"Claude, they are already worried about war crimes. They don't want any more trouble."

"You are saying they may destroy the evidence."

"You don't understand these people. They had orders to provide quotas and wagonloads and numbers. That's all finished. The SS are being withdrawn to defend the Fatherland."

Claudia gets up from the armchair. Her father is sitting at his desk, keen to get on with his papers. He looks crazy, his eyes burning, his face feverish.

"I am going, Papa."

"Please don't come to the house again. For your sake and Georges's sake."

"I understand."

She kisses him, but he is distracted.

Outside, in the corridor, she speaks to Fabrice. They whisper. Fabrice understands. She hurries off upstairs and Claudia goes down the back corridor and into the park.

44

Fairfax is leaving. I have offered to pick him up and take him out to the airstrip. By the mysterious bush telegraph he operates, a sort of serendipity that he relies on for his personal arrangements, he has been offered a flight back home with a pilot working for Save the Rhino.

I drive out to the coffee plantation sadly. He is ready, his cheap brown suitcase standing on the verandah. As I approach he raises himself with some difficulty. He is wearing brogues, which are shining unnaturally, like communion silver. The small, anxious steward immediately picks up the suitcase, as if it would be an affront to leave it earthbound for a second in the presence of the bwanas.

As I help Fairfax down the polished red cement steps of the bungalow I can feel his age and uncertainty pressing on my arm. I take it as a sign of trust, and my tricky heart moves like mercury in a barometer.

"Feeling a bit dicky today, I must say. Still, shouldn't grumble. Lots of chaps my age are pushing up daisies."

"What will you do at the other end? Will somebody meet you?"

"Oh, Camilla will be there, I should imagine."

He doesn't explain how his itinerary will be known to her, but I am sure he has his reasons. The steward stands clear enough to be useful if required, but not so close as to appear to be intruding. Fairfax climbs into the cab with a little help and we set off. He waves briefly at the steward, who clasps his hands together just below his chin as though he is praying.

"Nice chap," says Fairfax. "Not much of a cook, unfortunately."

The airstrip is deserted. We park under the single tree near the gasoline supply.

"He'll be along soon," says Fairfax.

"Tom, can I ask you this? Do you have any other information about Claudia that I could use? I have been to Paris and I know more or less what happened and in what order, but I don't really know much more. I need a few clues."

"I don't either. I regret so much of what I said and how I behaved. You do stupid things when you are in love. But she wrote to me from the ship and again from Paris, as I've told you, a few days before they were taken away, and she made it clear that she forgave me and wanted to come back. But I felt guilty for years. I could probably have prevented her going. I can't say for sure. I'll send you copies of the letters."

He speaks slowly. He is listless. His body seems to be uncomfortable, as though it were inflated, and his face is being tugged from inside, so that his features—to me, who has studied them—seem to be arranged in a new and unsettling way.

Sure enough, the plane is announced by the throb of its engine moments before we see it glinting. It lands without ceremony and taxis right up to the tree. The pilot jumps out. He is wearing a white shirt with epaulettes and blue shorts.

"Hello, Sir Thomas. All aboard."

He introduces himself to me and then stows the suitcase in the nose.

"Saved any rhino today?" asks Fairfax.

"There aren't any left. But for Chrissakes don't tell anybody or we'll all be out of a job. Right, let me give you a hand. Buckle up."

He climbs into the tin can and they taxi away. I can't see Fairfax with the dust rising and the sun playing on the windscreen. The last thing I can make out is a pictogram of a rhino on the tailplane.

He has gone, old and frail, leaving me desolated. I drive back to town slowly.

S. O. Letterman has bypassed Farwaggi. He has arranged to see Candice for lunch. He has not called her for four days and he is relieved when she accepts his invitation without question. But in the hours between the call and the rendezvous at the rue de Beaune he is having second thoughts. In the sexual realm, he has done things that might be considered shocking, if it weren't that there is a compact between men and women not to judge too harshly the irrational, infantile aspects of sex. Candice is, to all intents and purposes, a beautiful young woman, but now he feels his mother's fears of the untrammeled (Nietzsche was her bugbear) rising in him. Jews, because of their skepticism about an afterlife, have felt a greater need to make a go of this world. This excludes the option of mortgaging the soul in the search for consolation for earthly troubles. He has been brought up with this belief: worthwhile people, genuine people, successful people (there is a blurring of the categories) keep control of the animal, turbulent side of their natures. There are no hard-and-fast rules, but a consensus is quickly reached when a Jew has lost control. In Gentile society there is a sneaking admiration for this kind of failing because it suggests a contempt for the material world.

There was a poem his mother quoted: "Du hast das Nächste in dir selbst getötet." (You have killed what is dearest to you.) In America this was sometimes translated as "You always kill the one you love." What it means, however, is that you do not cause injury to your own nature. There is a depth below which you do not sink. Letterman thinks of deep-sea divers with the bends.

He walks down the rue Cherche-Midi. He passes a bakery, Poilane, where you can have a bread-roll baked with your name on it for fifteen francs. He stops and buys an open apple tart, which is made of pastry so light it takes wings in his mouth. On the other side of the road is a shop selling miraculous arrangements of dried flowers, perfect pyramids of bay leaves, mock hedges of lavender and wonderful stooks of wheat, tied with raffia. Decorators in Beverly Hills are probably on to this place already. He goes in and orders a miniature wicker fence decorated with miniature dried mustard-colored roses to be sent to Victoria in London. It costs three thousand francs. She has, for reasons he understands, asked him not to call. But he knows women.

Now he fumbles with the keys. The door into the courtyard will not open. He has forgotten the code. Fortunately, just as he is wondering what to do, the door opens with a click from the inside and a woman wearing a Burberry raincoat and escorting a pair of Yorkshire terriers steps out. He seizes the door before it can close and ignores her pointed pause and turn of the head. He crosses the courtyard, his feet feeling the raised cobbles appreciatively, and climbs up the stairs, which are in semidark. These hallways are the domain of the Portuguese concierge, who keeps them polished, embalmed, in accordance with a notion of propriety learned in the old Europe.

There are three locks on the door, opened with curiously shaped keys. Even in something as basic as this, the French have their own way of doing things. He opens the door eventually and turns on the lights. The apartment is slightly musty. He opens the main window, which looks down onto an antique shop displaying just one perfect chair in the window. In the bedroom he thinks he can still scent their last encounter four days ago. It hangs there. He tries to decide whether these perfumes are unnaturally exotic. He opens the bedroom window, too. It looks down onto a courtyard and behind that a school. The children are out in the courtyard, eating their lunch or playing. He feels a stab of envy. Do they realize the unreal beauty of their surroundings? In most of the world, if children go to school at all, they have to make do with industrial buildings in parking lots.

He undresses and puts on the bathrobe from the St. James's club that is hanging behind the door of the bedroom. From the school below comes the childish symphony, the babble, chatter and laughter rising up seamless. All schools, everywhere, produce this noise. Its timbre changes with the age of the children, but it always melds mysteriously into this music. A bell rings. He starts. The children outside pause in their games. And then, almost immediately, the buzzer sounds from down below on the elegant street.

"Come up," he says with as much casualness as he can summon.

"Okay," she says. ("Okay." It is cheery and girlish.)

He goes to open the door. He hears her coming up the three flights athletically. As soon as he sees her, he feels his worries depart. She is wearing a sort of beret and a very short polka-dotted dress under a long Armani or perhaps Versace coat; the whole effect is 1950s.

She kisses him in the doorway, pulling her coat open so that his rough bathrobe and her very flimsy silk dress come into shocking contact.

"Where have you been?" she asks, removing her coat. "I was worried."

She is wearing long white gloves that reach almost to her elbows.

"I have been having a hard time with the studio. And the writer asshole vanished in the middle of Africa."

She has her hand, still gloved, inside his bathrobe, stroking his treacherous zizi.

Du hast das Nächste in dir selbst getötet.

"Claudia," he says. His mouth is strangely parched. He believes he has said it to himself.

"C'est moi," she whispers. She thinks she's got it in the bag.

She opens her dress, offering her breasts as a prize. He wonders if they are real. He doesn't know, and now he doesn't care.

> You have killed what is closest to you
> So as to go shuddering after it with new desire
> And cry out with the pain of solitude.

Outside, from the playground, another bell sounds, and the childish noises are quickly stilled.

46

It is early morning, hardly light in the avenue Hoche. Léon Cohn-Casson's chauffeur pulls up. Cohn-Casson comes out of the house in his dark *ancien régime* clothes, his yellow star in place on his overcoat. He climbs into the car, the chauffeur closes the door and walks around to the front and they are off.

At the back of the house at the entrance that leads on to the Parc Monceau, Claudia is waiting. The maid, Fabrice, appears. She talks to Claudia briefly. Looking around, she hands her a small bag. She goes back into the house. Claudia walks briefly up to the gate of the park and returns, but the park is quiet. Only a very old man with a besom is visible, sweeping the gravel paths. Fabrice returns with Georges. He is in a coat, shorts and a large, floppy cap. The yellow star has been removed from his coat. He kisses Fabrice, as does Claudia. Fabrice hurries back into the house, and Claudia and Georges, hand in hand, set off across the park. The old man with the broom pauses and looks at them. They pass the kiosks that used to sell gingerbread, toy drums, barley sugar and roast potatoes. (In this park Proust, as an asthmatic child, used to buy a potato, not to eat but to warm his hands.) They pass an elaborate bower, a hillside with a romantic spring decorated with nymphs half-concealing themselves behind stone tree trunks, artfully sculpted with ridges of bark and twining ivy.

Georges is happy. He skips along.

"Where are we going? To Africa?"

"We're going to the country for a few weeks."

"Will you take me to Africa when the war is over?"

"Of course. I have a friend there you would like to meet. We will have a farm by a lake that is full of flamingos. And there are elephants in the woods."

"Are they vicious, elephants?"

"Not at all."

"And the Masai. How are they?"

"They are very tall and very beautiful. They don't wear many clothes."

"I want to see them. Are they sympathetic?"

"Very genial, once they know you. Come, let's go along here."

They wait at a bus stop. Soon a bus appears. It is crowded. Claudia leads Georges onto the bus. Georges wants to talk but she squeezes her lips gently together to indicate silence. He misunderstands and kisses her. The people on the bus are a mixture of the elderly and the poor, but one young man, unshaven, romantic, is standing near them.

Two Milice in their brown shirts, berets and ties get aboard. The bus is now crossing the Seine. The Milice start checking identity papers. Claudia tries to move toward the door as the two men come closer. Suddenly there is a confused shoving and pushing and shouting. The young man forces his way out of the bus and leaps off the open platform at the back. One of the Milice falls to the ground, stabbed. The other jumps off the bus and runs after the young man, but he has doubled back and jumped over a balustrade and is briefly seen running along the lower *quai* beside the river. In the bus the informed consensus is "Résistance." Claudia takes Georges away as fast as she can. They cross the river and enter the Métro, passing an armed German soldier at the barrier.

The Métro train arrives at Austerlitz. They emerge onto the platform. They go and wait at the side entrance, where they can watch the busy terminus. There is a great deal of activity among the German soldiers. (The Normandy landings are only six weeks away.) Some Milice in their sinister-buffoon clothes pass by.

"Come, Georges. Let's get on the train now."

Claudia is all prepared. She has her tickets ready at the barrier and they are soon aboard a waiting train.

"It's going in a moment."

But the train does not go. The station is garlanded with puff-balls and spirals and streamers of smoke. Now we see German troops jogging down the platform, backed up by French police and Milice. The train and the platform are sealed off.

"What's happening, Claude?"

"Don't worry, darling, it's just a check."

Her face is set. The Milice board the train, two to a carriage, while the SS wait on the platform.

"Madame."

"Yes?"

"Identity papers, please."

Claudia produces her papers.

"Is this your son?"

The Milice officer has one eye that is unable to direct itself at her. His idiotic fustian breeches are at her shoulder level.

"No. It's my brother."

"Please come with us."

Claudia and Georges stand up. They leave the train and join a small and growing gang of the detained, guarded by gendarmes on the platform. They stand there, nervous and ashamed, a wretched group that reminds us of the pitiful photographs of the arrests of Jews in the Warsaw ghetto. Particularly Georges in his cap and belted coat.

There is a whistling and flag-waving. The train pulls out of the station and the detainees are then herded out of the station into the street, where two green-and-white Paris buses are waiting to take them for questioning.

At the Israelite Hospital, Léon Cohn-Casson is in his office. He is discussing with his assistant how they are going to resist the latest SS demands.

"Hauptsturmführer Brunner wants to clear all the Jewish institutions. Every one. He is also trying to arrange a transport for two or three hundred children, Monsieur le Directeur."

"As you know, the most important thing with Brunner is to agree to everything, and then make problems. You know how much difficulty he will have. The Wehrmacht are not interested in transporting Jews now. There are no trains."

"But we have to supply ten people today. Today, sir."

"I will talk to them. Leave it to me. We can promise them that group from Dijon, but then discover they have diphtheria."

"After the paperwork."

"After the paperwork. Exactly."

Cohn-Casson has an assurance that calms his assistant.

"Thank you, Monsieur le Directeur."

"See if you can arrange a meeting with von Trenck."

"Right, sir."

The Israelite Hospital is a large building, once lavishly equipped but now stripped. The wards have been huddled together on one floor. Cohn-Casson steps out of his office to make his daily tour. He is accompanied by the head doctor and the matron. There is nothing grand about this tour, but it is conducted with dignity.

"How are the arrivals from Dijon, Matron?" Cohn-Casson asks.

"They seem to be in need of rest, Monsieur le Directeur."

"Apart from that?"

235

"Nothing serious, sir."

"Tests. They must have tests for suspected diphtheria."

"But, they——"

"They may need to acquire diphtheria by the end of the week."

"Yes, sir."

They enter a ward. It contains about ten mothers and fifteen children. The faces turn to Cohn-Casson and his staff.

"New admissions?"

"Twelve, sir. Including three children without mothers."

"One death overnight only."

A nurse comes up to them.

"Excuse me, Monsieur le Directeur, you should return to your office. Monsieur Jean says it is urgent."

"Carry on, Doctor."

Cohn-Casson makes the long walk down the empty corridors. He enters his office. His assistant is waiting.

"What is it?"

"Monsieur le Directeur, your daughter has been picked up by the Milice. And your son."

"Where are they?"

"They are at the Cherche-Midi."

"Get my car."

"My information, sir, is that you should leave Paris."

"Don't be ridiculous."

"Brunner has been looking for an excuse."

"That's absurd. I am going now. Tell them to proceed. Don't let the Dijon children be taken. I'll be back as soon as I can."

"It's not wise, sir."

"Are you suggesting I should leave Paris now, abandoning my family and forgetting my duty just as the Germans are about to leave?"

"Sir, they want to take some important people hostage. You are one."

"And my children? How important are they to the Germans? Get my car ready."

Léon Cohn-Casson carefully takes his notebook, his pens and his bags. He pulls on his overcoat, decorated with the word *Juif*, and sets off.

The Cherche-Midi military prison. Claudia is trying to calm Georges, who is frightened by the look of the other prisoners in the cell.

"Georges, let me wipe your face."

"How long are we going to be here?"

"Not long, darling. Don't worry. Papa will come soon. They all know Papa."

"Why did we have to go to the country house, then? Why couldn't I tell Papa?"

"Because Papa wanted you to continue at school and I wanted you to come on holiday."

"You think they are going to kill us all. That's the reason."

"No, no. Papa says they have stopped sending people to Germany. It's all over."

But Georges is terrified. He begins to cry again and Claudia wipes his face. In the cell the twelve other prisoners look like tramps and criminals. A woman, however, is lying on the floor moaning. Nobody is helping her for fear of the contagion of guilt or weakness.

At the headquarters of the Gestapo SD, Cohn-Casson arrives in his car. He is allowed to drive in.

Cohn-Casson is shown into an anteroom. He stands gazing out at the avenue Foch. He is summoned. Alois Brunner is sitting at a desk. He does not offer Cohn-Casson a chair. He is a youngish man, with dark hair and thick eyebrows. He is wearing the chilling SS uniform. He looks up with exaggerated distaste.

"Cohn. What do you want?"

"I want my son and daughter released. They have been picked up by some idiots. Probably Milice."

"I did not know you had a daughter in Paris."

"She is an academic."

"In Africa."

"Studying in Africa."

"And somehow she came back. Just now. I wonder why? I wonder who she has been associating with out in British East Africa?"

"She wanted to see the family. I would be very grateful if you could ensure that they are released. I have work to do."

"Could you wait outside for a moment?"

"I am sure that these are difficult times for everybody, but I would find it impossible to carry on my work if I was worrying about my son and daughter."

"I will speak to someone. Just wait outside, Cohn."

Cohn-Casson goes outside to the anteroom. He stands impatiently, a man with important matters to attend to.

Two armed SS officers come into the room.

"What do you want?"

One of them strikes him on the head with a rifle butt. He falls to the floor amazed, blood streaming through his hair.

"Warum?"

"Hier ist kein warum."

They get him to his feet and lead him out.

47

I am thinking about France in 1944, while looking out of my window at the scenes of makeshift butchery and light engineering, and beyond them the mountain that rises right out of the town. It is the Parthenon of this poor place.

Hier ist kein warum.

This is what I am thinking: There are no whys and wherefores. Claudia is arrested. Her foolish and snobbish father, who has worked with the Germans for years, who has worn his yellow star obediently and tried to help "our people" is beaten on the orders of an Austrian thug, Alois Brunner, and his family is sent to Drancy to await dispatch. General Leclerc is racing for Paris yet Hauptsturmführer Brunner, this human fuck-pig, this unspeakable piece of shit, moves heaven and earth to find a wagon to throw them in, a beautiful young woman, her eleven-year-old brother and her sixty-four-year-old father. *Kein warum.* There is certainly no why. There is no possible way to convey this in a movie. How do you make a movie about things so bestial? How do you make art— artifice—out of this? The only way you could begin to express this horror would be to murder a child actor on camera. Take an eleven-year-old boy and infect him with TB and then castrate him, and then, some weeks later, take out his spleen and his kidneys without anaesthetic, and then inject him with some unspeakable filth you have developed on other children, who inconveniently died, and then remove all his clothes, his empty scrotum not yet healed, photograph him for the medical record and then garotte him by hanging him on a hook to die in nine or ten minutes.

Kein warum.

My heart is drowning in bitter fluid, the bile that pours from the pancreas as the doctor, a trained doctor, slits open Georges's soft, capon belly. Outside they are butchering an unresisting cow, releasing a pent-up flood of unknown liquids.

Somebody knocks at my door. Mr. Shah enters.

"Are you all right, sir?"

"Yes, thank you."

"Would you like some tea sent up?"

"Yes, please."

"I'll be back in a minute. I have a message for you."

Mr. Shah and I have developed a dependence. Through me he feels he has reestablished links with the more glamorous outside world. It has been a hard struggle here, serving curried chicken and Coke, and a few samosas from the hot cabinet. The bedrooms have been mostly empty for the last thirty years. The few tourists stop only to have a piss. Once, for a few magical weeks, he had devised cocktails for John Ford and Ava Gardner. (Clark Gable and Grace Kelly made their own arrangements.) He had almost secured the contract for all the location catering. If he had, he would have made a fortune.

And me, what do I need from him? This is more difficult, but because of his enthusiasm and his sense of the importance of my work, I am under an obligation not to disappoint him.

He returns with the tea himself. He places it carefully on the spindly table and pours it. The teapot is made of steel, in a fifties style that has not endured.

"There is a man downstairs who wants to see you."

"A man?"

"A Masai."

He does not think much of the Masai, but he says "a Masai" as neutrally as he can, knowing my weakness.

The Masai is the laibon's son, Paramat. He is carrying his spear and wearing his dark blue robe. His hair is braided and held on his forehead by a little metal clip. He has made only one concession to urban tastes: in his left ear he has a new ornament, an aspirin container.

I greet him. He shakes my hand. His is so dry and rough it seems to be geological rather than fleshy. In my troubled state I think that if he were slit open, no more than a teacupful of vital fluids would emerge.

"How did he get here?"

Mr. Shah asks him.

"He walked."

"It's one hundred and ten miles."

"No problem for these chaps."

"What does he want?"

We are standing on the pavement, outside the hotel. Once, years ago, the colonial administration insisted that all shops and offices have a covered walkway and a drain in front of them. It was a practice developed in the Far East against the monsoon. This arcade still exists outside the older buildings, but the plan has not been followed through. Some buildings have, anyway, fallen down; between the hotel and the general goods store, for example, is a gap where goats make their way over the rubble and waste.

The laibon's son is talking. His face is grave. He is here on important business. His hair is tied at the back, too, with white, blue and red beads. Looking at him closely, I see that his whole head is an elaborate work of art; his hair is braided and adorned in four separate places, and his ears hold three decorations each, not including the aspirin container. His arms, his neck and his legs are host to bracelets and filigrees. I wonder if, when he looks at these dull people, these drones, who are so busy, or not so busy, with their town lives, he pities them. Or does he suspect that they are having a better time?

"He says his father wants to speak with you. Aai, these people . . ."

Mr. Shah does not complete the sentence.

"Could you ask him what his father wants?"

After a brief exchange, Mr. Shah, trying to keep patience, says, "His father did not tell him."

"How did he find me?"

"He made some inquiries."

"Will you tell him I can't go today? I must finish. Tomorrow morning early. He can come with me if he wants to."

Mr. Shah explains and Paramat nods gravely.

"He would like to. Are you sure you must go all that way back over there?"

"I am afraid so."

"All right. He will be here in the morning. I will pack some supplies for you."

"Where is he going to stay?"

"Don't worry about him. No problem."

"Go in peace."

Paramat walks off down the street. He pauses at a yard that sells corrugated iron roofing, but not for long.

Mr. Shah does not approve of my whimsy. He has seen the demands from Paris, the suggestions, the ironies: "Doctor Livingstone, I presume. Glad to hear you could make it back from safari. Casting run into problems. Studio still on side."

S. O. Letterman starts all his faxes in this staccato fashion, as if he were sending a telegram, a nickle or a dime a word. He soon forgets the economies and lapses into his free-fall prose.

I enter my room to try to finish my first draft. The mountain floats there above the trees, separated from us now by a low belt of cloud.

The butchery is complete, the skin pegged out.

Because he cannot properly understand the television or the advertising posters or the subtleties of conversation, S. O. Letterman feels that he has lost a vital organ in Paris. (He feels in this way solidarity with Candice.) Far from appreciating his street smarts and his finely tuned sensibilities, the French regard him as a sort of invalid. Americans, he realizes, are thought to be suffering from an incurable illness. Of course, there is a wide circle of Anglophone help and services. There are plenty of Americans in the street, some in native dress, others bounding unashamed into the various McDonald's in their ski wear, but they inhabit a netherworld in the Parisians' estimation.

He was invited to an evening of dance and music from a particular Moroccan village. Somebody explained to him just where the Atlas Mountains are situated, as Americans have no idea of geography. Like Dan Quayle. These wailing Moroccans, who looked like extras from *The Thief of Baghdad,* were the last word in ethnic chic. This meant that they were more charged with significance in Paris than in their own village or indeed in the rest of the world. As the wily musicians thumbed and plucked and bowed their instruments and sang through their noses in their mountain dialect, they looked down from the stage on an elegant gathering who were enjoying the performance on many levels, without that cheap jokiness Anglo-Saxons would bring to such an occasion. Far from it. They wore rapt expressions, swaying slightly to the snake-charmer rhythms, puzzling over the peasant musicians and the modern world. Letterman couldn't really be sure, however, what the audience made of this event.

This is why he feels bereft. His sensory organs have been sewn up. He has the numbness of the bereaved, made worse by his disordered sexual activities. He has still not told Candice that she is not going to get the part; each day he delays, promising himself to tell her later. His intense, painful lovemaking gives him some point of contact with life; in this at least there is a lingua franca.

Watching the turbaned ones, he confirmed something he had long suspected: he is an American. While the well-shod Parisians were feigning cultural uplift, he was more interested in inspecting their footwear. He had noted that all the men were wearing bulky black shoes, which spoke, in muted tones, of intellectual seriousness. His expensive Italian loafers with little bobbles on them were as conspicuous as the lead flautist's Ali Baba–tendency pink slippers.

For all his doubts, and self-doubts, it must be said he admires the French. Out of this self-congratulatory little city pours a torrent of evaluation. It is as if the French have been appointed the last tribunal, the court of judgment on man and the human condition. They are all Jews in a way, charged with making judgments. Some proposals to film in Auschwitz have provoked a storm of intellectual activity. There is to be a debate on filming the Holocaust, promoted by *Le Monde.* Here, French intellectuals and filmmakers, including Claude Lanzmann and Louis Malle, will debate the ethical issues. Lanzmann's film *Shoah,* a documentary about the Polish camps, is a towering work. Lanzmann spent eleven years on it. It is from him that Letterman has taken the idea of the endlessly moving cattle car. In *Shoah,* Lanzmann repeats endlessly the images of the hardware of the extermination camps, particularly the cars, to get over the enormity of the deed. Letterman agrees with Elie Wiesel that Auschwitz negates any form of invention. His movie is based firmly on the facts. From that the art can follow. Claudia's life and death are real. But the French have elevated the subject beyond reality, to a philosophic and intellectual plane, which—he now sees— absolves them from thinking about the reality. Sure, they know that Alain Resnais was forced to remove a shot of a gendarme at one of the French camps from his movie *Night and Fog.* But this is nothing to do with them personally; it is simply an interesting example of the way repression and progress are always at war, even in art. Choose your own protagonists. Join the debate. First, rush round to the rue du Dragon for the clumpy footwear.

"I'm pissed off because I am an outsider here. I'm like a wetback who's just swum across the Rio Grande. The only people who understand me don't have any clout."

"What is clout?" asks Candice. "I don't understand."

"It's pull. Influence. Weight. It's what you get on the inside."

"What is a wetback?"

"An illegal immigrant."

"We have got very many in France."

She purses her lips in the way he loves and lets them impel some air outward. It's a timeless French gesture of knowing disillusionment. It's curious how national stereotypes prove to have some basis. When she comes she says, "Oh-lah-lah."

"Hokay," she says, "let's fuck."

In her mouth the word is colloquial and unencumbered.

49

Drancy. The antechamber of death. The buildings, which were originally built as a housing project, are rundown. (It has been used since 1941 by the SS and their French auxiliaries to house Jews before their transport to the death camps. The Allies are advancing on Paris, yet there are still fifteen hundred inhabitants.)

Léon Cohn-Casson has been delivered direct from the avenue Foch to Drancy. In the processing area he stands aloof. He is well known. When a young man asks him to hand over the contents of his pockets, he refuses.

"I want to see the commandant immediately."

"Yes, sir."

Georges and Claudia are in the women's section of the camp. They are in the concrete shell of an uncompleted building, which nonetheless houses beds, suitcases and washing lines, although at the moment there are no other occupants. Georges and Claudia are summoned by an orderly. They emerge from the locked room and follow him through the squalor down long corridors into the commandant's office. Léon Cohn-Casson is standing there with the commandant.

"Papa. Papa has come to take us home."

Georges rushes to his father. Claudia kisses him too; he is stiff and proper, although his hair is still matted with blood, which Claudia notices.

"We can't go home immediately, but the commandant is trying to sort this matter out. He has seen my papers. Don't worry."

"They must go back to their quarters, monsieur."

"All right. Don't worry. You have a good night's rest if you can. Monsieur le Commandant has arranged a private room for you."

"When are we going home, Papa?"

"Soon, soon. Leave it to me."

Claudia and Georges are shown back to another room, where their possessions and mattresses are being installed by a trusty. Claudia tries to talk to her.

"How long have you been here?"

"I can't talk."

She is whispering.

"Don't worry, the war's nearly over for us."

"Madame, they are going to take us all away tonight."

Almost immediately after she leaves the room there is wailing and screaming and harsh German shouts in the corridors outside. Mothers and children are pushed and dragged down to the central courtyard, where assemblies for the transports take place.

"What's happening, Claude? Papa said we would be going home."

"We will, darling. This is not for us. Don't worry, my child."

Claudia tries to make Georges comfortable. She tucks him under a filthy blanket, a blanket on which hundreds of desperate, doomed people have left their marks. She lies next to him. Outside the corridors are still, but shouts and cries can be heard from the heart of the camp.

Very quietly, half whispering, Claudia sings in a high almost Arabic tone. She is singing a Masai lullaby. In this madhouse, it does not sound particularly strange. Georges sleeps. We see his face; his lips move and he raises his nose involuntarily as if gasping for air. It is a portent of things to come.

Claudia sings, her voice choking, her eyes drowning.

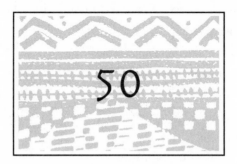

I catch sight of the laibon, near the fig trees, in his blue, bruise-colored tunic. He is accompanying a brown-and-white calf, blotched like a map of the continents, which he is guiding back toward the boma. He stops as he sees the Toyota. The calf stops, too. We drive up to him and climb out. He shakes my hand and his son's. He gives the calf into his son's care. The son smiles at me. We have a certain intimacy.

The laibon walks with me over to the watercourse, which has stopped flowing but is marked by large pools. He sits down on the trunk of a fallen tree. He is ready. I start my tape recorder. I have been summoned to hear a testament. This is what he says (translated by Professor Uitsmijter):

"I am dying. I have many children and grandchildren. I love to see the young wives and their children. I love to see my cattle feeding on green grass and becoming strong and content. I am a rich man. My father made me the laibon: he was the descendant of Mbatian. My brother who was hanged would have been the laibon. I asked you to come and see me again because I believe that you are a man who, like a laibon, has power to see. I dreamed after you and Fahfakhs left here that you would become a laibon among your own people.

"I know that you will always think about the Masai people. I see that you dream about the Masai. But what I want to tell you is that Ngai spoke to me. He said that I should tell you that there are many things we cannot understand. Just as our cattle sometimes die for no reason. I am going to give you a box now containing some stones."

Of course, as he is speaking I have little idea of what he is saying. He stands up and we walk back to the boma. The chairs are brought. The young mothers are suckling the small children. They don't seem surprised to see me back again. As a matter of fact I am not surprised either. I believe the laibon is giving me information I am going to need.

In the distance I hear cowbells. The laibon talks to me as the koko serves the oversweet tea. He sends her into the hut and she returns with the government forms. The payment for the boy killed by an elephant has been processed in the capital. It will be sent to the district office on such and such a date. I read the Swahili phonetically to them. One of the young mothers translates for the laibon. He listens to her, but he knows that the information is too important for it to make any sense to her. He accepts her familiarity with Swahili, learned at schule, as the sort of minor thing a performing monkey might pick up.

He speaks to the koko again. She has been expecting this request. She smiles at me. Her face brings to mind those fantastically lined portraits of W. H. Auden. Her earlobes swing as she stands up, but to me there is only dignity in her runnelled and folded features, and stretched ears. They are like the clothes aristocrats are said to prefer—old, familiar, and of good quality.

She returns with a small cylinder, similar to the one the laibon usually carries around his neck. She gives it to him. He spits on it and hands it to me. Then he speaks to the young woman who has translated. She turns to me, her eyes downcast.

"What is your age group?" she asks in Swahili.

I tell her that I am *il moruak botorok,* a senior elder. (Not as old as the title suggests.) She tells the laibon.

"The laibon says you may lie with me if you wish. My husband is *botorok.*"

I cannot speak. The laibon laughs. The laugh turns to a wheezy cough. The koko laughs, too, as bawdy elderly women do.

"No, thank you," I say.

"You don't like me?" asks the girl.

"I like you."

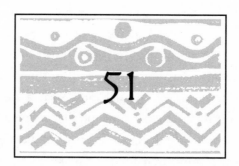

51

Drancy. The antechamber of death. This is written on the wall of a corridor by one of the departed. An orderly is painting it out. The camp is virtually empty. We hear footsteps echoing on the concrete. The footsteps immediately give us a sense of foreboding. Claudia and Georges are in their room. Claudia has washed some clothes and is hanging them on a line above the beds. Georges is playing a game that involves guiding a ball-bearing around a wooden maze. They are both wearing stars now, *Juive, Juif.* The stars are six-pointed, closely sewn to the left breast, so closely that an SS man with a pencil could not get the point underneath the yellow cloth.

Claudia is apprehensive when she hears the footsteps, but Georges jumps up eagerly.

"Papa is coming. We are going home."

Cohn-Casson enters their room flanked by orderlies. He is still immaculately dressed.

"Come, children. We are going."

"Are we going home now?"

"Not yet. It seems the Germans would like to keep me to negotiate."

"You will be negotiating with the Germans?"

"Well, no. The Germans hope to be negotiating with the Allies."

"Papa means that because he is so important he will be exchanged by the Germans for someone else after the war is over."

"What about us, Papa?"

"We must go now, Georges. Get your things. Will you help him please, Claude?"

Claudia begins to collect the washing. Georges realizes that all is not well. He stands, puzzled.

It is late afternoon, a summer day. Outside the Drancy complex a bus is waiting. As usual it is one of the Paris passenger buses. It is guarded by gendarmes in uniform. The Cohn-Casson family appear. They are guided onto the bus. Inside the bus there are about thirty people. A few more are brought on, some handcuffed. These are members of the Jewish Resistance. One man, in a light suit, sits by himself, almost completely untouched by what is going on. He is not mad, merely abnormally serene. Near him is a small group of expensively dressed elderly women.

The Cohn-Cassons are sitting together. The bus begins to move off into the streets. Five armed gendarmes remain standing. No talking is allowed, but children cry. Outside the windows of the bus, the streets pass by. They are ordinary Paris streets, conforming despite their variety to a comfortable pattern: *pâtisserie, épicerie, boulangerie, presse, boucherie, pharmacie,* all appearing again every few hundred yards.

The passersby do not let their eyes linger on the bus.

At Le Bourget station a train is waiting. It is not the conventional transport, but a troop train with one cattle car—*wagon à bestiaux*—attached at the end. The train has been positioned in such a way that the cattle car is just beyond the end of the platform. The bus is driven close to the track. We see the cattle car, open doors gaping. They bring to mind the ovens that are to come. We approach slowly, but before we can enter we see the passengers from the bus carrying their few possessions, embarrassed and ashamed to be treated like cows and heifers, herded brusquely by gendarmes—their fellow citizens—to the track. The German soldiers on the platform watch them. Perhaps they believe what is painted on the side of the car: JUDEN TERRORISTEN. This lettering has been ordered by Brunner. The reason is not that he necessarily believes it to be true, but that he wants to suggest to the uniformed officers on the platform that transporting this mixed bag of bourgeois Jews, indignant old ladies, captured Resistance fighters, an eccentric industrialist, tearful children and some previously scornful intellectuals is important war work, just as important as rushing home to defend the Fatherland against the apocalypse.

The group reaches the cattle car. Some of the older ladies—one is a Polish princess—have great difficulty picking their way over the rail lines. One complains that there are no steps, as if she were about to enter her carriage for a trot around the Bois de Boulogne.

The gendarmes are watched by five SS men, Brunner's personal troop, and a few Milice in their menial khaki shirts. It takes them a few minutes to load up this cargo, even though they have been used to as many as a hundred in a wagon, a thousand to a train. They want to get it over. It's degrading work, watched by regular soldiers.

The doors of the cattle car are closed and locked. It is not completely dark inside. Light comes through the gaps and a small high opening in one corner; nonetheless the effect of being shut in a windowless truck is frightening. Children scream. Two mothers, one with a baby at her breast, begin to cry, too, which frightens the children even more.

The Cohn-Cassons are sitting at the rear of the car. At the front end opposite them is a group of Jewish Resistance fighters, who are unshaven and defiant, handing around cigarettes.

Cohn-Casson stands up.

"I hope you will forgive me but I feel I must say a few words. I am Léon Cohn-Casson, director of the Israelite Hospital and a council member of the General Union of Israelites in France. I want to reassure you that with the war ending and Paris in the hands of the Allies, we have nothing to fear. I have had to deal with the German command for three years and I can assure you that although they are mad, they are not illogical. I have left word with the International Red Cross, the City Council of Paris, the General Union of Jewish—"

The Resistance fighters do not let him finish.

"Salaud. Collabo."

They call him a fucking collaborator and tell him to shut up. He tries again but they shout, "Sit down, you old cunt," and, worse, "Ferme ta gueule, Brune Yiddelach." In Yiddish they call him a Jewish brownshirt.

We see Georges with his pale, pampered face, his expensive clothes, his somewhat ridiculous cap. He is terrified. He has lost all composure. Claudia puts her arm around him and comforts him, but he cannot stop crying.

"Don't worry, darling. Papa knows what he is saying. They are just tramps and criminals. Papa is a leader."

Claudia's face, caught by a bar of light, a stray radiance that has entered between the planks of the truck, is turned to her brother. Cohn-Casson sits, as in life, a few fastidious feet away. He turns to Claudia and whispers: "These are the same people who supported the Nazi-Soviet pact. Heroes."

There is shouting in German and French from outside. The locomotive gives a long blast of its hooter, then a shorter one. Somebody blows a whistle and then, with a shuddering and clanging, the whole train lurches forward, that sickening, primitive motion, accompanied by the noises of a foundry.

On the platform Brunner watches and then turns to go to his car. He doesn't make any triumphal gestures. In his boots and breeches, holding a riding crop, he looks just like a Nazi in a movie.

We see the railway lines disappearing in front of the train, being eaten up on the road to hell.

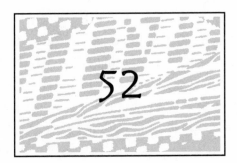

52

S. O. Letterman leaves Farwaggi with a task. He is to tell Candice Riberon that she will not be getting the part of Claude Cohn-Casson.

For once, Farwaggi demurs. Up to now he has done anything. It is part of the ethos of the movie business that producers and directors can make demeaning requests of their employees: sandwiches, cabs, hookers, postage stamps, cocaine—tasks of this order, which serve to show the underling that it is a hard struggle getting to the top and to demonstrate that the princes of the movie business are free of the normal constraints that apply to humdrum types. Success conveys powers and privileges that are as close to those of the Olympians as we are likely to see. Letterman is not quite up there, but that does not matter now. In the presence of the true gods, he would act differently. One of the privileges of his position—in fact, it is an obligation—is to be dismissive about actresses who the public foolishly imagines are securely established.

"What's the problem, André?"

"I don't suppose it should be coming from me, sir."

"Why not? You're my assistant, aren't you?"

"Yes, I know, sir, but Miss Riberon is a big star. Certainly she is regarded as a good actress. I am only an assistant."

"I regard her as a good actress. But I can't use her. It's nothing personal. It's the way these things pan out. Some very famous actresses have done humiliating things to get work. Do you know that Meryl Streep, the great Meryl Streep, wore a push-up bra to interview for *Out of Africa*? She popped her tits up like eggs Benedict because she had heard that the director saw Karen Blixen as sensual, practically a nympho. That's what happened, as true as I am standing here. I may be offending your Arab sensibilities, you may think it's not a man's job, I don't know, it could be anything. Maybe it's some sort of French snootiness, which, and I am going to compliment you, I haven't noticed much of up till now. Maybe it's something to do with Mademoiselle Riberon's medical history, which, I gotta tell you, is an absolutely false rumor, a canard. It is exactly as she says, a very small aberration of nature, nothing whatever to do with transsexuality. Never mind. I got an opinion from one of the finest plastic surgeons in the world, as it happens. He knows her husband. He knows the case, even. It began to bug me. It's not as uncommon as you might think. Anyway, what I am saying is that actresses, actors, directors, producers—all of us—are less important than the movie. That's the way it works. I'm not saying it's ideal, far from it. But there is no possibility of casting her in this role, whatever I may wish, and remember it's my project. It was me who read an article in some obscure goddamn magazine about Drancy. It was me who spent his own money getting it researched. It was me who wanted to cast a young, semi-unknown French actress as Claudia Cohn-Casson. As a matter of fact, it was me who hired you, too, when the biggest job you had ever had was scouting locations for a panty-liner commercial. I don't hold it against anyone. The deals have to be done. There's no rule in America, unlike in France, that obliges anyone to cough up money for pictures if they don't want to. This is—yes, I know I'm repeating myself—the way it works. You don't go sticking your cock on the block knowing it's going to be chopped off. Your *zizi* in the guillotine. No, I don't want to tell Mademoiselle Riberon myself. I want her to wonder if maybe she failed me in some way. If I call her and say, 'Look, you aren't going to get the part, it's impossible, they won't buy it,' she's going to ask me how long I knew this. The truth is, André, I knew it before I came to Paris. I'm telling you this for your education, no charge, because you are in the business and should know. I came here to stir up some interest in this project. That's all. Do you understand how it works? Ninety percent of what you read in the trades is bullshit. I signed her. Sure. Her agent can't read English. She's some old *madame* who knows her way around the Comédie Française—and the Molière was crap, by the way. The contract was just a PR release. She doesn't understand the term 'producer' or 'studio approval.' Why should Mademoiselle Riberon understand, when her *notaire* doesn't? You are thinking I should tell her myself, be a man, et cetera. It's nothing to do with that. I was born in Detroit, Michigan. I always wanted to be in movies. People who want to be in movies are basically crazy. They are trying to reach a certain level—*niveau,* to you—which is, of course, always changing or moving away. It's the Holy Grail syndrome. Do you know what I am talking about? Never mind. There are people in Hollywood who have lived there for twenty years, producers who have never produced a damn thing. Imagine a dentist who went to the office every day but never filled a tooth. Or imagine a man who had a shop in the rue de Beaune, a *traiteur,* making a salmon *en croûte,* or *en* jelly every fucking day for twenty years and never even sold a solitary *escargot.* These people, this deluded dentist and this crazy *traiteur,* would perhaps wonder if they were in the right business. But not a movie producer living in a friend's garage. No. He knows he is in the right business. What's the point of this? Why am I giving you this lecture? Because the movie business is not like any other business. To tell the truth, it's not like life at all. The people who get to the top, or even just survive, are a minute number. They have had all kinds of shit heaped on their heads on the way. Some people think this is one of the faults of Hollywood. But I think—and this is my conclusion after nearly twenty years of actually making movies—I think this is the whole point of Hollywood. That's why you are going to be the bearer of bad news, and not me. I don't need to do it anymore, because I have paid my dues."

Letterman delivers this monologue reasonably. He knows that Farwaggi understands only about half of what he is getting at. He doesn't care. He has enjoyed unburdening himself. For the past few weeks he has been speaking pidgin. What he really thinks is that this school of hard knocks, this fiendish survival course, ensures that American movies are seen by hundreds of millions, whereas French and British movies are seen by nobody. He also believes that it is impossible to make a great film out of this material if you try to apply a European sensibility. These Parisians don't seem to understand, despite their proximity to the time and the place, that this is their story. As a matter of fact it is everybody's story.

This is what he understands by Claudia's universal spirit, that we are all Jews, all Nazis, all Masai, all humans capable of anything. The movie must speak to everybody, not just people interested in historical dilemmas and dialectics.

But he has another reason for avoiding the beautiful Candice Riberon before he leaves for London: he does not want to see her again or hear her voice because he recognizes signs that have proved fatal for producers in the past, making them ridiculous and vulnerable in the eyes of their peers, the signs of obsession with unsuitable young actresses. This speaks loudly of a lack of seriousness. He can't go any further. He can't kill what is closest to him.

"Tell her tomorrow, after I'm on my way to Heathrow. Tell her I want her to come to Hollywood at the end of the summer. And call Trisha. Tell her to book a court at Queen's Club. I want a court every day at seven A.M. starting Thursday. Queen's. Trisha knows the number. Patricia. Pa-tree-si-aah."

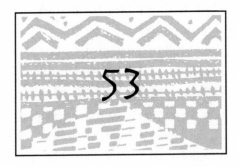

"The facts are wrong." That was Durkheim's reply when told that his theories did not square with the facts out in the field, or what we would call the real world. What he meant, I am sure, is that regarding the nature of human behavior we have many facts, but they don't confer understanding. In Alain Resnais' film *Night and Fog,* one of the most telling moments is the close-up of the scratches made by the victims on the concrete roof of the gas chamber when they realized that they were not, after all, about to take a shower. In order to reach the roof they had to climb up a pyramid of bodies. This is a fact but it explains nothing. Durkheim meant, I think, that his insights had an independent value and truth. I take it that the laibon is warning me about the limits of reason.

I am about to leave for London. My first draft is almost ready for dispatch to S. O. Letterman, although I need much more time. I have, I believe, filled in the gaps in our story up to the point where the trains arrive in Auschwitz and the selections are made. Beyond that point, through the gate marked ARBEIT MACHT FREI, I cannot go. I have seen movies where ten seconds of authentic footage from the camps was far more shocking than the previous two hours of drama.

But I am uneasy. There is a delusion among Elvis Presley fans and political groupies that they form, in some way, a vital part of their inamorato's life. Waiting to go down and eat my last meal in Mr. Shah's hotel, advertisements for which are already floating up to me, I allow myself the same delusion: I have seeped into their lives now. The famous osmosis has taken place. I cannot imagine them without me. In this way I imagine I am close to Claudia, too, but in matters the movie will never capture. In my hand, as I gaze at the mountain, I have the laibon's keepsake. It is a small leather cylinder, like a dice box, with a short thong attached so that it can be worn around the neck. The laibon has recognized me in some way. From his limited supply of artifacts, he has given me this box. In it are seven worn pebbles. As soon as I step onto the plane, a bland KLM flight, it will become nothing more than a trinket. In the wine buff's phrase, it will not travel.

As I was leaving Ol Doinyo Lengai, I saw the Masai girl, a young mother with her beautiful, slightly elongated head, her large eyes, her stretched and ornamented ears. She stopped chopping at a dead tree with a knife and smiled and waved at me cheerily. She knows the score. Women know. I could imagine Claudia seeing her Masai lover for the last time. The facts are simple and it's all recorded. I have seen the file. He was taken to the Fort and hanged on December 3, 1943. About nine months later, Claudia's train left Le Bourget station on an eight-day journey to Auschwitz.

I am not going to pretend that I agree with Proust that the last judgment is an artistic one. Nobody could write about or film such horror. But neither am I going to disagree with Émile Durkheim about the facts.

There are places, quite innocent places, that have had prominence thrust upon them by being drenched in blood. For example, Waterloo, Sharpeville, My Lai and, of course, Auschwitz. Some that deserve it have escaped the opprobrium: Drancy is one. Even Parisians hardly know its role as the waiting room for Auschwitz. Yet it hasn't had its name changed. There it is, boldly on the map, near Le Bourget: DRANCY.

The train rolls out of Paris. It loops back toward the center of town, seeking the Marne. Having found it, the train makes a haul of places with beautiful names, as only European countries have them—Pomponne, St. Thibaut des Vignes, Condé St. Libaire, St. Jouarre la Fêtre—names that do not just record topography and battles but have religious and historical origins, going back beyond Roman times.

It is night. Only the small children are sleeping. The adults are fearful. At last they know for sure what they already knew. But there is plenty of activity down at the *artisan,* Resistance, end. They have managed to conceal a large chisel. Perhaps it was smuggled to them by one of the gendarmes, who are, with the day of reckoning approaching from Normandy, assailed by second thoughts. The Resistance fighters are chiseling away at a plank.

Léon Cohn-Casson is writing a note with one of his many pens. Georges is silent now, but not asleep. His face is what is known as expressionless, but vividly expressive of incalculable shock and fear. Claudia has covered him with a coat. In a corner, the Polish princess is erecting a barrier with a piece of twine and a blanket. An elderly lady is defecating into the single bucket, her back turned. Two orthodox Jews are praying, standing.

"What are you writing, Papa?"

"I am writing notes to my colleagues. Every time we see a light or a station I am going to drop one out."

"That's a good idea."

"They must contact the Red Cross, to monitor our transport."

They can't see out, but the hay smells of *la douce* France outside penetrate the increasingly foul atmosphere.

The iron tracks are relentlessly vanishing under the wheels of the train, like pig-iron bars in a steel mill. A Resistance fighter, Mora, comes over to the Cohn-Cassons.

"We are proposing to escape from this train."

He has a Polish or Czech accent.

"I see that."

"Our comrades have been warned. They will blow up the line at Lunéville before Strasbourg."

Cohn-Casson appears to be offended.

"Why have you told me this?"

"I have told you because we will all have to get out in an organized way. You, Mademoiselle and the boy."

"We can't do that."

"You can't do that? What else are you proposing to do?"

"I can't do it because the war is almost over and I have my duty. I have written to the Red Cross and the City Council. We will undoubtedly suffer much discomfort and inconvenience, but we will soon be repatriated. You can believe me, the SS is now in disgrace. The Germans are in a state of disarray. We will get out."

Mora lowers his voice.

"There is only one way out. Up the chimneys."

Cohn-Casson is silent. He resumes his note-writing dismissively. Claudia reaches out her hand.

"I will discuss it with him. Thank you."

"I love the bourgeoisie. You have a nice discussion, please."

Mora goes back to the other end of the truck, stepping over the prone bodies carefully.

Georges speaks like a child talking in his sleep, blankly.

"Up the chimneys."

The Anglican vicar, Darren Wiggins, has invited himself to lunch. I have been avoiding him. Now he feels that his position permits this. He wants to see me off safely.

These are his words. I am fiddling with the last batch of papers to be sent off by Mr. Shah. I read the words I have given these people. I have used all the known facts, after a considerable amount of research, yet I cannot capture what Claudia experienced. Their conversations, spread over the six days it took to reach Auschwitz, as the universal spirit took the train to hell, would, I believe, tell me what I long to know. What is there in humanness that embraces and yearns for cruelty? All these conversations between the dead have gone. I imagine they had a banal quality. There are reports of families arriving in Auschwitz having somehow bathed and changed their clothes for the occasion.

Certainly the vicar, in his plumpness, is no help with ontological questions. He tells me that his mission here, his witness, has not been a success. I am appointed his confessor over the chicken. In London he was involved in radical Christianity (which I take to mean gay causes), and he felt he was losing sight of true nuts-and-bolts religion. These causes had taken over from religion itself, in which there was little interest. But out here he has not flourished. I wish he would shut up. He's come for a free meal and an airing of his contemporary, self-important kind of angst. I want to tell him to stop being presumptuous and go and administer the sacraments. At least in their mystery there is something to think about. But he fails to notice my irritation. The Larusa have not responded to his relevant, socially conscious Christianity. They want jobs and big pay. They want the address of Keele University so that they can study business administration.

Mr. Shah comes into the dining room, holding to his bosom the twenty pages he has not yet sent.

"There's a lady ringing you from Nairobi. She wants to speak to you urgently. Excuse me, Reverend. Lunch up to scratch?"

It's not easy to speak to Nairobi from here. We are alert to the urgency; Mr. Shah leads me importantly to his office, saying, "Excuse me, trunk call," as we go. Although I am pleased to get away from the vicar, my spirits are low and apprehensive.

It is difficult to hear. At the other end I hear a woman's voice, talking to someone else.

"Hello. Hello," I shout. "Are you there?"

It takes a while for her to realize that I am on the line.

"Oh, hello," she says. "It's Camilla De Marr here. Who's that?"

"It's Tim Curtiz. How are you?"

"I'm as well as can be expected. Look, Tom's back here now and I'm afraid he's had another stroke. He would like to see you if that's possible."

"Is he going to be all right?"

"I'm not sure. The doctors can't say."

"I'll get to Nairobi as soon as I can. Probably by midnight if the border is open."

Trisha has had the faxes transcribed in four hours: six typists from a script agency beat them into shape. Trisha has had no luck with men. In her youth she chose badly. Now in her middle thirties, she has a slightly demented cheerfulness that puts men off. They divine, correctly, the existence of a loopy maelstrom behind the accommodating front. But she is a tiger for work. She is passed from one visiting producer to another and tackles each project with complete and undiscriminating devotion. Film is a higher activity. Now she is "collating" the first draft into slim volumes, laying them on the floor of the sitting room that forms part of Letterman's suite at the club. She has installed a fax machine. She is wearing a bright blue sweater with stars appliquéd to it. The fax begins to hum and whir, an exciting noise.

S. O. Letterman finds the air easier to breathe in London. Trisha's bruised personality reassures him. London is a tolerant, slatternly place.

"Fax for you, S.O.," she calls out from her kneeling position on the floor. "Shah Holdings Pty Ltd."

Letterman reads the faint print.

"Can you fucking believe it? Tim's not coming. He's gone to Nairobi. He's gone to Nairobi for a few days on a personal matter. Who is going to make the changes?"

"Not too many, I hope," says Trish, but she is already warming to the certain prospect of late nights and rewrites.

"Are you kidding?" says Letterman. She is like a fruit, her pulpy, viscous center easily laid bare.

He picks up a page of the script.

"Listen to this: 'There are places, quite innocent places, that have had prominence thrust upon them by being drenched in blood. For example, Waterloo, Sharpeville, My Lai and, of course, Auschwitz. Some that deserve it have escaped the opprobrium: Drancy is one.' Jesus, he thinks he's writing a fucking Ph.D. thesis, not a filmscript."

"Bit depressing, innit?" she says cheerfully. "I can see what you mean."

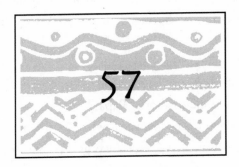

57

It is daylight. The train is stationary. The condition of the cattle car has worsened. One woman is now clearly mad. Her head is shaking. She is holding her baby, which has died in the night. There is no way to dispose of or lay to rest the tiny body.

Georges, with his plump face, his soft abundant quiff, his brown eyes, his already strong nose, is now smeared and dirty. Léon Cohn-Casson is slumped, defeated. Claudia holds Georges, who is swaying, staring.

"Papa, are you all right?"

"I'm so sorry."

"We must get out with them."

"We can't, we must stick together."

The Resistance men are, in contrast to the bourgeois, in a feverish state. They are men of action.

"They are going to stop the train in the night."

"Claude, these people over there, who accused me of being a collaborator, they are the same people, Polish and Czech Bol-sheviks, who supported Germany during the pact. Are you prepared to escape with them? To what? Do you want to go on the run with them?"

"We must get Georges out of here."

"It's too dangerous. He could be shot. He could be hurt jumping out. They could be betrayed. If we stick together we will be all right."

"You don't believe that anymore."

Cohn-Casson does not reply.

"I'm going to talk to them, Papa."

Claudia gently releases Georges, who lies down impassively. She makes her way over to the resistance group. She speaks to Mora.

"We want to come. When will you be getting out?"

"The train is late because of the stoppages, obviously, but our comrades will be waiting. If we are too close to the Rhine before night, we will get out anyway. Otherwise we will get out just before Lunéville. They are waiting."

"Will they take care of us?"

"They will do their best."

As they are speaking, a hand appears through one of the cracks with some water in a small cup. It is replenished several times before the train moves on. In that time notes are passed out, among them two from Claudia. As the train gathers speed the Resistance fighters sing "Le Chant des partisans." We hear the noise of planes overhead.

The wheels of the train, the pistons, the steam escaping, the relentless grinding toward the East, all gather pace.

Georges is sitting up, leaning against Léon Cohn-Casson. Claudia sits next to Georges.

"Do you want me to tell you about the Masai?"

Georges does not respond.

"They live in the savannah. In the distance are mountains full of monkeys. These monkeys have white tails, like horses' tails. The

Masai are very good walkers. They walk for many, many kilometers every day looking after their cattle. I often walked with my friend and I sometimes went a whole day without eating. Would you like to live there one day, Georges?"

"What is your friend's name?"

"Tepilit ole Saibol."

"Where is he now?"

"He is . . . He is there."

"With his cows."

"We will build a house by a lake, I know just the place. There are thousands of flamingos. They are pink with very long legs."

"You told me about them. Are the Masai cannibals?"

"Oh, Georges, of course not. They drink milk mostly and sometimes blood."

"Blood?"

"Cow's blood."

Tears are bounding down her face now. She leans back and holds him in her arms so that he cannot see her face.

The wheels of the train consume the track as her voice continues.

"They love cattle. Cattle are for them more important than anything else. That is what they want from life."

"Just cattle?"

"Cattle, yes. Cattle provide everything else."

"This is a cattle car, you know."

"Yes, I think it is."

"Don't they want to live in towns, like us?"

"No. They prefer the savannah."

58

The border is closed. I try to find someone to let me through, but the guards, a couple of sleepy young soldiers, say it is impossible. They point to the passport and customs offices, housed in a small cottage. They are dark. Across the border there is more blankness. The night is endlessly blank. For the first time in many weeks I feel trammeled by Africa. I feel a Western impatience.

"Okay. I'll sleep in the car."

"Thank you, sir."

"Look out for *shiftas*," I say. They laugh. Shiftas are bandits. I give them a few shillings. They seem to me too young, too thin, too impressionable to be equipped with lethal automatic weapons. Instead of conveying menace, they look to be in the employ of the guns. There are plenty of skinny young boys requiring a job, but very few expensive bits of hardware. The rifles are more valuable than they are.

I park the Toyota under a giraffe thorn and surreptitiously lock it before lying down in the back on an air mattress. I am soon asleep.

Triumphalist chickens wake me. The interval of sleep seems to have been very short. The border doesn't open all at once, but in reluctant stages. The flags have to be run up the poles. The keys have to be found, the rubber stamps retrieved from a Nescafé jar. I am the first one through. The road sweeps down into thick, drab bush country, which occasionally flares like peach blossom at the passing of Masai in their red cloaks. I think of them as my brothers. They, of course, have no reciprocal feelings.

"C'est un wagon à bestiaux, tu sais."
   "Oui, je crois."
   "Ils ne veulent pas habiter en ville, comme nous?"
   "Non. Ils aiment mieux les savannes."

I don't know if they said it. Who knows what they might have discussed?
   I am speeding down the road, with tears in my eyes. Kilimanjaro, snow-topped, is over to the right. The landscape stretches interminably in every direction. I am mortally tired.

59

The train stops. It screeches and shudders. The Resistance men rip the loosened planking aside. Up the track there is shouting and shots are fired. One of the men climbs through the hole. He returns in a few moments. Fog rises through the gaping hole in the wagon.

"Quickly, now. Everybody out."

The princess turns to Léon Cohn-Casson.

"Bolsheviks. I am not going."

Claudia pulls Georges to his feet.

Cohn-Casson immediately stands up.

"Where are you going?"

"We are leaving, Papa."

"No. I forbid it absolutely. It's suicide. You can't subject this child to the risk. Georges, you stay here. Look what happened when you left the house with Claude."

"I want to go, Papa."

"Georges, you may not go with these people."

The car is emptying fast. Georges, Claude and Léon Cohn-Casson stand locked.

"Papa, they are Jews like us."

Mora shouts, "Quickly, come now."

"We will be repatriated very quickly. I assure you."

Cohn-Casson holds Georges by the arm. There is a scramble to get out. The Resistance men are handing people through the hole. Arms from outside speed their exit. Now there are only nine people left, the Cohn-Cassons, the three elderly ladies, including the Polish princess, the two praying Hasids and the woman with a dead baby.

"Come, Georges. Let go, Papa. We must go."

Mora sticks his head back into the car, "Hurry, mademoiselle, quickly. The train is leaving."

Claudia tries to pull Georges to the opening. Cohn-Casson holds his arm.

"Please, Papa, let go."

Claudia pushes him, and they are free. As they move there are shots and shouts. They pause, fatally. The train begins to move again. Claude tries to drag Georges to the opening, where Mora's head is still visible, imploring them to hurry.

Cohn-Casson embraces Georges. He hugs him.

"Stay, Georges. We are French."

It is a moment of tragic absurdity. The train is gathering speed. Mora can no longer keep pace.

There they stand, the three of them, in the foul cattle car, fused unwillingly in an embrace, like disinterred victims of a volcano.

The rails are being consumed at increasing speed by the moving train. They suddenly cross an iron bridge that spans a dark river. The water can be seen gleaming for a moment. It looks, in this false light, like axle grease or congealing blood.

60

The house is built of brown stone on two floors, with a corrugated iron roof. It is somewhat rundown and overgrown, with ornamental trees that have gone native. There seems to be nowhere special to park, so I leave the Toyota on the lawn, at least what was once a lawn, now showing signs of the savannah coming through again and the termites rebuilding.

Three friendly spaniels greet me as I walk toward the front door. They are followed by Lady De Marr. She is wearing tailored khaki trousers, a long knitted cardigan and a pink sunhat. Her burnt old body gives the clothes unexpected angles. Her eyes are so blue and clear that they seem to have taken temporary lodging in her sun-baked and wind-dried face. The English girl she once was hovers there still.

"Did you have a bad journey?"

"The border was closed. That's why I'm only here now. How is he?"

"He's died, I am afraid. He died very early this morning."

"Oh, no."

"Come in. You look tired. Do you want some tea or something to eat?"

She has known him for sixty years. I have known him for a few weeks. We pass through into the hall, from which a staircase rises to a galleried corridor above. A huge painting of a horse being led into the winner's enclosure hangs over the fireplace. The whole house is strangely out of proportion. I follow her blindly.

"I always loved Tom. Everybody did, if the truth be told. Let's sit here."

We sit in two huge armchairs, covered in chintz so old and dog-worn that the rose motif looks like an ancient tapestry. An elderly servant brings tea almost immediately.

"He wouldn't tell you, of course, but he knew—we all knew—that he didn't have long to go."

"Why did you let him come down to me, then?"

"He liked you. He trusted you to make a good film."

"I am only the writer. And they will do whatever they like with my material."

"He won't know that."

She does nothing to restrain the spaniels, which are competing to sit on top of me.

"I've the letters which he wanted you to read, but before you read them I'm going to tell you something about Claudia. I don't believe you will put it in your film. If I thought you would, I wouldn't tell you. Of course Tom would be furious with me."

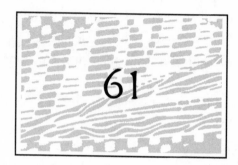

61

Somewhere along the way the car containing the nine who remained has been hitched to another train, this one made up entirely of cattle cars.

The nine are in a desperate condition. They have been in transit for six days. The train stops. The wheels clench, paring the rails. Claudia stands up, but her father lies motionless. The doors open. An SS corporal looks in. A voice addresses him from a distance.

"Wieviel Stück?" (How many pieces?)

"Nur neun." (Only nine.)

"Heraus. 'Raus. Das Gepäck lassen." (Out. Leave the luggage.)

The huge ramp, lit by floodlights, is waiting. The passengers stand up and stagger to the open doorway. Georges is now quite impassive. Claudia takes his hand. A multitude, over a thousand people, is gathering on the ramp. There are SS standing waiting in a line. Some of them carry whips. The men and women from the transport are being sorted with shouts and gestures into two battalions. Georges stands with Claudia. The useful men are soon marched away. An SS officer approaches them and asks for Léon Cohn-Casson. He is pleased to be recognized in this way.

"Don't worry. It will be sorted out soon. Courage, Georges."

"Quiet. Come."

Cohn-Casson, while filthy, is still wearing his starched collar and tie with a pearl stud. He is carrying a small attaché case, despite the order to leave all luggage behind.

Now a ghostly column of striped overcoats advances from the far end of the ramp. The people in this column are in rags. They wear berets on their heads. They wheel past the newly arrived at as great a distance as possible, not willing to engage their eyes. They enter the wagons and begin to sort the luggage left behind.

Claudia holds Georges's hand.

"What's happening, Claude? Why are they wearing those striped coats?"

"They are collecting our luggage for us."

"But how will they know where we are staying?"

"They know from the coaches."

"The cattle cars."

The group, into which they have been merged, is moving along now in response to shouted orders. As they start to walk toward waiting lorries, an SS officer makes a gesture with his cane and Georges's arm is seized by a Kapo.

"No, no. He's my brother. He must stay with me."

"Claude, Claude, help me."

"Viens. Tu n'es pas à la maison."

The officer speaks good French. Claudia is forced forward. There is no resisting the pressure. Her shouts to Georges join a cacophony. Georges is lost almost instantly. From a high position we see the multitude shuffling down the ramp. Already lorries are pulling away for the camp.

The main gate of the camp. Lorries are entering. Above the gate is the infamous slogan ARBEIT MACHT FREI.

Above the huge camp there is a glow in the sky, the sort of thing given off by an oil refinery or any industrial complex working through the night.

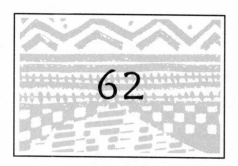

62

"Tom had been to Belsen. If I am honest, it only sank in when we saw the newsreel and the pictures in the *Illustrated London News*. It was the extent of it: we had no idea, particularly out here. Tom was determined to find out if Claudia was still alive. He interrogated a senior SS officer illegally. He beat him up. Tom told me this much later. He almost killed him. He found out that most of the French had been sent to Auschwitz. He traveled there. God knows how he got permission. But there was very little information available. Most of the prisoners had gone. He discovered that quite a number of French had been sent back to Paris already. He then took leave in Paris, inventing some mission or other. His regiment was supposed to be in Hamburg, but he had plenty of contacts."

"How did he know she had been transported in the first place?"

"She wrote to him from the camp in Paris and she also wrote from the train. She dropped letters out of the train. She wrote in Masai, phonetically, in one of them."

"It's incredible that the letters arrived."

"They arrived. Maybe she wrote a hundred. Two arrived. They were forwarded via people in Paris. Anyway, Tom asked friends in Paris to make inquiries after liberation. They confirmed that she had been transported, but of course they did not know the destination. Nobody did. But he left notes on the wall of a hotel, he told me, with her photograph.

"Somebody contacted him. This person thought she was still alive when Auschwitz was liberated. He had one hundred copies of her photograph made and distributed them about the place. He left the telephone number of a British liaison officer, I think it was, and returned to his regiment in Hamburg. This chap sent him a message three days later saying that someone had telephoned him saying she was Claudia. She said, 'Tell Tom I love my little heifer.' But she would not tell this man where she was. She said that she could not see Tom again. She was in hospital. Tom, of course, was not put off. He raced back to Paris as quickly as he could. He found out where she was. I don't know how. It was a small sanatorium in Fontainebleau. He was allowed to see her. He was shocked. She looked fifty-five. She weighed sixty pounds and was recovering from God knows what. Tom said that when she saw him she had convulsions. The doctors had to sedate her.

"Later, a few weeks later or possibly months, I don't remember, they were able to go out together to dinner in Paris. But she would not see her father or even let him know she was still alive.

"In November, or perhaps early December, anyway, when Tom was demobbed, I can't remember dates, they set off on the Union Castle Line via the Cape for Mombasa, but she jumped over the side two days out of Cape Town.

279

"Tom didn't want you to know any of this. You can understand why. I'm probably the only other person in the world who knows the whole story. Now Tom has gone, I'm next.

"And now you can have the letters that Tom wanted you to have. He wanted the story to end at the gates of Auschwitz."

I think, but I do not say, that this story will never end: it is in our marrow.

S. O. Letterman (only Victoria calls him Steve) thinks his legs are Old World. The rest of him is American, quite broad, without that slimness or etiolation that he thinks of as European. He is half a head taller than his father ever was and eighteen inches taller than his mother. But his legs are from another, pre-American, era. They are slightly short, with quite a lot of the calf bowing outward. At Queen's he plays tennis in a tracksuit.

In bed with Victoria he tries to keep these calves—he was once told they looked like olive trees—under the sheets. Not that she appears to care. He knows, without recourse to his intuitive powers, that he is the beneficiary of her disappointment that Tim Curtiz has made hardly any effort to communicate with her since he has been away. She has had only one, completely neutral, letter, faxed to her office.

"After all the fuss he made when he found out."

"Did you tell him"—he is sympathetic to the injured party—"that it was just the once?"

"Of course."

"Well, then?"

"Well, then, what? It wasn't all that many times."

But, of course, they both know there is a considerable difference between a one-off and three or four times.

Victoria is helping with the script. She has taken a week off from the ad agency. She has a talent for dialogue, somewhat better than Curtiz's, who tends to be a little heavy-handed. He also works in rather obvious philosophical points—memory, guilt, redemption, et cetera—whenever he can.

When they make love he finds himself comparing her hips, by no means broad, to the lean, mercurial back view of Candice, which still troubles him. But he likes her lips. They are full. He thinks for some reason of the mushrooms in little baskets on sale in the rue Cherche-Midi: *pleurottes.*

He has had some good news: Julia Roberts wants to read the script. She has told her agent that she would do the part for nothing, if the script is what she expects. ("Nothing" should not be taken too literally.)

"What are you going to do if Tim comes back?" Victoria asks.

"He's in breach."

"That's not exactly what I meant."

64

The grave has been neatly dug to a surprising depth, the spade-
work creating a pattern on this red earth so that the sides of the
hole, into which the coffin is to be lowered, are plaid.

I know nothing about the mourners. There are a lot of them.
They look embarrassed and exposed out here in the hot African
sun, listening to the black priest make a short almost indeci-
pherable speech at the graveside. These faded people in their
unfashionable clothes are interspersed with younger people, presumably grandchildren and so on, who are restless. Their sullen-
ness and impatience fight with the piety on their sun-shuttered
faces. The priest says, "He cometh up and he is cut down like a
flower." The phrase is brutally poetic. As the coffin, decked with
white canna lilies, trumpeting mortality, is lowered into the
grave, the priest assures us of the certain hope of the resurrec-
tion. He pronounces *certain* "suh-tun," with a long gap in the
middle. Lady De Marr smiles distractedly at this point. The
priest blesses us and I am stranded as the others move away from
the disturbed earth and form into little knots. The blue gum
trees that surround the cemetery are rustling, releasing a strong

odor of eucalyptus oil. But perhaps the smell is released by the mourners, walking on the fallen leaves.

Lady De Marr, wearing a long, dark dress and a poorly fitting pillbox hat, approaches me. Her body, all angles, looks like kindling, loosely wrapped.

"There's tea at the club. Do come."

"I won't. I'm sorry. I don't know anybody."

I feel as if I want to close the door on this intrusion of strangers. These dull, faded people are Fairfax's friends from his real life. I had never considered them.

I start down the dusty road from the church. My borrowed shoes are already powdered red. Then I remember the letters. I catch Lady De Marr just as she is about to get into her very old car.

"Are you coming? Jump in," she says, leaving off for a moment her search for a suitable gear.

"No. I was just wondering about the letters."

"Keep them. Tom asked me to give them to you. Are they going to be any use?"

"I don't think so."

"Goodbye, Tim."

"Goodbye, Camilla."

12 August 1944
My dearest Thomas,
We are being held in Drancy in the northeast of Paris. I tried to take my brother Georges away from Paris, believing that it would be safer to spend the next few weeks at our country house, but we were caught in an identity check at the Gare Austerlitz.

My father, who was arrested on the same day, believes that we will soon be released. I wish I could agree with him. In my heart I believe that we will be transported to Germany. Even now as the Allies are approaching Paris, more prisoners—mainly Jews—are arriving every day. My father is outraged that we should be interned with political prisoners, Jewish Resistants and so on, as if we were equal. I have tried to tell him that we are less than equal.

Thomas, my dearest memory is of the two of us together in our tent. I long to see you again. All around me people are saying that the Germans are going to leave us behind. Unfortunately my father is considered a valuable hostage.

I am trying to comfort poor Georges. If you are reading this you will not need to know that I love you. Ole sere, ole sere from your love, Claudia.

Ole sere. Go in peace.

The second letter has come from the cattle car. It is printed carefully on woven paper, which is lightly smeared with human misery:

17 août
Prière à la personne qui trouvera cette lettre de la mettre à la poste, adressée à Croix Rouge Internationale, Paris. (Nous sommes quatre, dans un wagon à bestiaux, destinés Allemagne.)

Fairfax's address is given, c/o King's African Rifles, War Office, London.

Darling Tom,
We are in a cattle truck, heading for Germany. The conditions are unspeakable. I am afraid that this is the end. I'm so sorry. Poor Georges. Tom, I will love you forever. Please tell the Masai that whatever they may think of me, they are always in my thoughts. I dream about them. Ole sere, pakiteng.
C.

Go in peace, little heifer.

I read the letters again, standing by the roadside. I return to the club and send a message to S. O. Letterman:

Steve—oh, yes—I am not coming back yet. Please feel free to use my material in any way you must. I leave any further payments entirely at your discretion. Tim.

Nobody is playing tennis, but in conformity with Fairfax's wishes, as relayed to Camilla, the mourners are having a few drinks. He has left some money for the purpose.

PARIS

The movie is nearly ending. You can feel it swelling to bursting point: the scenes on the station that served as Auschwitz-Birkenau (filmed in Czechoslovakia). The selection process. Georges torn away from Claudia. The figure of Claudia quickly lost in the multitude. The trucks arriving at the gate. The camera panning to find the ghastly, cruel sign above the gate, the sickest fucking joke in the history of humanity, and then rising up into the sky, which is glowing unnaturally. (I know from the adverse publicity that S. O. Letterman bought a surplus steel blast furnace to achieve this effect.) It is also the only color in this scene: the rest of the frame is black and white, a horribly unsettling effect.

Now the glow in the sky gives way to a massive sun. It is blood-red. It quivers. We have often seen this kind of image before, even though it does not exist to the naked eye. The sun is like a heart, exposed in surgery, beating away blindly although unaccustomed to public scrutiny.

The sun sinks fast behind the horizon. The camera holds the empty sky, which is catching fire from below. Now we hear the noise of a plane. It is approaching from the right of the egg cinema. But before it actually appears, as we know it will, we see that the apparently still sky is actually moving, which we discover only as Ol Doinyo Lengai, the Mountain of God, moves into the middle of the screen. At this moment, precisely the right moment, the tiny biplane appears from behind the mountain.

Now the sound track takes celestial wing. We hear, coming from all around the cinema, the Masai singing. It is a thrilling sound. All in one shot the camera pans down as the plane comes in to land and we find a large crowd of Masai warriors running toward the landing site. They run with long, loping strides on their flamingo legs. The plane touches down, bounding and skidding. The warriors run and run. They are in their finest, around their heads ostrich feathers, the plumage of smaller birds and lion manes. They are carrying spears and shields. They are painted in red ochre. Some have squiggly white lines drawn on their legs. (For a moment, I see Paramat, the laibon's son, running.) The warriors and the plane are converging. The magnificence of the scene is given poignancy by the knowledge we now possess. The landscape, the Mountain of God, the running morans, the dipping plane, the lingering glow in the sky, the savagery, all have a dreadful irony.

The plane finally halts and is swallowed up by the excited warriors. The pilot, Mel Gibson, removes his flying helmet and climbs down into the mass of ochre-and-animal-fat-decorated bodies.

At the head of a river of bodies, Fairfax/Gibson now walks across the savannah to the manyatta, where the cattle are also streaming home, driven by young boys. The laibon steps forward to greet him. The warriors and the women in their blue and red *marindas* close in around them. The laibon is wearing his hyrax cloak and holding his snuffbox. He says, in Maa: "You have come to tell us about our daughter, Khlodya."

(The subtitles are in French.)

"I have come to give you news of Claudia. She was killed in the war with the Germans. But she sent me a message to give to you."

From the pocket of his flying jacket, which is brown, with a lining of fleece, he takes a piece of paper.

" 'I am in the hands of the Germans. I do not know what they will do with me. But whatever happens to me, I will never forget you. You have taught me that we all share one universal spirit. Whatever happens to me, I wish that you may have many cattle and plentiful green grass. And wherever God takes me I will dream of you.' "

It is almost completely dark now. The darkness on the screen reaches into the cinema and we—the not-very-numerous audience—are plucked out of our seats. The singing rises, almost unbearably sweet and strange. The credits roll. The fires in the manyatta flicker and glow behind them. We can see nothing but shadows.

We have joined them up there under the mountain, on the screen.

ABOUT THE AUTHOR

JUSTIN CARTWRIGHT was born in South Africa and was educated there, in the United States and at Oxford University. He has lived all his adult life in London, is married, and has two children.

Masai Dreaming, Mr. Cartwright's fifth novel, was the winner of the M Net Award in South Africa. His previous one, *Look at It This Way,* was filmed by the BBC and shown in many countries around the world. His novels have been honored seven times.

In addition to writing novels, Mr. Cartwright has directed television documentaries for the BBC and other channels. He also writes for many newspapers in Britain.

ABOUT THE TYPE

This book was set in Perpetua, a typeface designed by the English artist Eric Gill, and cut by The Monotype Corporation between 1928 and 1930. Perpetua is a contemporary face of original design, without any direct historical antecedents. The shapes of the roman letters are derived from the techniques of stonecutting. The larger display sizes are extremely elegant and form a most distinguished series of inscriptional letters.